Corinthian Leather

Corinthian Leather

The Fourth Art West Adventure

Ben *and* Ann Witherington

PICKWICK *Publications* • Eugene, Oregon

CORINTHIAN LEATHER
The Fourth Art West Adventure

Copyright © 2011 Ben Witherington III and Ann Witherington. All rights reserved.
Except for brief quotations in critical publications or reviews, no part of this book
may be reproduced in any manner without prior written permission from the
publisher. Write: Permissions, Wipf and Stock Publishers, 199 W. 8th Ave., Suite 3,
Eugene, OR 97401.

Pickwick Publications
An Imprint of Wipf and Stock Publishers
199 W. 8th Ave., Suite 3
Eugene, OR 97401

www.wipfandstock.com

ISBN 13: 978-1-61097-3366

Cataloging-in-Publication data:

Witherington, Ben, 1951–

 Corinthian leather : the fourth Art West adventure / Ben Witherington III and
 Ann Witherington

 p. ; 23 cm.

 ISBN 13: 978-1-61097-3366

 1. Archaeology—Fiction. I. Witherington, Ann. II. Title.

PS3605 W55 2011

Manufactured in the U.S.A.

*This book is dedicated to Professor Mark Fairchild
whose wonderful pictures grace various of these pages.*

1

God Calling

ON THE SURFACE, PHILIPPA Philapousis looked like just another Greek grandmother. Walking with a slight stoop and always wearing black, she was indistinguishable from various other old women from her village of Nafplio (aka Nafplion), the ancient capital of Greece, located on the Argolic Gulf. But Philippa was far from ordinary, as she had been granted the gift of prophecy.

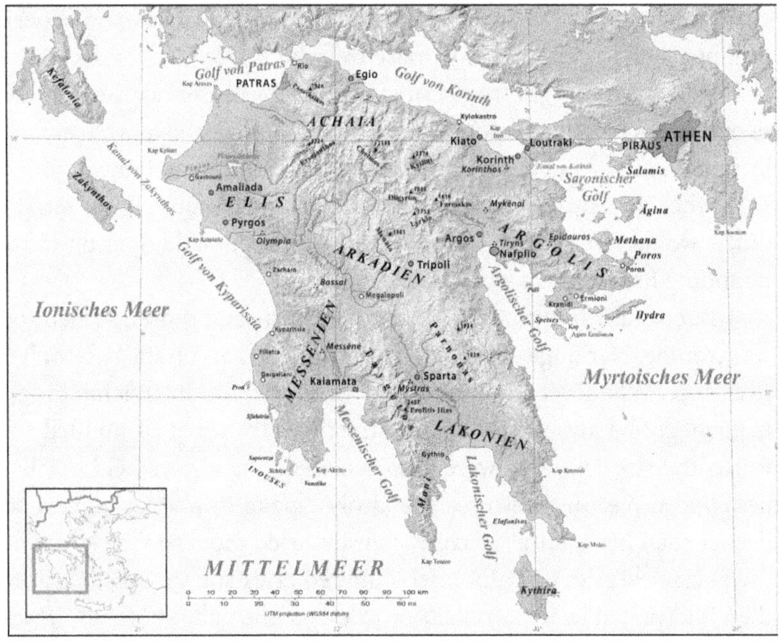

Born in the little Greek village of Kechries, once ancient Cenchreae, where Paul met Phoebe, Philippa grew up hearing tales of the Corinthian and Delphian oracles. This was only natural since Kechries had been and still was a little fishing village near Corinth's port on the Saronic Gulf, less than five miles from the ancient city of Corinth. In such a place, prophecy was a part of the local lore and, indeed, of the religious heritage, including the Christian tradition.

The local Greek Orthodox priests in Nafplio did not really know what to make of Philippa. At times, when she spoke a prophecy and it either was true or eventually came true, they felt a bit threatened by her. She had a source of spiritual power that they could neither domesticate nor dismiss, even though she was a woman untrained in the Bible or in Greek Orthodox theology. And it was not as though they could forget about her either, for there she was, week after week, Sunday after Sunday, standing through the whole Orthodox service, saying her prayers like all the other parishioners. Furthermore, she regularly wore a large Greek Orthodox cross whenever she went out during the day. She could not be written off as a liar, lunatic, or heretic. Indeed, she served as a sort of spiritual counselor to more people in Nafplio, especially the women, than the priests had ever served.

When questioned about her gift by friends, neighbors, and the curious from town (an article had recently run in the local newspaper), Philippa simply deflected any praise from herself to God, and said she had been given this gift from Christ himself for his service. Sometimes people would ask her to prophesy on the spot, and she always responded by saying, "The wind blows where and when it will. I can only prophesy when the Spirit prompts me. That is all. I cannot conjure it up, and if I did, it would not be from above." That usually put a damper on those hounding her for a late word from God.

But on this morning Philippa got up early and sensed something was coming. Her fingers began to tingle and the hair on the back of her neck rose. Whenever she spoke as an oracle several interesting things happened. She always stood very straight with her head uplifted towards the sky. Her eyes were always closed. She always held out her hands in a pleading gesture. She always spoke in a voice somewhat deeper than her natural voice. She always used modern Greek, unlike the ancient oracles at Delphi, who uttered cries and groans that were then interpreted by the prophets or priests of the temple. Finally, it was also Philippa's regular practice to stand up in Nafplio's *plaka*, the central square, and deliver her message only when a considerable audience of locals and tourists had gathered.

On this April day, the sun was shining and all seemed right with the world, but the prophecy Philippa had to unleash would quickly call that into question. Standing on a park bench to project her voice over the crowd, she warned:

DARK AND DANGEROUS
WONDEROUS AND WIDE,
THE EARTH WILL OPEN
WITH NOWHERE TO HIDE.

SHAKING YOUR PRESENT
REVEALING YOUR PAST,
THE LIGHTS WILL DIM
BUT THE SUN WILL LAST.

BEWARE ALL DOUBTERS
BEWARE INFIDELS,
THE CRACKS OF DOOM
THE DENIZENS OF HELL.

And as quickly as it began, the prophecy ended. Philippa stepped down from her bench and began to walk away. Bystanders were either puzzled or amused, thinking perhaps the old woman had imbibed too much ouzo, the ever-popular anise-flavored aperitif. But there was one local merchant, Aristotle, who had often heard Philippa's prophecies and learned to write them down quickly. He leapt from his café table, walked briskly over to Philippa, and tugged on her sleeve.

"When, Philippa, when? When will the great shaking come?"

The old woman herself was shaking at this point, and seemed in a daze. Aristotle had learned to give her a moment to clear her mind, and then asked again quietly, "When will the shaking come?"

"I do not know, but God always delivers his words in due season. You have been warned," Philippa reiterated, shaking her head from side to side.

Walking away, Aristotle muttered sadly to himself, "This does not bode well for tourist season."

2

On A Hill Far Away

THE LATE SPRING WEATHER in southern Greece is delicious. The air is cool and crisp, dew sprinkles the fields, and life is quiet even at the tourist sites. With the wind at his back, Art West poured over a map of ancient Corinth, a city built below the narrow band of land that joins the northern mainland of Greece to the southern peninsula known as the Peloponnese. Ancient Corinth had two ports, one on either side of the Isthmus: Lechaion served the western Corinthian Gulf while Cenchreae (a.k.a. Kenchreai, Kechries) served the eastern Saronic Gulf. People and goods flooded into Corinth from both sides. But it wasn't always so.

In 146 BC the Romans utterly destroyed Corinth. There are slim pickings for an archaeologist wishing to establish the presence of life in or around Corinth until 44 BC, when Julius Caesar (100–44 BC) rebuilt the city as his *Colonia Laus Iulia Corinthiensis*. The new city, built on a typical Roman grid pattern, flourished quickly and became a wealthy province and government seat. Acts 18:12–26 attests to its status throughout the time of the Caesars. The apostle Paul visited the city of Corinth around AD 51 when Gallio was the proconsul. According to Acts 18, he stayed approximately 18 months and became close friends with a married Roman couple, Aquila and Priscilla. Apparently, Paul returned to Corinth around AD 58 for a further three months (Acts 20:3; 2 Cor 1:15). At that time, he probably wrote the Epistle to the Romans.

Art West was also interested in the eastern port of Cenchreae, which in New Testament times had become a haven for Christians, including Phoebe, the first woman in church history to be called a deacon. So important was she to the fledgling church that Paul apparently entrusted her with his new Epistle to the Romans. In it he commends her in the most glowing terms, and insists that they "assist her in whatever matter she may have need" (Rom 16:1, 2). Obviously, Phoebe had been a hostess and patroness of Paul while fulfilling her diaconal role.

Cenchreae harbor

With his new, but still anonymous, funding, Art asked for a leave of absence from his professorial duties to spend the spring semester in Greece. Art had come alone to Corinth, but he had two old friends from school days, Doug and Barbara Zimmerman, who still worked at various sites in and around Corinth. In addition to her expertise in Greek tiles and icons, the effervescent Barb was well known for her watercolor renderings of southern Greece. Doug, in his spare time away from Greek manuscripts, entertained the locals by playing ragtime in many Greek bouzouki bars.

Art was also in touch with Nancy Bookides, whose work in Corinth was well known in archaeological circles. Corinth was one of those ancient sites where the American School of Archaeology could be justly proud of their fifty years of excavation. The results had been nothing short of spectacular, and now scholars and laypersons alike knew more about Corinth in the lifetime of Paul than about almost any other ancient city into which Christianity was introduced by the Pauline mission.

Standing in a field between two small Greek homes that overlooked the fenced area of the Ancient Corinth archaeological site, Art contemplated how he would approach this dig without repeatedly disturbing the neighbors. The goal was to finish unearthing a wealthy person's villa, which overlooked the old city and stood in the shadow of the Acropolis called the Acrocorinth. A start had been made on this site, and a beautiful mosaic had been uncovered five years before, but the ever-present nemesis of lack of funding had prevented the excavators from doing more at this location. Art intended to remedy this problem, without further taxing the Greek government's resources. The Ministry of Culture had been all too glad to give Art a permit to dig, knowing he would turn over any artifacts to Dr. Bookides. This was a reflection of the longstanding good relationship American archaeologists enjoyed with the Greek government when it came to this site so important to early Christian studies. Things were, on the whole, easier here than in Turkey, though there were numerous non-Christian detractors in Greece.

Art's finally official fiancée, Marissa Okur, would be joining him soon. Her current project, cataloguing the dig at Hierapolis in Turkey, was keeping her very busy.[1] E-mails and cell phones made the separation bearable.

On this particular day, Art was enjoying a walking tour of the area he was going to excavate. He had just procured lodgings right next to the site in a small but neat white-washed Greek cottage with electric-blue shutters, rented to him by one Elena Demetrios, a formidable elderly Greek woman who had lived her whole life in this same spot. She lost her husband to cancer some twenty years ago, and her children were all grown up and leading their own lives in Athens and Thessaloniki.

Elena, like the archaeological ruins in ancient Corinth, was rooted to the ground and refused to move. She had her routines: going to the market, visiting shut-ins, and attending the famous St. Paul's Greek Orthodox Church on the edge of the modern city of Corinth. Art had

---

1. About which you can read in the third Art West adventure, entitled *Papias and the Mysterious Menorah.*

a feeling he would be getting to know Mrs. Demetrios quite well, as she was a big talker, and loved to hear about the progress of the archaeological work. Her spoken English was not very good, but she comprehended the language well enough that if Art spoke slowly she could make sense of it all.

Art's own modern Greek was limited to some necessary words, but he could read the posted signs. The problem for him was pronunciation. Many, if not most, Greek words were pronounced very differently from how they would have been in New Testament times. He would never forget his surprise when he discovered, while eating at his favorite restaurant in Athens some years prior, that the word for "thank you," from the verb *eucharisteo*, is in fact pronounced *ef-feris-toe*, as opposed to the ancient pronunciation, *you-ka-ris-tee-o*.

Having finished his walking survey, Art could tell he would need to hire a lot of diggers initially, as he wanted to do some test soundings all over the site, or use his new imaging equipment to narrow things down quickly to particular plots where he and Marissa would concentrate for the summer's work. The mosaic floor piece that had already been uncovered suggested a large villa, probably with numerous out-buildings as well. From the Museum of Archaeology in Athens, Art had already rented the expensive sonar-like device that would indicate the location of large structures under the ground so he would not waste time digging in a dead zone that would reveal nothing but dirt.

Modern archaeology had gone high tech, which came with a high price tag. Thanks to his sizeable new trust fund, Art had not blinked when the Director of Archaeology at the Ministry of Culture told him it would be $5,000 to rent the equipment for a two-week span. He simply wrote the check, packed up the gear, and drove to Corinth. Someday he hoped to thank his anonymous donor in person.

Still standing on the hill, Art could hear the goats from a nearby farm making their presence known, the little bells around their necks ringing now and again as they moved to a new foraging spot. He also heard the sound of the children at the elementary school playground located down the street from where he stood. More distant was the sound of the traffic on the main north-south highway. Unlike many archaeological sites, this one was surrounded by civilization and the noises of day-to-day life, yet somehow this all made Art feel more at home with being here.

"Will you stand here all day, or be digging?" asked Mrs. Demetrios, who had walked up quietly behind Art and startled him out of his introspective mood.

"No digging today, Mrs. Demetrios, just surveying using this amazing device that lets me see underground. Here, look through this view finder." Art brought the instrument over and lowered it down so the 5′ 2″ Mrs. Demetrios could see through it.

"Is amazing! Shapes from underground. That is probably wall there." She pointed to the center of the screen.

Art figured that it would be a good idea to keep a cordial ongoing dialogue with Mrs. Demetrios as she was his ticket to familiarity with the local community, and would serve as his eyes and ears while he was in Corinth. Plus, Art wanted to learn more about the day-to-day life of a devout Greek Orthodox Christian, and Mrs. Demetrios was more than ready to share. She needed someone to talk to.

"When you finish looking through finder," she said, "come down to house for some lunch—soup, tzatsiki, vegetables, maybe little lamb, maybe even baklava, fresh from baker." Her eyes twinkled.

"With such a menu," laughed Art, "I promise to be there very soon!" Art had set up a deal to take one or two meals a day with Mrs. Demetrios. This had worked out so well in the four days he had been in Corinth that he had gotten an ear full on subjects ranging from local politics, to the state of the economy, to the problem with fishing in the Aegean these days, to the latest reports from the dig on the Acrocorinth, to what was in the vegetable market that morning, not to mention what was happening at church that evening. Art liked the family feeling that this dig site was giving him. It did not have to be all work, all the time. He could enjoy the culture and the people as well.

As she was walking away, Mrs. Demetrios' parting shot was, "And one more thing. Today, newspaper say earthquake coming according to Greek prophecy, so you best get to work soon."

"What?" exclaimed Art, "Now I've got to schedule around an earthquake? Well, maybe it will help with moving this earth."

"Is not laughing matter, since it came not from gossip columnist or weather man but from Philippa the prophetess, and she speaks truth."

Catching up to Mrs. Demetrios, Art asked, "And who is this Philippa? She sounds like a woman I need to meet sometime."

"She special woman who lives over in Nafplio and, yes, perhaps I can arrange meeting."

"Thank you," said Art politely as Elena continued on back to her cottage. But what he was really thinking while further wandering about the site was whether or not the voice of living prophecy could still be stirring in this part of the world. He found it hard to concentrate on buried artifacts when a living prophetess could be in their midst.

After showering, changing, and devouring a homemade Greek dinner, Art decided to get back to a project he had wanted to undertake while in Corinth, namely, roughing out a storyline he had hatched in his head about ancient Corinth in New Testament times. Art knew that his time here in Corinth could only inspire further reflection on those ancient events. Snuggling into a comfortable chair with his laptop on his lap, Art began to compose, attacking the keyboard with only his two index fingers.

3

Once Upon A Time . . .

*IT WAS A SPRING afternoon when Paul first arrived in Corinth, weary
from his journey from Athens. Having left Timothy and Silas behind
to return to Macedonia to check on the churches there, the apostle had
forged ahead on his own to the new center of life in the province of
Achaea, namely, Roman Corinth. Corinth, not Athens, was the hub of
Roman control in southern Greece. Paul intended to take advantage of
his Roman citizenship in order to get established in Corinth. One of the
first places to visit would be the synagogue, for Paul knew there had been
a large population of Jews in Corinth for many decades. Many Jews were
brought to Corinth as slaves after the Romans leveled the ancient Greek
city in 146 BC.*

*The Lechaion road was the main route into Corinth, and Paul man-
aged to reach the heart of the city by about three in the afternoon, footsore
and tired all over. He noticed at once the row of shops on the north side
of the city, including a leatherworker's shop. Since he was of the guild
of leatherworkers (with a specialty in making tents out of cilicium, the
famous goat's hair cloth) Paul thought he would check in to see if work
might be available. Fortunately, he had arrived at a time when prepara-
tions were being made for the biennial Isthmian games, and tents would
be needed to sell or rent out to the tourists coming for the games.*

*Walking into the entryway of the impressive dome-vaulted stone
shop, Paul saw animal hides hanging in various places on the walls. He
could overhear a bargaining session going on towards the back of the shop.*

"I'm telling you, friend Aquila, this tent you have offered me is surely not worth that many silver denarii. Why, just yesterday I bought one in Isthmia for only half that price."

"Ah, my friend, you probably did find such a tent," said Aquila, a short swarthy looking man with a strong accent. "I suspect that you bought it from Sosiper, who has even been known to make tents out of dog skin! You should know, Erastus, you get what you pay for. If you want a tent that will not shrink or leak when it rains, a tent that has been sown properly with double stitching, then you can have one of these tents at the discount price I have offered you. Don't make me call my wife Priscilla, who will regale you with stories as to how long it took to make this very tent."

Erastus sighed, knowing that he had reached the end of the haggling exchange and the bottom price Aquila would offer. "Well, there is some merit to what you have said, and there will be some more important visitors at the games wanting better accommodations. I will take the tent you have offered at your price, but remember I will be back later in the month to collect the rent on the shop," said Erastus with a knowing smile, indicating that there would be future bargaining sessions to come.

It was Aquila's turn to sigh, and then he rolled up the olive-brown leather tent and tied it tightly so it would be easy for Erastus' servant to carry back to the villa up the hill where the city treasurer lived. "Here you go, chairete [farewell]," said Aquila, "I see I have another customer waiting patiently behind you." As Erastus left he sized up the smallish man with the balding head and dark beard, looking like he had just had a long dusty journey on foot, and simply grunted as he went by.

"I gather your name is Aquila, and by that accent I would guess you come from some other part of the Empire," said Paul as an opening gambit.

"You are right, I'm from Pontus on the sea, but my wife Priscilla is from Rome, and of higher social station; you know how a man tries to better himself by marrying above himself," added Aquila chuckling.

"Only a wise man does that, as the Jewish Scriptures say," replied Paul with a wink.

"So are you a Jew then?" asked Aquila.

"Indeed, and a tentmaker like you, as well," said Paul. "My name is Saul of Tarsus, though my Greek name is Paulos. I wondered if perhaps you could give me some of your wisdom about where I might find lodgings at least for tonight."

"It seems that G-d has guided you to the right person and the right place, and I know my wife would be upset with me if I did not offer a fellow Jewish tentmaker some hospitality. Why not stay with us for a while? I could use some help here in the shop, as you can see."

"Why not?" said Paul as he extended his hand to Aquila, who gave him an embrace and a kiss of greeting on his dusty cheek.

"I have much to ask you," said Paul, "starting with the subject of the synagogue here."

"Yes, but first things first. You need to wash and then you need some food. I will send little Tychicus here back to the house to alert Priscilla I am coming with company." And with only a word in Greek to the lad who helped him in the shop, the boy set off running toward the tenement houses up the slope towards the Acropolis.

"Welcome to Corinth," said Aquila, "where there is never a dull moment."

"Indeed," said Paul. "I know the famous saying 'Not for every man is the journey to Corinth.'"

"But clearly you are the exception!" said Aquila, and they both laughed as they left the shop by the front entrance.

4

The Olde Waffle Shop

IT WAS LATE SUNDAY morning and some of the early church crowd had already poured into the usual breakfast haunt, the Olde Waffle Shop, an institution in South Charlotte. Old it certainly was, with metallic swiveling bar stools with red seat covers, and booths that various people shoehorned themselves into for a hearty but inexpensive breakfast. Behind the counter was Marsha, mistress of her domain, short-order cook extraordinaire, busily filling six orders at once from memory. Mopping her brow with the back of one hand while cracking six eggs into a bowl with the other, the orders just kept coming.

"I've got a pecan waffle, scrambled eggs, and hash browns with a side order of grits 'covered and chunked' [translation: with cheese and ham chunks on top]."

Marsha simply repeated what she had just heard in her good Southern drawl, concluding with "Coming right up," and never took her eyes off the ham-and-cheese omelet she was folding and flipping.

There was an odd trio of persons sitting at the counter together. First was an African-American man in a brown suit coat reading a local newspaper, combing it for some possible good news. The second was a very tall olive-complexioned man in a new black suit staring at the menu. Finally, there sat a little white-haired lady wearing her Sunday best Carolina-blue dress. She occasionally pointed to items on the menu being held by the second man. Names had been exchanged between these three while they waited for breakfast to arrive. Harvey

Pearson was the African American, just out of the A.M.E. church down the road; beside him sat Jake Arafat, budding star of the Charlotte Bobcats, fresh out of the early service at Myers Park UMC; and then "Aunt" Joyce West, who was gradually giving Jake the tour of various bits of true Americana, like a trip to the Olde Waffle Shop.

"So is there any good news in that Sunday paper you're reading? " Joyce asked Harvey.

"No, ma'am, just a couple of church columns of note."

"So how was church this morning?" Joyce persisted, leaning around Jake.

"Lively. More perky than a fresh cup o' java. How 'bout yours?"

"Well, more stately than a burr oak. You know, white folks' sort of church."

"Indeed, I do know. I don't know how you folks stay awake for that at eight thirty in the morning. Do the ushers bring coffee down the aisles?"

"I wish," claimed Jake, diving into the conversation, "But no such luck. At least Dr. Howell's sermon is usually interesting."

"Our preacher went on for forty minutes this morning," said Harvey proudly. "For some reason he was upset about all the media attention given to shows like *American Idol* and *Dancing with the Stars*. No one knows what a true hero or star is these days."

"Now that's one thing I really don't like about America—celebrity culture," said Joyce firmly. "It's a sign of sickness not wellness in our society if you ask me. *American Idol* about sums it up—idolatry!"

"That may be a bit harsh, but I catch your drift," agreed Harvey. "And speaking of drift, I smell coffee coming back this way. Could I have another cup while I await Marsha's treats?" Harvey asked the waitress, who was whizzing by heading for the end of the lunch counter.

"Sure enough," said the petite waitress with the teased red hair and coffee-stained white apron as she poured her fiftieth cup of coffee for the morning.

"Where would we be without coffee?" said Jake.

"That's an easy one," answered Joyce. "Still in bed, having missed church, which will not do!" And all three of them laughed simultaneously.

At this point another waitress appeared and plopped down: 1) a plate for Joyce with two scrambled eggs, whole wheat toast, and cheese grits; 2) the "ALL STAR" special for Jake, consisting of a ham-and-cheese omelet, raisin toast, grits with sausage, and a pecan waffle with warm syrup; and 3) Harvey's beloved grits with fried Neese's Liver Pudding, accompanied by two fried eggs and white toast with persimmon jelly.

"Shall I say a blessin'?" asked Joyce.

"You go right ahead, ma'am," encouraged Harvey. "This feast is already a blessin'!"

What went unnoticed by the three amigos were all the people sitting in the booths staring at the three. Some whispered questions like, "Is that really Jake 'the Cat' Arafat?" with the answer, "It sure looks like him, but what is he doing with those two?"

Life in increasingly multicultural Charlotte was a constant fascination, but some things never change—like a good Southern breakfast at the Olde Waffle Shop.

5

Having A Party, A Communist Party

THOUGH IT COMES AS a surprise to many American tourists, Greece has a long-standing communist party, called the Κομμουνιστικό Κόμμα Ελλάδας, (*Kommounistikó Kómma Elládas*), better known by its acronym, KKE (usually pronounced *koo-koo-eh* or *kappa-kappa-ep-silon*). Not only do they have a communist party, in fact it is the oldest political party in all of Greece, with a long and colorful history in the twentieth and into the twenty-first century. Granted, Euro-communism is not quite like the communism of Marx and Stalin, but nonetheless it is communism of a sort.

Oddly enough, this party was founded by a Jew named Avraam Benaroya, a teacher and labor movement leader in Thessaloniki. The KKE has experienced some severe ups and downs. For example, in 1948 just after WWII it was banned by the king of Greece, and its members were all declared spies for the Soviet Union. That put a damper on recruitment for some time. In fact, during the height of the Cold War in the 1950s, when fear of the Red Peril was at its peak in America, prominent members of the KKE were tried and executed, including Nikos Beloyannis in 1952 and Nikos Ploumpidis in 1954. The party did not entirely disappear, however.

Discrimination and prosecution against Greek communists were partially abolished with the re-legalization of the KKE in 1974, and prosecution was completely abolished in the 1980s. This was part of a larger attempt to restore parliamentary democracy in 1974, and allow all political parties to have some role in the Greek political process. However, there are various radical leftist parties, though too many for any one to be a major influence, and so at various times the KKE has waxed and waned with members defecting to either more leftist or more centrist parties. For example, in the early 2000s, a small group of major party officials, such as Mitsos Kostopoulos, left the party and formed the Movement for the United in Action Left (KEDA), which in the 2007 legislative election participated in the Coalition of the Radical Left. The party tried to recruit fresh blood by starting a youth organization targeting teenagers and young adults. Even so, in any given year the communists, while represented in parliament, have no more than about ten percent of the vote and representation.

Ordinarily, the Greek communists would be viewed as simply a small group of relatively harmless, easily ignored radicals, but sometimes the violent actions of a few of their members branded the KKE as a whole. For example, some of the KKE are what can only be called ultra-nationalists, violently opposed to: 1) peace talks with Turkey over disputed land, and 2) any kind of compromise or treaty with the US or the UK. These tendencies accelerated among those who saw Greece's joining of the European Union as a disaster. On the other hand, some members of the KKE saw joining the EU as a chance to be allied with other Euro-communists in a common cause.

All of this is quite relevant for understanding Nikos Alexandros, a thirty-five-year-old member of the KKE from Corinth, who was hard to ignore at 6' 4". Nick, as he was called by his friends, saw himself as a watchdog in his region, always on the lookout for foreign influences at odds with the socialist causes he favored. There is little love lost between most devout Greek Orthodox Christians and secular communists in general, not only because of Marx's anti-religious views, but also because communists were infamous for suppressing Orthodox Christianity in Russia and elsewhere. Interestingly, secular communists sometimes see themselves as the true nationalists in their country, preserving its ancient, especially pagan, heritage.

Nick was just such a person. He saw the Orthodox Church as a bad influence on the Greek people, and saw himself as a watchdog protecting Greece's pagan past. He frequently patrolled the grounds of the ancient Corinth and Acrocorinth archaeology sites eavesdropping on Christian tour groups, American Christians, Turkish Christians, etc.

His level of concern would rise meteorically if he discovered Christian scholars involved in excavations and work in Corinth.

The Diolkos road connecting the two
harbors on the Isthmus

On this particularly beautiful morning, he haunted the ancient Lechaion Road in the middle of the Corinth site and learned from the ticket taker that a famous American Christian archaeologist was soon to begin a new dig up on the hill overlooking the Temple of Apollo and

the ancient city. His early warning system went off, and he became quite irate about the matter. "That American School of Archaeology has been nothing but trouble for many decades here and the bane of my existence as a Corinthian, but this really makes things worse—allowing another Christian to dig at our sacred shrine! They have no right to be here!" Muttering to himself, he went on fulminating about American fundamentalist Christians for another five minutes before finally quieting down when the lady watching the back gate at the archaeological site gave him a good scowl for some of his remarks she had overheard. He would need to be more careful he told himself, as you never know who's listening. He promised himself he would give a call to Athens and consult with his superior in the party. He would know what to do next.

6

Putting Papias To Rest

T HE PUBLICITY THAT THE Papias findings garnered was sufficient to convince Abdullah Koroturk, the director of all archaeological work in Turkey, to leave Papias' remains in the little Hierapolis museum, which then merited an upgrade. The manuscripts were headed for the Istanbul Museum, with realistic copies displayed in Hierapolis. The originals were just too precious to leave under minimum security in Hierapolis. Marissa was tending to these last-minute details, but her mind was elsewhere, namely in Greece.

As a Turk, Marissa had never been to Greece. Indeed she avoided that country like the plague. The ongoing rivalry and hostility between Greeks and Turks had touched her own family's life; one of her relatives living on Cyprus was killed by rioting Greeks. As she pondered heading to Greece in a few days, fear and trepidation stressed her. She told herself that as long as she was not wearing a sign saying, "Hit me, I'm a Turk" she could blend in relatively well. "Keep your head down, and work, work, work!" became her mantra. Marissa's parents, having just gotten used to the notion that she was engaged to an American, were now coping with the idea that she was off to Greece for a few months.

"A few months!" exploded her father on the phone. "For sure something bad will happen to you if you stay that long. And you are going to Corinth to dig? Don't you realize that the ruins on top of that little mountain are Turkish fortifications? Don't you remember when Turks controlled a good deal of Greece? What are you thinking?"

"Father, I appreciate the concern," replied Marissa, holding the cell phone away from her ear when her father started yelling. "We live in ever-changing times, and besides Art will be there with me, and together we will be alright. We will keep a low profile I am sure."

"It better be so low that you are digging underground," replied Zafer Okur. "I do not want to read about you being abused or thrown in jail just because you are Turkish. Mark my words: too much time in Greece is not good for a Turkish girl like you. And don't even get me started on how Greek men disrespect women, especially foreign women." Zafer served his time in the military on some of the islands off the coast of Turkey that belonged to Greece but which Turkey also claimed. Fear and prejudice ran deep.

"Yes, Father," said Marissa wearily. This harangue only fed her nearly overwhelming fears about the trip to Greece. "I promise I will be careful and uncontroversial. I will not look for trouble."

"No, I am confident of that, but it may come looking for you, unexpectedly. Do watch your back," sighed Zafer.

"I will, I promise. Love to you and mother." Marissa hung up. There was a part of her that knew there was some justification for these warnings.

But Bishop Papias was calling her, and she needed to make sure the new signs next to the glass case where his remains lay in the Hierapolis Museum were properly worded, with proper spelling and grammar in both Turkish and English. She always winced when she saw a lack of attention to these details, which are seen as telltale signs by educated English-speaking tourists of a lack of education in her native land. There were too many signs and pamphlets at archaeological sites full of bad English. "We have got to work harder at being cultural ambassadors!" she laughed to herself.

Soon she would be doing her best to blend into a rather similar culture, but with different national biases and agendas. Marissa, whatever her other strengths, knew that blending in and being unobtrusive was not her strength.

7

In the Limelight

G RACE LEVINE COHEN, WHILE taking her husband's name after her
marriage, continued to go by the name Levine in the academic arena to prevent confusion in regard to her published work. As Professor
of Ancient Semitic Epigraphy at Hebrew University in Jerusalem, she
had never been one to shy away from controversy, and this day was
no different. Though she usually had a cordial working relationship
with the Israeli Antiquities Authority (IAA), the recent comments of
the judge at Oded Golan's trial (namely, that the prosecution needed to
give it a rest) had prompted her to make a public comment in agree-
ment—that it was time for the IAA to acquit Mr. Golan. Grace even
quoted an old Kenny Rogers song: "You gotta know when to hold 'em,
know when to fold 'em, know how to walk away, know when to run . . ."

This story had been plastered all over the front page of the
Jerusalem Post ("LEVINE TELLS IAA, PACK UP YOUR TENT AND
GO HOME") and *Ha'Aretz* ("LEVINE PREDICTS DECLINE AND
FALL OF IAA CASE AGAINST GOLAN"). Naturally this led to a swirl
of controversy as TV stations and radio commentators sought interviews. Fortunately, Grace could retreat to her gated home along the sea-
shore in Tel Aviv. Despite their schedules, Friday lunch was becoming
a routine at home, and Grace was now searching for salad ingredients.

Grace's husband Manny, a multimillionaire who owned a successful tech company and a pro basketball team (Maccabee Elite),
frequently used a media consultant. So he coaxed Grace into doing a

further press release to keep the yapping media hounds at bay. "I don't really want to do this," complained Grace. "It's too much like admitting you did something wrong and apologizing, which I didn't and I'm not."

"Well, dearest, this is called damage control," said Manny as he munched on his lunch, a Reuben sandwich and fresh fruit. If you want the story to evolve their way, you say nothing. If you want the story to die a rather quick death, then you take charge and speak out through a press release."

"Alright, alright . . . so how about this: 'While the trial of Oded Golan is still ongoing I have no desire to render a personal final judgment on the matter, or to pre-empt or influence any of the due process owed to both the plaintiffs and the defendants. The judge's comments speak for themselves, and suggest that it may be time for the prosecution to reconsider whether they want to continue prosecuting Oded Golan. On a related front, I think it's time the court released the James ossuary so that my colleagues and I can resume an epigraphical study of it. I will not be doing any further interviews on this matter.'"

"Well, you didn't back down, and hopefully you won't stir up more trouble—a good balance. My team can polish the press release," promised Manny as he grinned at his new wife. Life as a married couple had settled into a good routine. On most weekdays they would head off to work in opposite directions, but midweek they would lunch together and plan their future, near and far.

"So do you have any thoughts for the weekend?" wondered Manny.

"I could head up to Tel Dan to see some of the new inscriptions uncovered up there, which are apparently quite interesting according to Marc Bar Yonah, the director of the dig. How about you?"

"I really should go to Athens. There's a computer expo being held there, but I don't have to be physically present until maybe Tuesday. Would you like to join me for a few days in Greece? The jet is fueled and ready!"

"Absolutely!" cried Grace. "Can we get away tomorrow or Friday? Just strolling the Plaka and eating moussaka with baklava for dessert sounds great to me right now! And, if I'm not mistaken, Art just arrived in Corinth to start work at a new dig. That's a short trip from Athens."

"Amazing how your mind works!" admired Manny. "A side perk of this trip—it should keep you out of the all-seeing eye of the Israeli media for a few days."

"Right, my media mogul," quipped Grace.

One could tell by the banter just how much these two enjoyed each other's company and respected each other's judgments and work. Camelia, Grace's mother, who now lived just down the street in her own seaside bungalow, had marveled at how well these two Type-A personalities meshed.

After a kiss goodbye, Grace headed to their workout room complete with weights, treadmill, and a TV hanging from the ceiling. Grace tended to turn off the TV and pump up the radio, listening to music while she jogged and sweated away. With all the high-calorie dinners she was now attending with Manny, she and the treadmill were becoming well acquainted. Changing the dial, she found the local classic rock station, which was playing "Hot Blooded" by Foreigner. Grace starting jogging at a good pace, singing along to the music. Life was good, and even the recent run-ins with the press could not spoil the feeling that she had reached a high point in her life.

8

Hoop Hysteria

As some of the sports pundits at the *Charlotte Observer* had been predicting, Jake "the Cat" Arafat had become a bona fide star in the NBA. The lowly Charlotte Bobcats had suddenly become a team competing for a playoff berth, though they had miles to go before they caught up with Boston, San Antonio, or Los Angeles. But still, better was better, and "the Cat" was the talk of the sports fans in Charlotte, putting lots more bodies in the seats in the downtown arena.

Riding down Tryon Street in his Highlander Hybrid with the sports talk radio station blaring, Jake was surveying his domain, and liking what he was seeing. Slowly but surely a change had come over his demeanor, from hopeful to confident. The voice inside his head kept saying, "Yes you can!" to almost any question he posed to himself. The only things keeping him grounded were "Aunt" Joyce, as he now called Art's mother, his time at church, and the occasional conversations with his real mother, who was now living and working in the monastery near Jericho.

With some coaching from Aunt Joyce, Jake began to pick his friends more carefully, and be alert to the telltale signs of sponges—those who would drain him dry and give nothing back. Jake was a kind and generous person, which made him an easy target. Thus far, he had managed to avoid signing any bad contracts to do ridiculous marketing for some product, and Michael Jordan easily persuaded his own agent to take Jake on as a client. But Jake resolved not to make any business decisions without first spending time in counsel with his coach, Aunt Joyce, and his minister, James Howell. Still, there was no stemming the rising tide of demand for his attention, services, interviews, and the like.

One outlet that helped immensely in keeping him focused and levelheaded was his work at the Bethlehem Center for underprivileged children, an outreach ministry of the United Methodist Church started in 1984. Every time he walked into the main center and saw all those children and every time he saw the word Bethlehem over the door triggered memories of his hometown in the Holy Land. Jake not only remembered to thank God for all the good that had happened to him since his brother Issah's horrible murder, but rededicated himself to living a life like his brother lived—a Christlike life. Self-sacrifice, not self-indulgence, came to mind when he walked through the doors of the Center with his new pal Charlie Brown.[2]

Charlie was a pretty normal local guy, despite his name. He grew up in Charlotte, graduated from UNC–Charlotte, and was now working for a bank downtown. Charlie had two passions in his life: his Christian faith, and sports. His job in the international banking department paid the bills on his first home outside town in Monroe, and he made sure his Saturday mornings were free to go with Jake to the Bethlehem Center. Being only 5' 9" and sporting strawberry-blond hair, when he was together with the 6' 5" swarthy Jake they looked like an old vaudeville team.

"Hey, Charlie, guess what?" said Latoya, a young girl who spied him walking through the door and who loved to play board and video games with him.

Grinning from ear to ear, Charlie replied, "I give up, what?"

"The Center just got the new edition of the classic Trivial Pursuit game, so I was thinking we could try it out."

Jake laughed and said, "You go ahead, Charlie! It's obvious that you're the most popular gamer around here. I'm heading to the back court to shoot some hoops with my posse." Kids of all genders, sizes, and shapes at the center loved to try and beat Jake one on one in a game of HORSE or a free throw contest. One such devotee was Jamaal, who was hanging out by the backdoor listening to Kanye West on his head-

---

2. This story is told in the second Art West adventure, *Roman Numerals.*

phones. With dreadlocks, a baseball hat on crooked, and a couple of chains hanging off his military pants, which were pulled down too low, you would never know he was also an A student and a good basketball player as well. When he looked up and saw the Cat striding across the floor towards him, he nearly dropped his MP3 player.

"Time to hit the court, Jamaal," hollered Jake. "I'm challenging you to that free throw contest you keep telling me about."

"For real?"

"Yes, for real! Get a ball and let's go," replied Jake. And so a morning filled with games and talk and lunch would pass quickly for Jake and Charlie.

Jake did not know that he was being observed the whole time through the fence by members of the Kings, a street gang who hung out primarily in West Charlotte. Considered one of Charlotte's two largest gangs, this group was called the Westside Kings. Selling crack, stealing, breaking into cars, and hanging with their girls, the Queens, were typical "fun" activities. For now, Jake was merely a "person of interest" to them as they watched him move about the court. But already the leader of the gang, Ahmed, was planning his own moves. It would take more than petty theft to rise in the ranks of the Kings or even break into the biggest and baddest of the gangs, the Mara Salvatrucha 13 (MS-13). He was thinking big time, and he smiled a crooked smile as he watched Jake Arafat school another would-be challenger on the b-ball court.

9

A Sad Secret

MARISSA HAD BEEN WORRIED for some time about something she and Art had never discussed—because Art knew nothing about it. She continued avoiding the subject because she was afraid of how Art would react. Truth to tell, she was even somewhat afraid he would break off the engagement if he found out. But now, when it had become clear that they would be making a life together soon, she had to tell him—but how?

Art was a pro-life evangelical Christian. In fact he was consistently pro-life right across the board—he opposed abortion, euthanasia, capital punishment, personal firearms, and war in general. It was the first item on that list that had Marissa worried. When she was still a teenager, after a brief fling with another college student she became pregnant. Panicking that this would ruin her chances to get into her dream profession, archaeology, because all the men at the top of the Turkish government hierarchy just looked for excuses not to hire qualified women, she went out without the knowledge of her family or her boyfriend and had an abortion in Istanbul, well away from any of her close associates in Ankara. The abortion had gone well, without physical complications. Psychologically, it was another matter. Alone and demoralized, she planned to remain single—that is, until Art came along.

But how could she tell Art about the baby? It was bad enough fretting about being in Greece as a Turkish woman—*that* she could face. But she could not face rejection at the hands of Art West. At night she would toss and turn or lie still, flat on her back feeling like she had a massive stone on her chest. Could he possibly understand? Would he forgive her? She knew she had to take the chance and tell him, because otherwise her secret would poison the well of their relationship. And she would not let that happen. She would rather lose Art now than have a time bomb go off in the relationship later, perhaps even after they were married.

And lastly, there was another concern. Though Art was pushing fifty, Marissa was ten years younger. What if he wanted children? Of course her biological clock had been ticking for years, increasingly louder as the years rolled by. Could she still have children? It was another fear preying on her mind. So, she had resolved that as soon as she got to Greece she would have a heart-to-heart chat with Art, right after they got settled. Then, she could and would deal with the consequences.

Rehearsing all this in her mind, while sitting at the bar at her hotel, the Pammukale Palace, she had gone through one dry martini and was now ordering another. "Bartender, make it a double this time."

"Are you sure, Miss Okur?" asked Hakim.

"Trust me, I am sure," she said. "I plan to sleep the sleep of the dead tonight."

"A nightcap then," said Hakim with a smile as he expertly tossed the shaker full of gin, vermouth, bitters, and ice.

10

Athena's Airport

THE FLIGHT INTO ATHENS can be spectacular *if* one swoops in very early before the haze of pollution and heat settles over the capital city. Flights from the east glide right over the Acropolis with its iconic Parthenon before circling back towards the east to land. Both commercial and private planes were landing at the new Athens International Airport, which opened in 2001 to replace the now-closed Elliniko Airport. The new aiport was named after Elefthérios Venizélos, the prominent Cretan political figure and Prime Minister of Greece, who made an outstanding contribution in the Cretan uprising against the Ottoman occupation of Crete in 1896. The very name of the airport would set off alarm bells for a Turkish person.

Turkish Airlines offered only one flight a day from Istanbul to Athens, but even this was an improvement over the old days when a Turk had to take a ferry from the Turkish coast out to an island like Samos, and then fly Olympic Air to Athens. Art West stood waiting beyond the checkpoint where passengers would emerge from baggage control, praying that Marissa would not be hassled at passport control. He had sent the required letter of invitation to come and work with others at the Corinthian archaeological site, and it had her name right in the first paragraph. This ought to expedite matters considerably. Any minute now he was sure Marissa would emerge, but as the door opened Art's jaw dropped.

Sporting a white fedora, Manny came waltzing into the lobby with a Louis Vuitton case in tow. Right behind him, in white linen, red heels, and lots of bling, strode the well-tanned Grace Levine Cohen. Art immediately raced over and blurted, "You two look like movie stars!"

Grace got a big grin on her face. "You must be the reception committee. Who told you we were coming?"

"No one; not even the media! I'm here to collect Marissa— if they ever let her through security," answered Art with a worried look on his face. Recovering, he added, "What's your excuse for being on this shore of the Mediterranean today of all days?"

Manny butted in. "We are going to the computer expo in Athens, but we thought we would surprise you in Corinth just to see if you were spending your grant money wisely."

"Aha, so you are admitting that you are my anonymous benefactor!" accused Art.

"Sorry," replied Grace emphatically. "We could and maybe someday we would, but we didn't."

Shrugging his shoulders, Art probed further, "So when are you coming to the dig? I'm eager for you both to spend more time with us. We've barely seen each other since your wedding last summer."

After a few more minutes chatting, Manny and Grace promised to come see Art and Marissa for the weekend, and Art handed Manny a business card for a quaint seaside hotel in Corinth, right on the Isthmus. Turning back towards passport control, Art could hear an argument going on in the non-EU line. The voice was all too familiar.

"I assure you sir, I am here strictly for business, and would not think of overstaying my welcome. I just need an entry visa for the summer months, and will be returning to Turkey in September."

Marissa was enduring an inquisition with the passport control officer, and even the letter of invitation in Greek had not convinced him to quickly stamp her passport and insert the visa into it. As time went on, Marissa's anxiety and Turkish temper began to get the best of her. "Miss Okur, I must ask you once more, is there someone who can vouch for you, someone authorized by the Greek government's archaeological bureau?"

"It's *Doctor* Okur, and that's what the letter of invitation is all about!" retorted Marissa.

"Yes, but how do I know it is genuine. It could be forged," he challenged.

Suddenly, from behind the control officer's head, another voice took charge. "It could be, but it certainly is not since I obtained this letter personally from Nancy Bookides, the head of archaeology at the Corinth site," intruded Art.

Swiveling around in his chair, the guard asked, "And who might you be?"

Flipping open his passport, Art spoke in slow and measured terms. "I am Dr. Art West, authorized to dig at Corinth by the Ministry of Culture. I will vouch for Dr. Okur, especially since she is my fiancée," and Art finally lightened up with a big smile.

"Alright," groused the guard, "I guess I should let you in *Miss* Okur, but I must say Dr. West you could have picked a Greek woman for your fiancée if you want to dig here!"

At this Art could see Marissa turning bright red and reaching for her purse to bop the man over the head. Art immediately mouthed "NO!" to Marissa, at which point she calmed down and settled for angry glaring as they both left the office.

"Thank you, Sir Galahad, for preventing yet another chapter in the Turkish-Greek border wars," muttered Marissa.

Art took Marissa by the hand, wrapped his other arm around her waist, looked her right in the eye and said, "We will be just fine now." His lingering kiss resulted in mixed emotions on her part. "We have other battles to fight in Corinth. It's time to get on the road south."

Still stewing, Marissa complained, "But that male chauvinist pig was beyond rude."

"I completely agree, but maybe he was trying to goad you into doing something you would regret so he would have a good reason to deny admission. Did you think of that? In the future, don't take the bait. You know that some authorities here would just love an excuse for a good fight. Admit it, so would you—resist the temptation!"

Marissa finally flashed her famous smile. "Did you get us a sports car to run around in?"

"As a matter of fact, I did," grinned Art as he steered her toward a "stormy blue" Mazda Miata ragtop. "Yes, we will put the top down for the drive south, so you can let your jet-back hair blow in the breeze.

I hope you packed all sorts of fun-in-the-sun outfits along with your work duds."

"Oh yes, not to mention the bikini," said Marissa as she wiggled her eyebrows and winked at Art, who promptly blushed.

"What would my Momma say?!" replied Art in mock horror.

"It's about time!" And Art and Marissa both laughed as they loaded her gear into the trunk.

"Remind me to tell you about the recent prophecy that there's going to be an earthquake in southern Greece," said Art cheerfully.

Marissa's mouth fell open, but what came out was "Whaaat!? You said 'fun-in-the-sun.' I was already having my own visions of an idyllic time! We had more than enough doom and gloom during last year's dig at Hierapolis."

"Right—let's think good thoughts. No secret chambers. No underground gas pit. No skeletons. Let's just imagine a quiet, above ground, stable time of digging, relaxing, more digging, eating, more eating . . . " said Art with a Cheshire cat smile.

Standing on a little knoll overlooking the parking lot was a swarthy looking man with a pair of small binoculars, focusing right on the kissing couple who were quite oblivious to his presence. When he saw they were headed for their car, he hopped into his small black sedan and revved the engine. He didn't intend to let them out of his sight.

11

Go East, Young Man

Promptly following his UNC–Chapel Hill graduation, Arthur West, BA, packed up all his belongings, carted them back to Charlotte in an already old station wagon, and set out to fully enjoy his graduation present—an all-expenses-paid, two-week trip to Greece courtesy of his mom and dad, who had saved their pennies for a long time. Art's father was an accountant with NCNB in downtown Charlotte and his mother a piano teacher; their resources were not vast. Art's dad expected him to get an MBA, but Art chose a very different path, namely, pursuing an MDiv in New England. His college Bible professor, Dr. Bernard Boyd, instilled in Art a great love of archaeology, especially at New Testament sites. Working every summer to pay his tuition meant never joining a summer dig. And without the now taken-for-granted Internet, it was a lot of work to get news from the American School of Archaeology in Athens. The Biblical Archaeology Society, founded in 1974, was his best source of news with its bimonthly publication of *Bibilical Archaeology Review* (*BAR*). Ironically, Art was now one of *BAR*'s best sources!

So it was on that very first trip to Greece that Art met not only Charles Williams, who was then in charge of the dig at Corinth, but also a colorful character named Spiros Spandexikos. Spiros was a man of many parts, most of them portly. He was built something like a bowling ball, though his friends preferred to call him "the cannon ball" because of his love for jumping off high diving boards in the cannon ball mode. Spiros was, among other things: 1) a world-class bouzouki player, famous in all the clubs in Athens for his drinking and chain-smoking; 2) a gossip columnist for an Athenian underground paper, *The Owl*; 3) a member of the Greek communist party, though in 1977 and thereafter this was kept very quiet; 4) an ardent Greek nationalist; 5) a former Olympic athlete in the hammer throw; 6) an employee of the Greek government; and finally 7) a famous lothario, or as he preferred to call himself, a lady-killer.

Williams himself introduced Art to Spiros in the Athens Museum. Spiros's alarms sounded immediately when he discovered that Art was a conservative Protestant American who seemed to believe that the archaeology being done in the Christian sites in Greece confirmed the truth of the Bible. Imagine that! Spiros did not like the Christian heritage in Greece, never mind the Greek Orthodox Church, and he certainly did not like the notion of archaeology supporting Christianity. He had made it his mission to block Christian artifacts from being displayed in the National Archaeological Museum. He saw himself as the protector of the ancient, pure Greek heritage. The initial encounter with Spiros left quite the impression on the impressionable newcomer, Art West.

Art was only twenty-two at the time and Spiros twenty-eight, but Art was negatively impressed with this brash but miniature figure of a man. What he did not know then, or later, was that Spiros was perhaps the most famous of all the communists in Greece who did not hold some official party office. Rather, Spiros was their spy, their source of insider information, their watchdog. Some of that inside information would lace Spiros's gossip columns, where he did his best to subtly undermine persons he did not like, i.e., those who opposed communism in Greece. He loved to tell stories of philandering wealthy Greeks, capitalistic entrepreneurs ripping off the Greek government, or Christians just behaving badly. He especially loved to dish the dirt on Americans in general.

Young Art West had not thought much about his brief encounter with Spiros, though it alerted him to the fact that there were those in Greece who did not like Christianity and its influence. He knew this because Spiros had taken him to a back room in the museum to show him the various statues of phallic symbols. He railed against the censorship imposed by the Greek Orthodox Patriarch when it came to the public display of such items. "Narrow-minded Christian meddlers" is what Spiros called people like the Patriarch. Art left realizing that there were all sorts of political and ethical points of view in Greece.

It was with some surprise then, when Art arrived in Greece this very spring, that he learned from the newspaper that Spiros Spandexikos was now high in the ranks of the Ministry of Culture. His position allowed him to oversee many of the national museums and archaeological sites. Spiros had objected to giving Art West a permit to dig, but he was overruled when the Patriarch interceded with Spiros's boss, Petros Thanatopsis. This caused a large bruise on his oversized ego. So it was that Spiros was determined to have Doc West watched during his whole stay, and this determination was reinforced when one of his fellow communists from Corinth, Nikos Alexandros, sounded the alarm that a Christian was digging at the ancient site. Spiros would bide his time, and if the opportunity presented itself he would attempt damage control through his gossip column.

At this particular moment, Spiros was sitting at his desk, sneaking a little retsina, the Greek milky-colored, pine tar alcohol, and looking at the photo that had been e-mailed to him by Nick from the airport along with the brief message, "Check this out." It showed Art West kissing an olive-skinned woman who had just come through passport control. Who was this woman, and what was her relationship to West? Spiros's senses were tingling and he had an inclination that this might be important. His first call would be to passport control to get a name. Hopefully, the Internet would reveal plenty more about the dark-haired lady.

12

The Gerasene Fanatics

THE ANCIENT CITY OF Gerasa, modern-day Jerash, in modern-day Jordan, is certainly one of the most important tourist attractions in all of Jordan, second only to the wildly popular site of Petra. Just a little over thirty miles north of Amman, the capital city, nestled in the Gilead Mountains, Gerasa boasts impressive ruins from the Greco-Roman era, not least because large portions of the old agora, forum, and colonnaded streets have been carefully preserved and restored. Here, if anywhere, one can get a clear visual image of what a Greco-Roman city from the New Testament era would have looked like.

Gerasa began its history in the fourth century BC as none other than Alexander the Great himself developed the site into a massive city. By the time of Jesus, Gerasa was one of the ten cities of the Decapolis, the ten cities near the far-eastern border of the Roman Empire. It is unlikely that Jesus ever visited Gerasa itself. However, the district of Gerasa seems to have extended from the city to the eastern shores of the Sea of Galilee. Thus, when the fifth chapter of Mark's Gospel refers to a visit by Jesus to the region of Gerasa and an encounter with a Gerasene (Gadarene) demoniac, it is this eastern region that the author had in mind.

Today more than the usual number of tourists were plentifully scattered among the ruins. It is festival time, a two-week Jordanian cultural extravaganza! Kahlil el Said and his daughter Hannah had joined the excitement by watching the afternoon Roman Army and Chariot Experience (RACE) at the hippodrome. Legionaires in full armor proudly re-enacted Roman army drills and battle tactics. Gladiators dazzled the crowds by heroically fighting "to the death." Hannah especially was awed by the Roman chariots competing in a seven-lap race around the hippodrome—the reality of it all played in her mind, convincing her for a time that she really was in the first century. And she realized it was no place for the weak-hearted.

Now, strolling down the colonnaded street in the center of this immense archaeological site while holding a little guide book, Kahlil el Said, antiquities dealer and retired millionaire, was fulfilling a life-long dream to see the archaeological sites in Jordan. Hannah, who now ran their antiquities shop in Jerusalem by herself, was still reliving the chariot race in her mind.

"Can you believe this street? I feel like we have walked right into the past. Look! There goes a Roman gladiator on the way to the arena," marveled Kahlil. "And that theater we visited earlier—imagine an orator standing on the rostrum announcing that a new play by Aristophanes was about to begin. Come to think of it, I believe there is a play listed for tomorrow evening! So much to do here during festival!"

"Art was right," replied Hannah rather dreamily. "Gerasa is a wonder and well worth the visit. According to our guidebook this city was favored by Pompey in 63 BC when he named it one of the ten great cities of the Decapolis. It received all sorts of imperial patronage after that time, which explains some of these impressive buildings."

"What it doesn't explain are those parachutes landing in the forum back there!" said a bedazzled Kahlil.

"Father, we came deliberately during the annual festival just to see all sorts of entertaining things. But I must admit, the ancient residents never saw a parachute! Remember, tonight we will see King Abdullah and his wife Queen Rania," replied Hannah excitedly.

"I well remember the intrigue there—Abdullah was appointed heir only on King Hussein's deathbed. His brother, Hassan, as Crown Prince was supposed to take over despite being the younger brother! Some things about court life never change it seems."

Hannah countered. "But how different the modern world is from the ancient world, where it was believed that a religion could only be true if it was ancient, or a family could only be royal if it had a long noble genealogy. Three of King Hussein's four wives were foreign-born, I believe. I remember when the former Queen Noor, an American no less, converted to Islam upon marriage."

"The more I study the ancients and their world, the more respect I have for them," said Kahlil. "They had enormous skill and artisanship, much of which we have lost, it would seem. And it gives the lie to the idea that the latest is the greatest and the newest is the best. I could stay here for weeks and become a real fanatic! But for now, I am feeling something else familiar and ancient as well—hunger! It's time to go find a good Jordanian restaurant. I like modern Jerash. Most of the people are Muslims like us, but many Christians now live there I am told. Art might like living in this town, but you say he is in Greece."

"I thought you were so busy consuming all the sites that you had forgotten food altogether," teased Hannah.

"Not a chance, not a chance. My nose is leading us back over the bridge to downtown Jerash towards some kebabs. Let's find a great buffet." And with that, Kahlil's love for things ancient lost out to things recently cooked over an open spit.

The battle plan was to spend three days and nights in Jerash during the festival, which transforms the city into one of the most lively and spectacular cultural centers in the world for two whole weeks. In truth, commerce, art, and culture have blended perfectly in this city for over two thousand years. However, in 1981, then Queen Noor Al-Hussein inaugurated the festival to showcase Jordanian artists, dancers, orators, actors, artisans, and musicians. By day, skilled craftsmen and women demonstrate the making of rugs, jewelry, ceramics, embroidered clothes, scarves, and other wares in glass, metal, and wood. For two weeks, there is no darkness—floodlights brilliantly illuminate the colonnades, plazas, temples, churches—in fact every square inch of the site becomes an exciting meeting place for artists and the public from the four corners of the world.

If they didn't succumb to extending their stay, Kahlil and Hannah planned to drive south to Mt. Nebo and Medeba on the way to Petra. Kahlil and his daughter were enjoying the freedom financial independence had brought them, obtained by the sale of what was now the most famous menorah in the world.[1]

---

1. A story told in the third Art West adventure, *Papias and the Mysterious Menorah.*

$$13$$

True Confessions

After lunch in the Plaka and a short stop at the museum, Art and Marissa realized they needed to head to Corinth. Marissa seemed a bit distant all afternoon, but Art chalked it up to being apart for so long and needing time to get back into familiar territory. But as they wound their way out of Athens and into the countryside, Art could see that something was indeed bothering Marissa, but he could not figure out what it was. Rather than let her stew any longer, he decided to gingerly open a conversation. "So, honey, what is causing you to look like you just bit into a rotten apple? Trouble at work, trouble with your family?"

"Am I that transparent?" she asked with worry in her voice.

"Given the beautiful scenery all around us, now that we are out of the Athens traffic, and the fact that we are finally together, you should be all bubbly! But all I see is worry written on your face. Now you may have noticed that I'm not heading directly to the canal just yet. In fact, we are heading to a special spot by the sea—the exact destination will remain a secret for now. Meanwhile, can I bribe you with a drachma for your thoughts?"

"This is hard Art, because I care so much about your opinion of me, so let me start by saying, I have done some stupid things in my life."

"Welcome to the club. As the T-shirt says, 'Christian under construction,'" reminded Art pursing his lips.

"No, you don't understand. I'm not talking about merely making a mistake like telling a lie. I am talking about a decision that cost someone's life," said Marissa with emotion in her voice.

Art noticed the tears starting to roll down her cheeks, and so he realized he needed to be very careful. Something very painful was on his fiancée's mind. "I'm going to pull into that rest area overlooking the valley. Right now, you deserve my undivided attention," promised Art as he steered into the deserted parking area.

For awhile they sat in silence as she looked out over the sheep pastures. Finally, she continued. "When I started my PhD at Bilkent University in Ankara I was a pretty liberated lady, fresh from college in Izmir, and pretty wild as well. Bilkent was opened in 1984—all new and shiny—with a growing archaeology department. Students were coming from their own schools all over the world to take courses, work at digs, and just enjoy field trips. It was all cutting edge, as you say. I sort of put my fledgling Christianity on hold and was enjoying the party life. And there was plenty of it even in this Muslim country."

"You are not telling me anything surprising. Carolina was the same way. I was just too much of a bookworm to be much of a party animal," claimed Art.

"But what I did at college and what you did cannot be compared in at least one respect." There was a long pause, and then Marissa quietly said, "I became pregnant. I panicked because I knew my career as a woman in archaeology would be over. So I went and had an abortion." All this was stated rather matter-of-factly at this point, but Marissa's mind was reliving events that occurred nearly twenty years ago.

Art's mouth opened, but no words came out for the longest time. But then it was his turn to weep. "No, Marissa, tell me you didn't do that to your unborn child!" Art said in barely a whisper.

"That is what I did, not quite twenty years ago now, and I have lived with the vivid memories ever since. At first I was sure I would never tell anyone—not even you. But my conscience kept telling me that we must be totally honest with each other. And now I've lived with the fear of how you will react. To tell or not to tell—either choice is a terrible burden."

The day was beautiful and the breeze was blowing through Marissa's hair, but suddenly Art could hardly look at her. It was hard to tell who was in more pain at the moment, Marissa or Art. Still staring into the distance, Art quietly said, "Marissa, it is not for me to judge you. Seek forgiveness from the Lord."

"Many times have I prayed and asked for forgiveness, and yet, still to this day, I feel guilty. I wish it had never happened. I wish I could take it back, but there is no going back."

"I agree," said Art. "So the question is, how to go forward? Marissa this *does* surprise me, and I will be honest, it hurts pretty bad. So I am sure that Jesus' word to both of us is 'neither do I condemn you—go and sin no more.' Did the procedure go well? Are you physically okay?"

"The doctors say that I am fine, although I have often wondered whether or not I can ever have children. There's really no medical reason why I couldn't. Women my age are having children even in their forties." Marissa took a deep breath and tentatively said, "This sort of opens up uncharted territory for you and me, doesn't it?"

All these revelations were a bit too much for Art to take in all at once. "Marissa, at this point I know you will enjoy my planned detour," said Art suddenly as he put the Miata in gear again and headed down the road.

"Where are we going?" Marissa asked with some concern.

"Check your map. We are heading south and east, not west, toward the Aegean, home of Neptune. Should I give you any more clues?"

Marissa began to smile. "I'll wait until we get there and then tell you if I'm right."

"If you are right, then we should end up at one of my favorite meditation spots." And as the sun began to set, the emotion-filled couple drove to Sounion at the southernmost tip of the Attica Peninsula to the Temple of Poseidon. They parked the car and sat down together on a bench to watch the sun go down. Sometimes the beauty of one's surroundings can overcome the sadness in one's heart.

The sound of the ocean waves of the Aegean crashing against the rocks below was clear and insistent. And the couple sitting on the bench was taking in the beauty of it all in complete silence, holding hands. Art finally broke what seemed like an eternity of silence and said, "Let's pray for a moment, before we talk. Heavenly Father, you are the author and giver of every good gift, including the gift of life. But now we come before you because of the taking of a human life that you had begun in Marissa. Lord, my heart is aching over this, even though it happened so many years ago, and I don't want to make any decisions abruptly like a shot fired in anger or pain. Marissa has borne already the guilt for this act for many years, and still without release even though she has asked your forgiveness, so Lord, I ask now that you give us a strong sense of that forgiveness here and now. Forgive me for being tempted to judge, and forgive her for what she has done. Lord I don't want this to become a wedge that drives us apart, so help me overcome my emotional reaction to this news." At this juncture Marissa interrupted.

"And Lord please help me stop making fear-based decisions in my life, afraid of what might happen, when I know I can't control the future anyway. I love Art, and do not want to disappoint him ever again if I can help it. Help me to be a better Christian."

"Me too," echoed Art, "And Lord I would ask you to go on blessing this relationship and lead us in the paths of righteousness for your sake. Amen."

"Amen!" dittoed Marissa with emphasis.

No words seemed necessary after that, so Art and Marissa just sat quietly for a while. In the distance a ferry could be seen coming from Paros towards the mainland, packed with tourists and commuters. The boat seemed to float along as if by magic—Art and Marissa were too far away to hear the hum of the motor. The light played on the waves, which seemed to be receding at this time of the evening, or at least landing on shore with less force. Somewhere a horn from a tug boat could be heard, likely guiding or pushing a tanker. The couple, mesmerized by the beauty of all they saw, snuggled, took deep breaths, and let their cares roll away.

"And as the sun sets slowly in the west, we are happy it is not setting on the relationship of West and Okur," said Art trying to lighten the mood a bit. And with that they kissed again confident that no one else was around at this hour to watch. But in fact, discretely around the corner was a little black sedan waiting rather impatiently for the couple to hop in their car and head south to Corinth.

Art suddenly jumped up from the park bench and said, "Marissa, we need to get ourselves down to Corinth for a very late supper. My housekeeper, the formidable Mrs. Demetrios, will be waiting on the doorstep. I suspect she will set herself up as chaperone as well."

The Mazda roared into life, and the couple headed back to the main highway, oblivious to the fact they were being trailed over the canal and all the way into Corinth.

14

In The NBA without An MBA

JAKE "THE CAT" ARAFAT was collecting names. He was born Ishmael, took the name Yakov at his baptism, which became Jacob or just Jake for the Americans, and now sports commentators were calling him "Koby" since Yakov was often abbreviated as Koby by the Jews and since his game resembled that of Kobe Bryant. And to complicate things further, one writer for the *Charlotte Observer* had taken to calling him "Koby B" as opposed to "Kobe A." By whatever name, Jake was struggling with his finances despite having Michael Jordan's own agent as his financial advisor. Jake was only slowly learning about the world of high finance. Everyone said money must be invested—but in what exactly? Unfortunately, Jake was discovering that his money was being invested in things he didn't believe in, things he found morally unacceptable. He certainly didn't want to offend Michael, so Jake found himself in a real quandary.

Munching on a cinnamon raisin bagel with cream cheese while sitting with Aunt Joyce at the breakfast table, Jake was mulling over his options.

"On the one hand, I do not want to offend the man who gave me my chance to be an NBA player and who has been my idol since I began to play basketball. But on the other hand, I think I need a Christian agent. What do you think?"

"How we spend our money reflects our core values, and hopefully our Christian values. What concerns you most about your investment portfolio?"

"Well, for one thing I am invested in companies that promote gambling, casinos, and probably prostitution. I am invested in whiskey and bourbon. I am invested in military weapons and companies that make rocket launchers. I am not happy about this but I don't know what to do. I mean on the one hand, there are lots of Christians who drink, work for the military-industrial complex, and even gamble for fun—does bingo count? Only prostitution seems like a clear-cut thing to avoid on the list, but I am not comfortable with supporting these other things in a big way. In short, I am also not comfortable with making money off of people's vices, much less their misery."

"Good for you!" said Joyce, and she thumped her hand down on the table. "I like the way St. Paul put it: 'Whatever is not of faith, is sin.' So whatever you can't do in good faith, you shouldn't do. Now apply that to your investments!"

"That helps," said Jake, with relief on his face. "But how do I tell my broker this? Do I just go to him and tell him I want to change my portfolio? I have some ideas. Maybe I can invest in 'green energy' companies or Christian businesses."

"Sure, why not? It's your money, Jacob. And you're responsible for how you spend it. So why don't we have a prayer, then you can call your adviser, and simply tell him you want a meeting to make some changes in your portfolio. The only difficult bit might come when he advises you against abandoning some of those bad investments, in which case, you tell him that it's a matter of principle for you. He should respect that at least. If he doesn't, then you'll have to think about getting another financial adviser. But I'm betting in this economy it won't come to that. He won't want to lose a star client like you."

"Which reminds me, I'm starting to get calls asking me to support local products. One thing's for sure: I won't ever be sponsoring Nike! That gig has belonged to Michael since 1984. Even I wear Air Jordans! Michael was one of the first professional athletes to be endorsed by sponsors. Imagine! He makes more money from sponsoring products than he ever did from shooting hoops! In the locker room, the players talk about TV commercials, print ads, website endorsements, voiceovers, radio spots, infomercials. I don't know what half of that stuff is," moaned Jake.

"All the more reason you need to talk to the right people before making any decisions. Otherwise, you'll be a lamb sent to the slaughter for sure!" said Joyce emphatically.

"And speaking of slaughter," continued Jake as he unleashed yet another idea floating around in his head, "I could get creamed on the court. I can't play ball forever. Then where will I be? We don't exactly have a good retirement plan. Some of the guys want big salaries so they can save the cash for a rainy day. For others, it's obvious they just want the big bucks to squander on bling. How much is enough? How much is too much? If I make more, I could donate more to the Bethlehem Center and Art's work and so many other good things. But I don't want to be greedy—that's just not Christian."

"Whoa," cried Joyce. "How long have you kept all this pent up in your brain. Some of these ideas are way beyond my simple understanding of 'save your pennies.' I lived through the Depression and can remember what a spool of thread cost—and I saved up for even that. I know I'm out of touch with the world of high finance."

"And I hear too much about money in the locker room. I just want to play ball. But all I hear is the commercial side—celebrity, product, image. Like I said, it's a new ball game," said Jake calmly, finally running out of steam.

Joyce quietly suggested, "Let's talk to Dr. Howell and see if any of the committed Christian business folks at Myers Park can help with some of these really deep financial subjects."

Jake brightened up and said, "Aunt Joyce, you're the best. Where would I be without you," he said laughing.

"Probably still in bed since I woke you up with the vacuum cleaner," said Joyce.

15

The Corinth of St. Paul

B Y THE TIME PAUL arrived in Corinth sometime around AD 50 it had become a crucial and powerful city in the Roman Empire. Made a Roman colony city where soldiers were mustered out and settled, the city was set up to run according to Roman jurisprudence, and the laws favored those who were Roman citizens. It's no accident that Paul, a Roman citizen himself, chose this city as a place to stay and invest considerable time for the sake of the gospel. Here he had instant clout and credibility as a well-educated and articulate Roman citizen who knew the Greek language and understood its culture. By the mid-first century AD, Corinth was well on the way to being the wealthiest and most prosperous city in all of Greece. After all, it had the best of all patrons—the Roman ruler himself.

With its two port cities, facing east and west, Corinth was the ultimate crossroads town. Here was the place that slave traders would offload their cargo—Jews, Scythians, Egyptians, Ethiopians, and "barbarians"—to be sold as field laborers, domestic slaves, and even tutors for children of the wealthy. Here was the place where sailors made port and found entertainment and sexual pleasure. Here commercial competition was a cutthroat way of life. The Roman poet Horace is quoted as saying, *non licet omnibus adire Corinthum*—"not everyone is able to go to Corinth." On the upside, people also came for healing at the temple of Asclepius or for answers to life's difficult questions by consulting an oracle or prophet or priest at the ancient temple of Apollo, the god of prophecy. Here people came every other year for the Isthmian Games, the second most popular games in all of Greece after the games at Olympia. And for some of the same reasons, here is where Paul chose to lodge himself for over two years.

Paul was a leather worker, a trade he learned from his family. Jews, unlike patrician Romans, had no problems with the idea of working with their hands. They saw such work as noble and necessary. Paul, though born in Cilicia (now part of southeastern Turkey), grew up in Jerusalem. His family worked with *cilicium*, or goats-hair cloth, and hides to make tents and leather goods. A tentmaker and leatherworker would be much in demand in Corinth, especially during the games, when people needed to rent tents to stay for the celebrations. Thus it was that Paul was able to practice his trade in the old city, to make friends and converts in the process, and to establish a Christian presence there with the help of one couple named Priscilla and Aquila, who practiced the same trade. Corinth's artisans had a reputation for producing high-quality work, especially in bronze. Paul was able to plug into that market when he arrived. It may well be that the way Paul met Priscilla and Aquila was through the guild of leatherworkers in Corinth.

One of the myths that Art West in his scholarly work had long sought to dispel is the idea that the Christian church was largely composed of illiterate women, children, slaves, and a few male plebes. The New Testament attests that at least the leadership of the Christian church by the middle of the first century was literate, something one could only say of perhaps fifteen percent of the general populous. Many were multilingual and some were of notably high status.

Art was particularly interested in Erastus, an aedile of Corinth during the time that Paul was there. In front of the theater built in the first century is an inscription that Erastus placed there in his own honor. Why? Because he laid the stones in the area in front of the theater as a "liturgy," a public service to the city, but also so he could obtain the office of aedile.

The inscription reads, "Erastus for the office of aedile paved this place." The aediles were responsible for maintenance of public buildings, regulation of public festivals, and even enforcement of public order. It is highly likely that this same Erastus is referred to by Paul in AD 57 when he writes to the Roman Christians: "Erastus, the city's director of public works and our brother Quartus send you their greetings" (Rom 16:24). There were indeed high-status Christians who were some of the leaders of the early Christian movement in Corinth and elsewhere. One can readily imagine Paul sitting in his shop when Erastus came to collect the rent, an encounter that may have led to more than the city official had counted on, namely, a change in religion.

Art West had long wished to find evidence of high-status Christians in Corinth, other than the famous Erastus inscription. At a minimum he figured digging an ancient villa like the one he had been licensed to uncover more fully could help fill out our picture of what a house church setting might entail, and thus what early Christian worship might have looked like. All this Art had been sharing with Marissa during the last hour of their trip to Corinth.

"You see Marissa, it was not so easy to dismiss Christianity as a 'superstition' of the illiterate and ignorant if there were high-status, well-educated Christians and even some Roman citizens like Paul and

Erastus. One of my goals is to provide further evidence about the literate leadership who produced what we call the New Testament."

"So, you think Corinth is a prime spot for finding rich Christians," said Marissa succinctly.

"I really do. And I'm very excited about our dig this summer," smiled Art as they crossed the bridge over the Corinth Canal.

"It always surprises me how long it took to finally build a canal here in the late 1800s. I'm trying to remind myself that this canal just didn't exist in the first century. Imagine ancient ships sailing the extra 250 miles around the peninsula to get from the Aegean to the Adriatic and vice versa. And just look at this narrow canal. Really big ships can't possibly squeeze through. It might be fun to take the four-mile trip in a small tourist boat, though. Even our Turkish newspapers report the occasional tremor and rockslide. This thing needs an overhaul!" exclaimed Marissa.

The little blue Miata was bumping along the cobblestone streets of Old Corinth heading up the hill towards the house of Mrs. Demetrios, which stood next to the even smaller house that Art had rented. Teens were still playing basketball under the street lamps in a small court nearby. Basketball is enormously popular in Greece, second only to soccer. And as Art pulled into a little dirt driveway, Mrs. Demetrios appeared instantly.

"Is about time you get here. I have warm special dinner waiting too long!"

"Sorry, Poseidon sidetracked us along the way," claimed Art. Just as quickly, Marissa was introduced to her new landlady.

After dinner, Marissa, now exhausted as much by the emotions of the day as the travel, excused herself to unpack and go to bed. Art savored the last bites of his honey-dripped dessert, walked to his own cottage next door, sat down at the computer, and began writing again. Hopefully, creative writing would take his mind off the day's revelations.

16

Once Upon A Time II

*T*HE FIRST TWO MONTHS *in Corinth went well, and when spring turned to summer Paul had become a fixture in Aquila's shop. Plus, he was now the talk of the Jewish community with his preaching and teaching in the "synagogue of the Hebrews." Paul quickly learned that Aquila and Priscilla converted in the forties to the new Jewish sect called "The Way" when they lived in Rome. Priscilla was a freedwoman in the Priscillan gens or family, and one of the first high-status converts to the new faith. Literate, industrious, friendly, articulate, Priscilla was well liked. She had learned much from her patrician mistress Domitilla, whom she served for some years until she was freed to have a legal marriage to her fellow Jew, Aquila.*

Several of the prominent synagogue members had been won over by Paul. Stephanus had even been baptized. However, while the synagogue leaders had been initially quite receptive to Paul's reading of the scriptures, conflict arose over his new message about a Jew from Nazareth being the Messiah. Most of them could not swallow the notion of a crucified Messiah and so the arguments had become heated.

By the time Silas and Timothy arrived in Corinth, the situation had become intense, not only because of Paul's insistent message about a Christ crucified, but also because Paul had actually won over several prominent Jewish leaders. The day finally came when the Jews opposed Paul so strongly and became so abusive that Paul shook out his clothes in protest and said to them in a stern voice, "Your blood be on your own heads! I am clear of my responsibility. From now on I will go to the Gentiles."

If that were not enough, Paul left the synagogue and went next door to the house of Titius Justus, a worshiper of God. There, Crispus, the synagogue ruler, and his entire household were persuaded to believe in the Nazarene as the Messiah. Daily, many other Corinthians believed and were baptized. But this created more, not less, furor and Paul began to receive threats on his life. He seriously wondered if he should leave Corinth, at least for a while. However, one night the Lord spoke to Paul in a vision: "Do not be afraid; keep on speaking; do not be silent. For I am with you, and no one is going to attack and harm you, because I have many people in this city." So Paul resolved to stay, with the help and support of people like Priscilla, Aquila, Titus Justus, Stephanus, and Crispus. In fact, as things turned out, he would stay in Corinth for eighteen months, despite the opposition. He enjoyed increasing support, especially from a high-status convert—Erastus, the city official!

On this morning Paul was chatting with Erastus: "So you say that being an aedile is not all it's cracked up to me. People don't like tax collectors, and the public works projects always involve more dilemmas than is apparent at the outset."

"You are so right Paul, but if I had not come to your shop to collect the rent from Priscilla and Aquila, I might never have met you, or more importantly, learned of the Savior of the world. I don't mind telling you that your preaching has made my job more difficult. Now I have to ask myself awkward ethical questions about how much money to take from this person or that person. You know very well that as city treasurer I am given something of a cart blanche when it comes to collecting money. As long as I collect the fees I agreed in advance to pay into the town treasury, I am allowed to take as much as I like beyond that for myself. Somehow, that doesn't seem right or fair any more. Now my calculations are more difficult."

"Well," said Paul smiling, "Jesus never said it would be easy to handle money as his follower, and he did say render unto Caesar what is Caesar's, but at the same time Jesus said a workman is worthy of his hire, so you must figure out what a fair wage would be for the amount of effort and hours you put into your job."

"What a novel idea, linking the number of hours I work to how much I remunerate myself, rather than just bilking people according to my own

wants and needs. Salvation may be free initially, but I can tell you, it keeps costing me at the bank!" And on that note the two new friends both had a good laugh.

17

"The Game's Afoot"

IN BASKETBALL, FEET ARE everything. If you can't jump, you are not likely to play in the NBA unless of course you are 7′ 5″ or thereabouts. Jake, or "Koby," Arafat was only 6′ 5″, but he could jump out of the gym, and so not surprisingly the kids at the Bethlehem Center loved seeing him dunk the ball. One time Jake jumped up and put a quarter on the top ledge of the backboard, and then from a standing start jumped up and took it back down. He had a forty-four-inch vertical leap. When Jake was around, the grapevine quickly brought the local teens who hung out in the neighborhood of the Bethlehem Center. Some even sauntered onto the court to challenge the Cat to a game of HORSE, a great way to show off trick shots. Most were at a distinct disadvantage since they wore baggy, way-too-low-slung jeans.

"Dude, I am taking you to the rack," boasted Jamaal as he eased his rapidly growing, tough frame onto the court. A good kid, he had so far escaped the lure of the gangs. Jake had been seeing him more often at the Center.

"Alright big man, bring it!" replied Jake. Jamaal also had some serious hops but when he tried to leap, Jake went up to block his shot, and the two collided in midair. Falling fast, Jake tried to jump sideways to avoid planting his feet on Jamaal's chest. With a yelp of pain Jake crumpled into a heap below the rim.

Jamaal jumped up, and stared down at the fallen hero. "You alright man?" asked a worried Jamaal. "I wasn't looking to send you to the injured reserve list."

With a grimace, Jake replied, "Help me up, Jamaal. I need to sit for a bit and see if my ankle swells up."

"Swell," echoed Jamaal, "Just when I was going to school you, you come up lame. That's lame, dude."

"No lie; it hurts bad," said Jake, at which point Jamaal stopped posturing and preening, and put his arm under Jake's shoulder and helped him hobble into the Center.

Across the way two members of the Kings were grinning. "Yo, did you see that? Don't be laying down any bets on the Cat and the Bobcats for a while. I'm thinking that brother is in for a few small repairs soon."

"Yeah, not good, cause we set up our betting racket based on him. He better get well soon, or there will be no dough from that source."

"For real. But there are other ways we could use him, maybe. You know that ole scam where you get someone to sign an autograph on blotter paper, and then you transfer it to something else. I was thinking we could at least sell some autographed basketballs and apparel outside the stadium down town."

"Sounds like a plan, but we need to wait until the next time he comes down here."

"Unless the team is travelin' he's here every Thursday about now."

"Yeah I noticed. Let's check back then."

"Righteous." And with that the "boys from the hood" sauntered off down Baltimore Avenue, one of them carrying a boom box with the latest Snoop Dog CD playing at top volume. Deep down they all knew they would never pull off that scam, but it made them feel tough just thinking about it.

Meanwhile, Jake's ankle was looking red and swollen, and Jamaal had run off to get a towel full of ice. Jake called the team doctor. His next stop would be the ER.

"Just great," said Jake. "And the playoffs start next Monday."

18

Corinth Times Four

GRADE SCHOOL WAS STILL in session in the village of Old Corinth, and Marissa awoke to the sound of children chatting while walking up the street to the local elementary school. Marissa sat up in bed and watched the parade through the lace curtains in her bedroom. Wearing little blue and white uniforms and tiny backpacks, they looked so cute and so much like school children of that age in her own native land. Marissa sighed when she thought about all the centuries of animosity between Greece and Turkey, and yet what mattered was that human beings are all loved by God. Why was it so hard for everyone to just get along?

Mrs. Demetrios was stirring a huge pot of hot porridge while the sweet smell of cinnamon rolls filled the air. Jumping out of bed and washing her face, Marissa put on her comfortable khakis for work at the dig this morning.

"Is time you got up! Planning on working only half a day today?" she scolded, and then winked at Marissa. She reminded Marissa of her own grandmother, the rock of her family for so many years.

"No, Mrs. Demetrios, I am not accustomed to being a lady of leisure, but thanks for letting me sleep in this first morning. I was worn out."

"Best knock on Dr. West's door; breakfast is ready."

"Good idea. I'll be right back." Walking up the hill only a few yards, Marissa opened a little gate, stepped one-by-one on the dozen long-embedded stones leading to the bright blue doorway, and was about to rap on the door when it opened of its own accord. There was her smiling fiancée, who gave her a quick kiss. "Good morning, sunshine," said Art. "You're looking fetching this morning."

"And what I'm fetching is you; it's time for breakfast! Mrs. Demetrios has been slaving over a hot stove for quite awhile."

Breakfast turned out to be a culinary adventure—stewed tomatoes, scrambled eggs with Greek olives, porridge, cinnamon rolls, and cherry juice to wash it all done. Neither Art nor Marissa were used to such a huge breakfast, but they knew enough to politely sample all that the little Greek woman had prepared.

"You two are not farmers! You eat like little birds. You need strength for day's work. What is day's work?"

"Marissa will begin to survey the site with the gadget I showed you. Then she will draw up a grid plan for the dig, to designate the most promising spots. Meanwhile, I am going to work on uncovering the villa floor that was discovered some seasons ago."

"Good. Is mosaic," said Mrs. Demetrios. "I remember when first discovered, my neighbors groaned because it meant digging up their garden between houses. Now they are happier since government paid them money. Most expensive tomato patch in Corinth, if you ask me."

Trying their best, Art and Marissa attempted to do justice to all the food Mrs. Demetrios had prepared, and finally Art patted his stomach and said, "I'm stuffed like those olives. Thank you so much for all the good food. This was a good hearty breakfast."

"Was needed. You two cannot live on romance alone."

Marissa just laughed and said, "You are so right. We should also tell you that we will have company this weekend—friends of ours from Israel."

"Is fine. Maybe we have picnic lunch outside."

"Don't go to any trouble, Mrs. Demetrios," replied Art. "We do want to take them to one of the fish restaurants down by the canal."

"Try Zorba's. Is always fresh fish."

"Will do." And with that Art and Marissa arose from the table. Marissa offered to help clean up, but Mrs. Demetrios shrugged her shoulders and told her to get busy at the site instead.

After picking up the sonar-like device and the shovels and trowels, Art and Marissa climbed up the dusty cobblestone street. Art was content. "It's nice to be able to stay in the village of Old Corinth and not have to commute from the big city of New Corinth. I would like to take you there, however. New Corinth is quite the modern seaport, complete with ships trading in olives, veggies, wine, and so on. Which reminds me; we need to revisit that prophecy I mentioned earlier! It's all about the earthquakes after all! New Corinth got its start after the 1858 quake destroyed Old Corinth, and it was rebuilt in 1928 after yet another big one. Maybe a third is on the way. But let's not worry about that now. We can survey the ancient Corinth site today and maybe drive up the Acrocorinth this weekend with Grace and Manny. From up there we can see everything!"

"One thing for sure," mused Marissa, "When you use the word Corinth, you better explain. So far I've counted four different spots that qualify as Corinth! That could be confusing to the locals, let alone the tourists! But the village is beautiful. Look at the flowers! Lots of capers are in bloom already, plus the cliff roses, and of course the ever-blooming bougainvillea, my very favorite flower, even if it is a Brazilian import!"

19

Food For Thought

MUNCHING AWAY ON HIS gyro stuffed with spiced lamb and a special cucumber sauce resembling tsatsiki, Spiros was just finishing up his latest blockbuster gossip column, dishing the dirt on a Greek movie star on drugs, and the philandering of a famous Greek playboy named Andros Andreos, and concluding with a rant against the downturn in the American economy caused by "greedy capitalistic pigs on Wall Street." That downturn hit the Greek economy hard, especially the tourist industry. Spiros fully expected to have a sympathetic audience for this column. He liked to think of himself as the champion of the ordinary person in Greece, the blue-collar worker who inevitably got the shaft when times were economically tight. Of course Spiros had made a career by capitalizing on other people's misery and making it must-read material in the Athens underground paper known simply as *The Owl* (*Ho Otos*), named after the companion bird of Athena.

As he put the finishing touches on his column, the fax machine across from his desk began making its usual squawks and odd noises. Pushing his portly frame back from the computer desk, he whirled his wheeled desk chair around to the fax machine and grabbed the page before it fell into the tray. It was a brief message from Nick, his contact in Corinth. "Turkish woman with Art West is Dr. Marissa Okur, archaeologist from Turkey. See attached picture from lecture event with West in Istanbul last year. Could she be the sister of Mehmet Okur, the basketball player?"

"Now this is interesting," said Spiros, licking his lips to get the sauce off them from his last bite of gyro. "We have an American and a Turk digging in Corinth. That scenario is begging for tabloid trouble. I'll just have to spend some time doing my own version of digging. I'm sure I can turn up a spadeful of dirt on those two."

Meanwhile, the smell of lamb cooking on an open grill was overwhelming as it wafted into the hotel room where Grace and Manny were staying right off the Isthmus of Corinth. They earlier opened the windows hoping for a sea breeze, but instead got a souvlaki breeze. It was nine o'clock already on a beautiful Saturday morning. They slept in late because they arrived late. Manny failed to get directions, took a wrong turn, and ended up in Nafplio. Grace was hopeless at navigating in her own country, never mind a foreign one. Despite this they managed to get to the charming seaside hotel called Poseidon's Pleasure before midnight.

"Let's have something to eat, and then we can wander over to the archaeological site," suggested Manny. "Art and Marissa shouldn't be too hard to find, and we can always resort to the cell phone."

"Sounds like a plan," replied Grace. Suddenly they heard a foghorn sounding loud enough to wake the dead as a small freighter was about to enter the narrow Corinth Canal. Scrambling to find their sandals, they walked down the lane to see the spectacle of a huge boat ever so slowly navigating its way through the man-made ravine.

"Do you know the story about Nero and the Isthmus?" asked Grace.

"Well, no. I've lived a deprived life when it comes to ancient history. That's why I have you along," said Manny, feeling pleased with himself.

"Nero was the one who first planned to dig the two-mile canal through the Isthmus, and they actually began the task but never finished it."

"Why not?" queried Manny, watching the gray and red freighter slowly squeeze itself through the seventy-foot-wide space.

"Because some priest told Nero that the waters of the Aegean on the east side were higher than the waters of the Adriatic on the west side. So, if he dug the canal without the blessing of Poseidon there would be massive flooding that would wash away the Isthmian Games being held in Corinth. Now Nero couldn't have that because he had just won the poetry prize there. That was the end of the canal digging until the nineteenth century."

"What a shock—Emperor wins his own poetry contest," added Manny sarcastically.

"Sad but true. Let's head for the café for a quick bite. At this rate we will get to Art's dig right about the time they are quitting for the day."

"As you wish!" Manny and Grace sauntered across the small street to the restaurant where fish, lamb, and all manner of other things were smoking or simmering on a grill. It was going to be a hot day, so they chose to sit in the shade under an awning near the canal where they could feel the breeze. There was something beguiling and calming about sitting and eating near the sea with the sea breeze in your face, and the Cohens enjoyed it immensely, but they knew they needed to get up to the archaeological site soon.

20

Riding The Pines

THERE IS HARDLY ANYTHING more frustrating for a good basketball player than being told to sit on the bench when he knows he can make a difference in the game. It is doubly frustrating when riding the pines is your own fault. Such was the plight of the glum "Koby" Arafat, who had a third-degree ankle sprain and was wearing a protective boot on his right foot. There would be no leaping and dunking for him for a little while. He was just fortunate he had not broken the ankle. The swelling had gone down, but when he first told Coach Brown what happened he got a stern lecture about not taking unnecessary risks, especially on the cusp of the Bobcats' first playoff appearance.

"It's bad enough that we have to play the Celtics in the first round of the playoffs, but it's even worse when our rookie-of-the-year guard injures himself when he wasn't even in a real game!" The frustration just oozed out of Coach Brown. And even worse was the cold shoulder he had gotten from some of his teammates with the unspoken message, "Stupid rookie!" Jake wanted to crawl under the bench, but Aunt Joyce reminded him that it wasn't the end of the world.

"Maybe your teammates will up their game in your absence."

"Maybe," said Jake. "But beating the Celtics is a tall order. We just have to win a couple now for me to get well enough to play at least one game down the road!" There was no consoling the inconsolable Mr. Arafat. So Aunt Joyce concentrated on feeding him some of his new-found favorite comfort food—barbecue, fried okra, and hush puppies.

The first playoff game ever in Bobcat Arena produced a sellout crowd, and an apprehensive bunch of Bobcats did not want to be embarrassed before the home crowd. They had already lost the first two games of the series in Boston, and so this game was crucial. They would have to play tight defense and maximize their offensive opportunities.

"We can do this!" shouted Raymond Felton, the likable point guard and graduate of the UNC 2005 championship basketball team. He found it difficult to play on a team that lost more games than it won, but this year, with the help of his backcourt teammate Jake the Cat, the team had earned a 42–40 record for the regular season. Raymond knew that Koby, as he called him, was not enjoying his bench seat. Jake, on the other hand, was determined to be the best bench-seat cheerleader he could be for his team.

The Bobcats got off to a good start largely due to the energetic play of Felton and Gerald Wallace. When the buzzer sounded after the first twelve minutes the score was 28–25 in favor of the Bobcats, but the Celtics hardly looked worried. They had been down this road before. Ray Allen had not even begun hurling three-pointers.

The second quarter involved some physical play, mostly on the part of the Celtics, who were trying to intimidate the young Bobcats. But it cost them: by half time, Paul Pierce, Ray Allen, and Shaquille O'Neill had all collected three fouls each. Meanwhile the Bobcats were making most of their free throws, so there was a glimmer of hope when the refs blew the halftime whistle and the score was still in favor of the Bobcats at 51–45.

The third quarter was a different story. The Celtics came out highly motivated, scoring the first ten points of the quarter and threatened to take a double-digit lead. But Pierce got his fifth foul while charging the lane, and the resulting free throws by Wallace cut the lead to five, where it remained until quarter's end.

The fourth quarter proved to be a surprise to everyone. The Celtics made bad passes, missed free throws, and in general gave away the game! The Bobcats held on to a three-point advantage to take their first playoff win ever.

"It's hard," explained Ray Felton in the postgame interview, "to establish a winning tradition when you've been the doormat of the league. But this is a giant first step, and it's good we have two days off before the fourth game with Boston. Who knows? Maybe Koby Cat will reappear and give us a hand. For now, I'm just happy we finally got a playoff win. As the big-ticket Kevin Garnett said after the Celtics won the championship a couple of years ago, 'Anything's possible!'"

21

Shake, Rattle and Roll

PHILIPPA AWOKE SUDDENLY BEFORE dawn on Saturday morning, her eyes wide open, with one word throbbing in her head—Σήμερα—TODAY! Like a beating drum the word Σήμερα just kept flashing before Philippa's eyes, over and over and over again. Getting dressed in a hurry and quickly drinking a cup of her morning coffee, she walked rapidly to the town square and assumed her special spot. Only the street sweeper kept her company. By seven thirty, however, as the shopkeepers drifted into the square, Philippa began to plead her case—a two-word message, repeated over and over. "TODAY—BEWARE!" The local police were called, but Philippa stood her ground, repeating the message again and again. She would not get down from the bench, and she would not be quiet.

Most of Greece sits in the middle of what has been called a seismic box, a quadrant of land surrounded by numerous fault lines, which in turn makes Greece, like Turkey, prone to numerous earthquakes. So prevalent are the minor earthquakes in Greece that many buildings, even homes, are built to withstand the stress of the smaller quakes. In addition, active volcanoes still exist. Many are watching the volcanic island of Nysiros in the Aegean, which has erupted at least thirteen times in recorded history. The most famous, however, is the volcano on Santorini. Its 1600 BC eruption probably gave rise to the legend of the lost city of Atlantis. Explaining all this tectonic excitement is the idea that the African plate is slowly flowing northeastward and diving under the Eurasian plate.

Earthquakes and volcanoes in Greece are tracked by the Greek Institute of Geodynamics and duly reported in the English-language Greek paper *Kathimerini*. Because most such quakes begin under the sea, the ancient Greeks attributed these events to Poseidon's wrath against some human folly or sin. Given the hundreds of reported quakes each year, both the locals and tourists seem to go on blithely ignoring the dangers. But on the very day Art and Marissa and Manny and Grace were about to explore the site at Corinth, something would happen in southern Greece that could not be ignored.

It was nearly noon by the time Manny and Grace headed towards the site of ancient Corinth. Art was up earlier than usual and spent the morning surveying the site, marking locations on his schematic for digging, taking notes about curious things seen through the viewing device, all the while singing to himself, "If I were a rich man . . ." Marissa helped Mrs. Demetrios with some Saturday morning chores, including grocery shopping, which she hoped would lead to a few Greek cooking lessons. The two roasted eggplants and then mashed them with olive oil, lemon juice, and seasonings to produce *melitzanosalata*, the Greek version of baba ghanoush. Today's picnic lunch feast would include flat bread (pita) with the eggplant dip, fresh tomatoes, and lots of Kalamatas, the dark, purple olives grown exclusively in Greece. Art's favorite cherry juice was chilled and ready when he sauntered over to the cottage. Marissa and Mrs. Demetrios had decorated a wooden table in front of the cottage with flowers and food. At about the very minute Art entered the door something strange happened—the tea cups in the little cupboard over the stove began rattling a bit, but this quickly stopped, and was quickly ignored when they heard a car horn honking nearby.

Art and Marissa were beginning to wonder where their friends were, when up the little cobblestone street came a bright yellow car with two tourists talking loudly. One was clearly saying, "I'm sure Art said it was a little street overlooking the ancient site. I just don't know which one!"

"You never know which one, darling, when it comes to directions" replied Manny with a devilish grin.

Art flagged down the Cohens, and directed them to park across the street in a dirt alley. Marissa and Mrs. Demetrios came out to meet the unlikely duo, and after greetings and introductions all around, all five sat down around the flower-and-food-filled table. The Cohens were too polite to tell Art and Marissa that they had in fact already had a late breakfast.

After the last coffee was poured and the conversation wound down, Art coaxed his charges up the hill. The tour was going well enough, with questions flowing freely from Grace and Manny. Just as Art finished showing them the lay of the land, the earth moved, shifted, buckled, and suddenly opened up beneath Grace! In a split second they were all on the ground, except Grace, who screamed and disappeared into a large crack in the earth, leaving behind only one red boat shoe!

The radio in Mrs. Demetrios' kitchen, where pots and pans were flying off the hooks on the wall, announced, "There has just been a sizable earthquake, 4.3 on the Richter scale, northwest of Kalamata off the west coast of the Peloponnese, less than one hundred miles from Corinth. Take cover immediately!" Fire alarms went off at the local school. Sirens blared as EMT squads responded to one call after another for help.

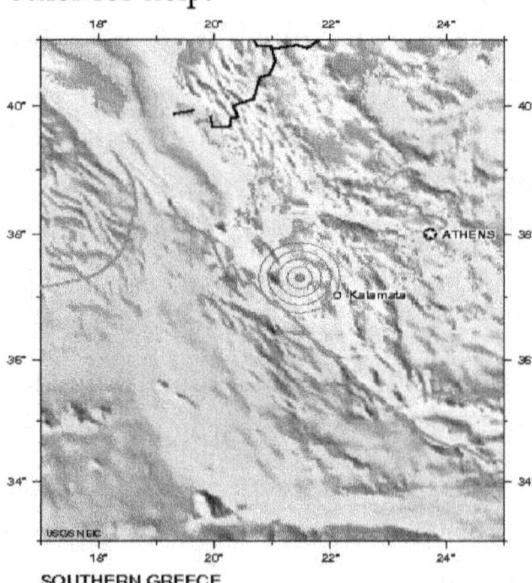

SOUTHERN GREECE

2009 05 07 15:31:48 UTC 37.31N 21.47E Depth: 66.7 km, Magnitude: 4.3
Earthquake Location

Trembling in fear, Mrs. Demetrios crawled out from under the table, kicked aside some errant pots, and bolted out her front door. Her first sight was a group of school children now standing in the road looking bewildered and covered with plaster dust. Some were whimpering, some crying, but some were screaming for their teacher.

Heading up the street, Mrs. Demetrios could hear, "Help! Call the police! Call an ambulance!"

22

The Rock Rolled

OUTSIDE OF ISRAEL, ONE of the top tourist destinations in the lands of the Bible is Petra, the ultimate rock city. Petra began as the sixth-century BC capital of the Nabataeans. Here the Spice Road passed through on the way north to Israel and Syria. Here Hellenistic rulers built elaborate burial vaults, temples, and shrines. The wise men may have passed through here on their way to Bethlehem.

Here may have been the place where Paul first tried out evangelism on non-Jews, for something must explain the fact that he went away into Arabia after his conversion. We hear the tale both in his letters and in Acts of how Paul escaped from King Aretas' henchmen in Damascus by being lowered in a basket over the city wall. What had so angered King Aretas that he had Paul trailed all the way back to Damascus? Likely it was Paul's attempts at evangelism within Aretas' kingdom.

But to most modern tourists who are biblically illiterate, Petra is the city of Indiana Jones fame, from the third and best of those movies, *Indiana Jones and the Last Crusade.* Hannah and Kahlil knew why Petra was famous then and now.

At this moment, Kahlil, Hannah, and their guide, Abdullah, were winding their way down the eastern entrance into the city though a narrow half-mile-long gorge called the *Siq* (shaft). Other tourists were being led on horses hired at the beginning of the passageway, but Kahlil wanted to savor the colors and formations of the natural sandstone that rose up over 250 feet on both sides. All of a sudden the ground moved, and Hannah looked up in time to see a boulder bouncing down from the sandstone wall. "Father, look out!" shouted Hannah as she pushed him out of the way of the incoming rock. The tremor was brief, but unsettling on many counts. One spooked packhorse galloped by without its rider.

Dusting himself off while being helped up by Abdullah, Kahlil asked excitedly, "What in the world was that? I know the signs read, 'See Rock City,' but I didn't notice any fine print saying 'and get stoned'!"

"We are all the time having little tremors. That was very small." For now, however, all thoughts of the minor quakes were put aside as they came out of the Siq and into the light of the canyon. Facing them was Al Khazneh, the so-called treasury, the most famous building in all of Petra.

"Abdullah, do you believe it was a treasury?" asked Hannah.

"No, but the Bedouins were convinced it must contain some treasure somewhere inside. Look up high and see the bullet holes in the rock carvings! People thought they could shoot holes in those structures and treasure would pour out. But those urn-like structures are solid."

Kahlil and Hannah were stunned by the sheer magnificence of Al Khazneh, carved out of solid rock of a pinkish-red color characteristic of Petra. At this point earthquakes would not keep them from seeing Petra, a World Heritage site, which actually extends some twenty miles into the ever-widening valley. Fortunately the main attractions are within walking distance—unless, of course, you prefer to ride. Hannah more than once turned her head only to find herself staring into the eyes of a camel. Finally, in exasperation she said to its persistent owner, "Get that camel out of my face!" After that Abdullah waved away the many camel venders seeking their business!

There were also small children, dark-skinned gypsies, hawking postcards and trinkets, flitting about like gnats. Kahlil and Hannah were well aware of their street-smart tactic—how young children are used as diversions while the teens steel wallets from back pockets. He and Hannah always carried their passports and money under their clothes. Sure enough, when he looked behind him two boys were planning their attack. Abdullah yelled, "Go away little urchins! Leave us alone."

"I must apologize to you," said Abdullah. "The venders are bad enough but the children just swarm about. There is good money to be made as a pickpocket; tourists need to be smarter these days. Let us move on to the amphitheater." As they rounded the bend, they saw the amphitheater, surrounded on three sides by rose-colored rock walls. The amphitheater was cut into the hillside and into several tombs during its construction by the Nabataeans around the time of Christ. The Romans later added rows after they conquered Petra in AD 106. In its heyday, it held up to four thousand people. Hannah found it hard to imagine sitting in a theater—surrounded by tombs!

Petra was one of those places that, when you got there, you realized you had booked far too little time in the local hotels to really see the place properly. It would take at least four or so days to do so! Nevertheless, Kahlil and Hannah were savoring every moment at the place in the valley known as the Rose City.

23

Walled-In on Wall Street

THERE IS PLENTY OF fear on Wall Street on any given day of the year, but when the stock market is tanking the pressure becomes enormous on stock brokers and others who deal in economic commodities subject to market fluctuations—stocks, bonds, gold, pensions, endowments, trust funds, 401Ks, to mention but a few. The brokerage firm of Gaines and Galloway (G&G) Investments had been feeling the heat for months, but the brave know that the market will eventually recover. G&G, however, had put too much "stock" in hedge funds and pyramid schemes, and the results had been nearly disastrous. Reassurance that the market would recover was all they could offer to their investors at the moment. The party line was to offer a rosy future to those who stayed the course with G&G.

Ben Grimes, a sharp young G&G accountant, was not convinced that the promises being made could ever be kept. A graduate of UNC with a Harvard MBA, Ben found his current job on Monster.com. Staring out his ninth-floor window at the Manhattan traffic below, he was trying to find the words to deal with the two clients now on the phone.

"No, Mr. Arafat, I am not saying that the million dollars Michael Jordan's agent invested through us has been irretrievably lost. I am saying that it's out there, but can't be recouped all at once. I understand that you want to invest in companies other than what has been the case with your portfolio thus far, but we can't make changes until we recoup your losses. Mrs. West, as for your pension funds, I am afraid that things are even more tenuous. You invested in American Bank shares, and their stock value is minimal at this point."

"And whose fault is that?" said a peeved Joyce West, who had little patience with people who played fast and loose with other people's money or investments. "My husband worked for that bank for decades and it had a sacred trust with people like us, which, so far as I can see, it has violated. It gave us this stock as part of our pension, and now, right when I most need the stock, it is virtually worthless. Is that what you are telling me son?"

"Well, in a manner of speaking, yes, Mrs. West. We live in hope that American Bank stock will recover with the market in general. There is no point in selling these stocks as low as their value is now. You simply must stay the course and be patient. And Mr. Arafat, my advice to you is the same. Once the market recovers and your portfolio is back to being more robust, we can make the changes you desire."

As if in unison, Jake and Joyce said, "I guess so." And Joyce added, "But we will be calling regularly. No funny business like using our money to pay off your own firm's bad debts. I expect you to be fiscally conservative and responsible with our money!"

Holding the phone out from his ear and adjusting his collar, Ben replied, "Yes ma'am, you can count on a Tar Heel like me to have your best interests at heart."

"I want the best interest on my money not just in your heart, though I appreciate the sentiments. We'll be calling back to check on our investments."

"I'll be happy to give you updates any time," assured Ben, all too glad to finish this difficult phone call. It had been this way all week. The more he learned about the questionable business practices of his firm, the more he got depressed. Shaking his head as he walked off to the water cooler, he muttered to himself, "What have I gotten myself into?"

24

Cracked Pots

ART WAS FLAT DOWN on the ground reaching into the large gaping hole and yelling, "Grace, we need to get you out of there! There could be more aftershocks. It's not safe down there—wherever you are. I'm just glad you didn't fall all the way to Hades!"

"Being the Christian you are, you wouldn't let that happen to me. All I did was get a little crack on the cranium. And speaking of cracked pots, I'm sitting on one! Reach way down. I'm handing up a piece of pottery." Stretching his arm as far as he could, Art drew up a rather large handle, a piece from an amphora, a jar meant to hold wine.

"This explains everything!" cried Art down to Grace. "You were obviously looking for the wine cellar of the villa—and you found it! Now give me your hand!"

"Come on Grace, you might have some broken bones or cut feet. One of your shoes is still up here! I'm going to throw it *at* you, if you don't let us hoist you out of that cellar," pleaded Manny.

"In a minute! I'm just doing a little shopping down here," explained Grace whose fall had indeed been broken by the now-broken amphora she was sitting on. Looking to her left what she saw caught her quite by surprise. A shaft of light entering the chamber was bouncing off a small glass object. "Here Art, grab this little perfume bottle. Don't you just love the greenish color of the glass? Too bad it's empty!" And Grace handed up a nearly priceless object.

"I can't believe Grace is thinking only about ancient perfume bottles at a time like this," said a somewhat befuddled Manny. Finally Grace stood up, tested her legs, felt a rising lump on her forehead, and held out her hands.

"You know I'm thinking that archaeology-by-earthquake is an underrated practice. Art, next time you dig, you ought to think about getting one of those big earth-shaking machines and see what happens when the ground opens up," said Grace, now standing beside the hole. Her dress and arms were covered with dirt, but otherwise she looked pretty good. "It's only appropriate that an egghead like me should have a goose egg on my head!" At this Grace broke out into an old Carole King song: "I feel the earth move, under my feet, I felt the sky tumbling down, tumbling down, and I just lose control . . ."

"Okay, that bump on the head has jarred you in more ways than one! I have *never* heard you sing before," said Manny as Art and Marissa stared at Grace.

"Well, Carole King is a nice Jewish girl just like me," assured Grace. And at that moment Mrs. Demetrios arrived huffing and puffing from running up the hill to the site.

"Everyone is safe?" she asked with an anxious look on her face.

Art turned to her and said, "Not to worry, Mrs. Demetrios. Apart from discovering a new candidate for American Idol, we are fine!" And with that they all marched slowly down the hill to the cottage, where cold compresses and colder cherry juice were administered as needed.

Grace and Marissa tidied up the cottages while Manny and Art headed off to the schoolhouse to see what could be done. Ambulances had come and gone, but the villagers were there cleaning. Pitching in, Manny and Art worked side by side, sorting through broken glass to salvage desks and chairs, chalk and pencils. Only a storage out-building had totally collapsed.

After dinner, Art extracted his special battery pack for his laptop since the power was not yet fully restored, and he resolved to do some more writing on his "Paul in Corinth" project.

25

Once Upon A Time III

*T*HE HOUSE CHURCH MEETINGS, *first in the home of Priscilla and Aquila, which quickly became too cramped a quarters, and then in the house of Erastus, who had an ample villa for such meetings, were lively. The Corinth converts included Jews and Greeks and even Romans, like Erastus. With a majority of the "assembly" being Gentiles, a new dimension had arisen in the worship times, namely the sharing of inspired messages from God, prophecy, and then interpretation of prophecy as well, not to mention the increasingly frequent speaking in tongues. Corinth had always been a city famous for its association with Apollos, the god who sponsored prophecy, including at Delphi up in the mountains. But there was a problem.*

The Gentile Christians all expected Christian prophecy to look much like pagan prophecy, and so there was an expectation that one could ask questions of the prophet before or after he or she prophesied. But this was not the way prophecy worked among members of The Way, the new Christian religion. How was Paul to explain this to his converts, and how especially was he to explain this to women like Priscilla who had strong gifts of prophecy and teaching? Paul had no wish to quench those gifts. He would have to ponder this.

In the meantime there was the further problem that Erastus was such a congenial and convivial host that he was always inviting all sorts of people to the Christian meetings in his house. Some were leaving with reports that wild ecstatic utterances were taking place in the meeting, something both some Jews and some Gentiles disparaged.

And then there was the further problem that some of the Gentiles had approached baptism as if it were some sort of magical ritual, a ritual that could even benefit the dead. Baptism was even thought to impart some sort of special spiritual bond between the baptizer and the one baptized. Factions resulted. Some were bragging they were "of Paul," whereas other new Christians, who had been baptized by Apollos when he came through town and was evangelizing Jews, claimed to be "of Apollos."

Finally, there was the most recent meeting of the church, which involved celebrating the Lord's Supper, except that some mistook it as an occasion for a full drinking party. Indeed, some had even come to the fellowship meal and celebration of the Lord's Supper already somewhat inebriated.

So many problems, so little time. What was an apostle to do? On top of all that, at the last meeting during the prophecy time, the ground had begun to shake, and the glass vials and cups in the nearby dining room had started rattling, and some had taken this as a sign of God's anger with something that had been said during the time of the prophesying. How was Paul to reassure his frightened and somewhat superstitious converts that there was probably no connection between the earth shaking and the content of those prophecies? Running his hand over his balding head, he resolved to write a little letter to Timothy asking him to come and help for a while. The apostle was a bit overwhelmed by all that was going on in his lively congregational meetings, not to mention in the town itself.

26

Quaking in Delphi

H E WAS UP IN the mountains of Parnassus in central Greece when the shaking began. A large marble stone rolled right up to his feet. Nikos Alexandros was at his second favorite ancient Greek spot, Delphi, when the earthquake hit. Oddly, he was reading an inscription on a column about how the oracle at Delphi once predicted a natural disaster involving earthquakes in the age of Alexander. Right when he got to the full description of what happened, sure enough the earth began to move! Stones teetered and one or two fell off their pedestals.

From the eighth century BC until nearly AD 400, Delphi was the place of pilgrimage to which thousands went every year to get answers to their deepest questions about marriage and childbearing and wars and property acquisition and a host of other things. The oracle of Delphi was always a woman, probably chosen from among the temple priestesses. She is always depicted as sitting on a three-cornered chair. Some sources believe she spoke in a drug-induced gibberish that had to be interpreted by others; some believe she was quite lucid. Regardless, she relayed messages that were gratefully received—for a fee.

Some sources indicate that her answers were often puzzling. For example, the Pythia once told one of the great kings of Greece, when he asked if he should go to war with Persia, "If you go to war with Persia, a great victory will be won." Unfortunately, she did not specify the winner!

Nick was not in the mood to stay at Delphi if the tremors continued. He was surrounded by rocky terrain and rickety ruins. Getting into his tiny black car, he headed south. His trip to New Corinth would take at least four hours, not least because of the traffic jams he would encounter the closer he got. Of course, the canal was closed down—and there were some questions about the integrity of the bridge. Police were monitoring the traffic flow even as engineers surveyed the underpinnings.

When he arrived home, he was thankful his apartment building in New Corinth was made of reinforced concrete, which withstood the quake rather well. The power was down and Nick could not get online. Since he relied on Skype to talk to Spiros and his other communist buddies, Nick was pretty much in the dark in every way possible. His cell phone was not charged either. For now, he decided to wander the streets and talk to folks about the day's events. Brooms were busily sweeping up broken flower pots. Cars were avoiding glass and cracks in the road. Most of the café patrons were standing on the sidewalk enjoying a drink and a reason to talk to anyone and everyone who passed by. Maybe tonight he would get lucky with the ladies by offering his manly services in more ways than one. All work and no play made Nikos a dull boy, or so he thought. In truth, all the play and alcohol made Nikos less than the sharpest knife in the drawer.

From his office at the Culture Ministry, Spiros Spandexikos briefly spoke to the authorities at the Corinth site. Fortunately, no one was hurt during the quake, but the site was now closed to tourists until further notice. Most of the staff had gone home; some were still salvaging broken pieces in the museum. Every inch of the ruins would be inspected for safety reasons.

Spiros also tried to reach Nikos to no avail. So he turned his TV first to the news, which he didn't find very interesting despite the on-the-scene earthquake reports, and then to the Explorer Channel, which turned out to be quite fascinating.

After introductions by an Israeli woman, there was Art West in Turkey talking about the recent finds at Hierapolis and Laodicea. This was a rebroadcast with Greek subtitles of the lecture and news conference Art and Marissa held in Istanbul the previous year. When Spiros recognized who was speaking he nearly choked on his coffee! His temper worsened when it dawned on Spiros that West was sharing the stage with the same Turkish archaeologist that was now with him in Corinth. Even more interesting was the fact that Dr. Grace Levine, a specialist in ancient languages, came all the way from Jerusalem to introduce him. Maybe he should step up his surveillance of Art West. It seemed as if West had contacts everywhere except in Greece itself. There would be no international conspiracy under his watch! The very thought of such a thing gave Spiros such indigestion he popped two antacids into his mouth and slurped them down with his caffeinated coffee.

Flipping channels back to the news, Spiros discovered an old Greek woman being interviewed in Nafplio. "Yes, God told me this earthquake was coming! I warned everyone, but hardly anyone listened. The living voice of prophecy is still alive and well!" she stressed.

"Great!" growled Spiros. "That's all we need! Greek pseudo-prophetesses claiming they know what's next for Greece. When will all this religious superstition stop bedeviling my country?" Spiros knew the answer—no time soon.

27

When The Dust Settled

THINGS WERE BEGINNING TO get back to normal in Corinth. By five in the morning the electrical power was finally restored. Grace woke up with a headache and her forehead looked as if Manny had hit her with a frying pan, but the black and blue lump was going down.

"You might want to hide that bruise with a hat, or else the police might question me for battering my wife," suggested Manny.

"I might want to cover it up just because it looks so bad! Obviously the concealer I used this morning isn't working. Unfortunately, the Greek police and fireman are far too busy checking on everyone else. The morning paper is full of reports of collapsed buildings and gas fires."

True to form, Mrs. Demetrios used the quake as an excuse to clean up her entire house. She was ready to receive her brunch guests. Grace and Manny were coming over one more time to say goodbye before they returned to Athens and then Israel. Art planned a brief walking tour of the ancient site before they left so they could see what had been accomplished in Corinth over many years of painstaking archaeological work.

Marissa was up early that morning to take a long walk around the town, which ended at Art's cottage. "Are you ready to go down for brunch?" asked Marissa.

"I guess I'm as ready as I shall ever be, considering you can't make a silk purse out of a sow's ear," replied Art.

"You are hardly a sow's ear!" retorted Marissa. "In fact you look just fine—your skin is so tanned you could pass for a local."

By the time Art and Marissa arrived at the blue-shuttered cottage Manny and Grace were busy chatting. "So, have you lived here your whole life?" queried Grace.

"Not yet," said Mrs. Demetrios with a twinkle in her eye, and everyone broke into laughter. "Been here *only* fifty years. Was born up road in Nafplio on the coast. You should go see. Many nice icon shops."

"You come from a beautiful port city! I took a wrong turn and we ended up in Nafplio—and I'm glad we did! We must confess that we *drove* up the back windy road to the old Palamidi fortress. Most of the tourists were bravely climbing the staircase. The views of the gulf are extraordinary from up there!" gushed Manny.

Mrs. Demetrios smiled in remembrance. "Ah yes, I climb those thousand stairs in my youth!"

And so these two unlikely couples sat down with Elena Demetrios for an elaborate Greek brunch featuring souvlaki and a salad with feta cheese. Dessert was a new treat—*revani*—semolina cake with orange sauce. After coffee, the two couples piled into Manny's rental car and drove down to the parking area across from the entrance to the ancient Corinth site.

The earthquake halted the flood of tourist buses that would normally be parked along the little street with all the souvenir shops. A few authorized individuals were going into the site, and a few locals were sitting in their shops talking to friends, but otherwise all was very quiet. Art was allowed immediate entrance. He spoke briefly with Nancy Bookides, promising to note carefully any on-site problems, and to return later to help with identifying any misplaced Christian artifacts. For now, however, it was a perfect time to see the site without interruption and distraction. Art chose to take his intrepid band across the street first to see the famous Erastus inscription that lay in a field in front of where the theater used to be.

"In case your Latin is rusty, this says 'Erastus for the office of ae-dile paved this place.' He's talking about the 'liturgy' or public service work he performed in order to obtain the office of aedile, director of public works. In short, Corinth was a 'you scratch my back, I'll scratch yours' society. But why am I showing you this? I think it's entirely likely that this same high-status person is the one mentioned in Romans 16. There's no doubt that Romans was written from Corinth. Paul sends greetings to the Roman Christians and Erastus is said to be the city's director of public works or treasurer. This is too much of a harmonic convergence to be a pure coincidence. No doubt, early Christianity was led and sponsored by various high-status Christians who pro-vided their villas and funds to keep the movement going. Who knows? Maybe Erastus collected funds from Paul who was selling tents and leather products in a shop. Maybe Paul shared the gospel message with him. After all, Paul was a well-educated Roman citizen. He would have shared things in common with a guy like Erastus."

"And they say archaeology can't confirm biblical facts," mused Grace with a smile on her face. "Who are those people that say these things?"

"Who indeed," replied Art, beginning to get downright riled. "Whoever they are they don't know what they're talking about. Let's walk across the street into the ancient site itself." After walking down the Lechaion Road only a short distance, Art stopped at an area of re-constructed shops.

"Welcome to the mall! You can almost picture Paul and Priscilla and Aquila working away in this shop over here, and then one day Erastus comes by and gets more than he bargained for. I can hear the conversation now . . .

Erastus: So what line of work are you in?

Paul: In tents. I have an in-tents interest in working here since the Isthmian games require lots of tents when the tourists come to camp out for the games. So that is my in-tent, to get them in-tents.

There were audible groans from Marissa, Grace, and Manny.

Art continued without skipping a beat. "Just over here from the shops is the famous *bema*, or judicial high seat, where Paul's case would have been thrown out of court by the proconsul Gallio. Did ya'll know that Gallio was the brother of the famous Stoic philosopher Seneca?

"Now look down on the left. We are coming up on the only thing left standing after the Roman general Mummius leveled this town in the second century BC. This temple and the one at Delphi were closely associated with Apollo, the god of prophecy. I have no doubt that the Greco-Roman ideas about prophecy affected the way the new Gentile converts in Corinth understood prophecy. It explains so much, including why women were asked to cover their heads when they prophesied. No self-respecting Greco-Roman oracle would be caught dead without her head covering!

"Up here to the right are the springs and fountain of Pirene. Even better, this is the location of the meat market that Paul talks about in 1 Corinthians 8–10. The ancients were wise enough to hang their meat over the cool streams running under the portico here as a means of refrigeration."

The group of friends chatted together for an hour while walking in the heat of the day. Now was a good time to head back to the newly remodeled Corinth Museum.

"I want you to see the sort of mosaic floor I expect to uncover up on the hill this summer," promised Art.

Marissa was enthralled with the patterns. "So many of these beautiful mosaics remind me of Turkish tiles. The workmanship is intricate and amazing. We underestimate the interior design skills of these so-called ancients. Who wouldn't want a floor like that!"

Manny turned to Grace. "Do you think we can redo the dining room in those colors? Sure fits our Mediterranean décor."

"Speaking of décor," laughed Art as he led his band into another room off the courtyard, "look at these remains found in the *asklepion*, the ancient version of a hospital or healing temple. Notice all the different body part molds—even molds of genitalia. The molds were like offerings either soliciting cures of those particular body parts or thanking the god Asklepius for healing the same. And you probably know that the famous image for medicine—the snake on the staff—comes directly from the cult of Asklepius."

Manny interrupted. "I think I'll draw the line at hanging body parts on the dining room wall—especially the X-rated ones. I'm guessing they suffered from sexually transmitted diseases in those days too!"

"A wise decision," said Grace with a look that said ugh.

"I've saved the best for last," claimed Art as he led his group into yet another room of the museum. Carefully labeled inside strong glass cases was a stunning collection of glass artifacts in shades of green and earth tones. The quake had knocked a few over, but no large-scale damage had been done in this new earthquake-proof building.

"Considering how often I break a glass at home, it's a miracle these pieces survived yesterday's quake, let alone centuries of abuse," marveled Manny.

Marrisa added, "Grace's find in the wine cellar will be in good company here. And we need to earn some points with the Greek authorities, some of whom are not thrilled with this Turkish-American duo of ours!"

"Art, this personal tour was great! All new for Manny especially. And I often get too wrapped up in old manuscripts. But tomorrow, we all get back to work. I'll learn a little more about Manny's computer side, and you two can go find that floor. Promise me you will scrounge around some more in the wine cellar."

"Yes, indeed, we promise to make that wine cellar a high priority. But tonight, Marissa and I are going down by the Isthmus to a little fish place Mrs. Demetrios told me about to have a quiet evening together— if they are open."

"And if we follow the map more closely, we will go straight back to Athens tonight!" laughed Grace, turning to Manny. "Are you up to the challenge?"

"Madam, if I can manage the challenge that is you, finding the road and driving to Athens is a piece of baklava, to coin a phrase." And with that they all had a good laugh.

28

The Cat and The Celts

J AKE ARAFAT WAS CHOMPING at the bit. Coach Brown kept him on the disabled list as long as he could so the ankle could mend, but desperation was setting in with the Bobcats, who were now behind three games to one in the series. The Celtics were looking to close things out. It was the second quarter and the Bobcats were losing 28–21. For the Celtics, Ray Allen and Paul Pierce had been in vintage form, and the Bobcats were lucky to be only seven points behind.

Coach Brown roared above the crowd. "Jake! Now's the time and now's the hour! Give it your best shot! We've got nothing to lose but another game at this point. If you boys don't want to start your summer vacation early, then get out there and do something about this deficit!"

"Yes, sir!" said Ray Felton, the point guard. "Jake is going to give us the boost we need."

Jake Arafat was what they called a "tough cover." He was too tall for the point guards, too quick for the forwards, and too agile for the shooting guards to defend. Initially Ray Allen would attempt to cover him, but he would need help.

The whistle blew and Jake came into the game with little fanfare. The Boston faithful had heard of Jake's ability, but in the one regular-season game the Bobcats played in Boston Garden, Jake had a mediocre game—ten points, three rebounds, two fouls. On this occasion, on the biggest stage, the NBA playoffs, Jake was determined to do better. On the first play from scrimmage Jake saw a crease to the goal, and when

Felton bounced the ball in his direction he grabbed it with one of his enormous mitts, elevated directly up over Ray Allen, and dunked the ball. The whistle blew as Ray fouled Jake in the act of shooting. All that weight training was paying off with more upper body strength.

"And one!" yelled the ref. Jake trotted to the line. With the sound of a swish, the gap was cut to four.

As the teams were trotting to the other end, Kevin Garnett started trash-talking Jake, which Jake ignored as long as he could. But when Garnett said, "Even your momma has a better scoring average than you," Jake replied swiftly, "You better leave my momma out of it! She's out of your league!" And it was on.

To say the rest of the game was hotly contested would be an understatement. There were personal fouls, technical fouls, two Celtic ejections (for protesting calls), and when the smoke cleared the Bobcats had managed a three-point victory on a three-point buzzer-beater by none other than Jake the Cat Arafat. It was back to Charlotte for game six!

In the locker room, with high fives all around, Coach Brown said, "Remember boys, we are still behind three to two. But this game put the Celtics on notice, and the Cat is back in action. We'll see if we can cook up some Irish stew next Tuesday when we get back to home cookin.'" And with this Coach Brown shook Jake's hand and said, "Welcome back, Jake! And need I say, no more pick-up games for a while!"

29

Trouble Calling

Professor William (Bill, to his friends) Arnold was a careful scholar and he liked to be sure before he delivered any bad news, especially if it might compromise a person's scholarly reputation. In this case, he had checked and double-checked his facts. What he discovered both confused and dismayed him. The goateed gentleman from Kentucky strummed his fingers on his desk, weighing the pros and cons, and decided to act.

Dr. Arnold was an expert in ancient inscriptions and coins, but particularly ancient Hittite inscriptions, a field in which there were few experts. Others had published papers on the finds at Hattusha in Turkey, and William now had the evidence to suggest not only that the author's translation was wrong, but also that the author had distorted the facts. The paper's author was Professor Marissa Okur.

Being Art's friend, Bill knew Art was now engaged to Marissa. This certainly complicated matters, but he decided to contact Art anyway. Nervously he punched in Art's number—and failed to take into account the seven-hour time difference.

At precisely five a.m. Corinth time, Art's cell phone rang, sounding like a fire alarm to the startled and sleepy Art. Knocking his Bible, his glasses, and his drink cup on the floor, Art finally located the pesky device, opened it and said "Hulloooo" in the drowsiest voice imaginable.

"Hello, Art, is that you? I hope I'm not calling at a bad time," said Bill.

"Well, for me, anytime before dawn isn't the greatest time!" moaned Art.

"Oh man! I forgot about the time difference. I'm so sorry! It's ten at night here in Kentucky. I certainly managed to catch you before you went off to your dig!"

"You caught me alright. In the middle of a delicious dream about good ole NC barbecue, but that's a story for another day. What's up?"

"I don't know how to break this to you gently so I will just come right out with it. I have evidence that a paper written by Marissa inaccurately translated an important Hittite inscription from Hattusha, and worse, possibly falsified the translation to make a point in favor of the Hittites."

"What!" exclaimed Art, now wide awake, "You're saying she committed academic fraud? I flat don't believe it!"

"Well, she is the expert in Hittite scripts. She published most of the work after her excavations at Hattusha at the Lion's Gate and elsewhere—right?"

"Right. But tell me more about what the problem is here. Couldn't it just be a case of bad translation?"

"I wish that were the case, but no. The letters of the inscription are clear, and they can't be translated as they are in the article. Indeed, they say pretty much the opposite of what her translation reads, if it is hers."

"Go on. Tell me exactly how it reads and how it should read."

"First let me explain. There's a rock in a central position in the Upper City of Hattusha that has a lengthy inscription at its base. The relief was very low and it is almost worn off; only some of the words have been deciphered. It is written in Luwian hieroglyphs, Luwian being a language that could be written both in cuneiform and hieroglyphic characters. It became very common in the last phase of the Hittite Empire. Archaeologists attribute the inscription to Shupiuliuma II, the last of the Great Kings of Hattusha, and it probably lists his accomplishments. Here is the crucial bit.

> I fought the great Ramses at Kadesh and won a great victory.
> He sued for peace, as the green stone at Hattusha shows.

Now this could be propaganda in part, as royal pronouncements usually were, but if I'm reading the script right, then it reads

> I fought great Ramses at Kadesh and he won a great victory.
> I sued for peace and won it, as the green stone at Hattusha
> shows.

That's a story with a different ending, don't you think?"

"I see," agreed Art. "So the author is claiming the home boys, the Hittites, whipped the Egyptians, but in fact it is the reverse."

"Exactly!" exclaimed Bill. "I'm not sure it's right to come to you and not Marissa—she is a professional after all. Actually, I did send her an e-mail but I got an out-of-office reply. So it was easier to talk to you first and get your opinion."

"At least I can explain the communication problem. Marissa arrived here just recently, but obviously she needs to check her e-mails. I will try to lay out the facts impartially. As you said, she is a professional, so I'm sure she will contact you personally. Does that sound fair?"

"Absolutely," assured Bill amicably.

Scratching his head, Art got out of bed despite the early hour. Sleep would not return. A cold shower didn't clear his head either. For a long time he simply mulled over how he was going to approach Marissa. Finally at about six thirty Art peered out his windows to see whether or not Mrs. Demetrios was up and about. As luck would have it, he spotted her in the garden picking fresh herbs and flowers. He padded barefoot over to the fence. "Mrs. Demetrios, could I come in for some early coffee? If it's too early, I can wait."

"Is too early. You look terrible. Take a walk; see sun rise. Come back at seven thirty, and I have breakfast and coffee for you," she replied sagely.

Art laced up his hiking boots and headed up the hill to his archaeological site. The sun was steadily rising over the ruins, and Art sat among a patch of weeds to watch the progress. Finally, he decided to check out some of the cracks in the field left behind by the earthquake. The one that nearly gobbled up Grace would need a lot of work; the second was just an empty fissure, but the third crevice slashed the land about four feet deep into the ground. Sticking up from the bottom of this crevice was an object that looked like a laundry rack made of greenish metal. What in the world could that device be? Whipping out his camera, Art took several shots and then headed down the hill to the house for breakfast. He was now eager to see Marissa. They would have a lot to talk about this morning.

30

Petra through Rose-Colored Glasses

KAHLIL AND HANNAH WERE having such a good time at Petra that they decided to extend their stay. Their guide told them they must see el-Deir, the so-called monastery, and that he would review for them the history of Petra during their walk to the monastery. On this morning their guide, Ibrahim, would escort them to the so-called back door of Petra, not the main entrance through the Siq. Kahlil voted for a very early start since it was bound to be a hot day. Ibrahim agreed.

At seven a.m. sharp, the car pulled up to the modest hotel on top of the Siq, and Ibrahim found himself knocking on the hotel door. He was somewhat surprised to find the el Saids ready and eager to go. Most tourists would still be sleeping away when the sun rose, but not these two highly motivated people.

"Are we ready then to see more of the great Rose City?" asked Ibrahim.

"Indeed," Kahlil replied jauntily. "As you can see I already have my rose-colored sunglasses on." Hannah was so thrilled that her father was actually relaxing and enjoying himself this much. The trip had been good for the both of them.

"Let me start by telling you some modern history," began Ibrahim. "The site remained unknown to the Western world until 1812, when it was introduced by Swiss explorer Johann Ludwig Burckhardt. It was described as 'a rose-red city half as old as time' in a prize-winning sonnet by John William Burgon.

"Well, time is relative, so we will only go back to 100 BC, when the Nabateans constructed part of Petra as their capital city. The Nabateans were an interesting people. They spoke Aramaic just like Jesus and other Jews in Israel. They were Semites so they were cousins of the Jews. In any case, Petra is the place Paul calls Arabia, which is where he went for a while after his conversion. If you ask me, he traveled to Petra because he wanted to try out his message on non-Jews, the Nabateans being sort of halfway between Jews and Gentiles for him. We do not know how that turned out, except he tells us in 2 Corinthians that King Aretas' henchmen were after him in Damascus."

"Yes," said Hannah, "a tale also told in the book called Acts. We have lots of Christians come into our antiquities shop, so I have studied their Bible stories."

"Just so," said the impressed Ibrahim. "My guess is that Paul was run out of town and went speedily back to Damascus."

Just then the car pulled up to the back entrance to Petra and the three hopped out, ready for a considerable walk down the hill and into a rather wide, sandy valley surrounded by remarkable tombs, monuments, and the so-called monastery.

Ibrahim paused before the stunning structure. "The casual tourist often mistakes this building for the treasury; the architecture is certainly similar. We know it was a Nabatean temple, not a monastery. Carved entirely out of the red sandstone of the mountain wall, the temple is

50 meters wide by 45 meters tall [165 x 150 feet] and has an 8-meter [26-foot]-tall entrance door. Inside the single empty chamber, which is 12.5 by 10 meters [41 x 33 feet], the walls are plain and unadorned, except for a niche in the back wall with a block of stone representing the deity Dushara. The chief deities of the Nabataeans were Dushara, Al-Uzza, and Allat. The name Dushara means 'He of the Shara,' referring to the Sharra Mountains on the northern border of Petra. Dushara was symbolized by an obelisk, or standing block of stone, and his symbolic animal was the bull. The Nabateans were not monotheists, so far as we can tell."

"What amazes me," said Kahlil shaking his head, "is how this huge building could ever be constructed in this desert in the first place!"

"Truly the Nabateans were ahead of their time," said Ibrahim with a great deal of respect in his voice. "They learned to control the waters—turning this desert place into an oasis city. You may remember seeing the long Roman water channels built into the walls of the Siq when you were touring yesterday. Even before that, the Nabateans had a system of catching and then storing the water that came from the storms and flash floods during the rainy season. This was crucial since there is no rain from about May until October. The archaeological evidence demonstrates the Nabataeans controlled these floods by the use of dams, cisterns, and water conduits. These innovations stored water for prolonged periods of drought, and enabled the city to prosper from its sale. Water is the most precious of life-giving commodities in a dry and weary land."

Hannah added, "That's true today. Many refer to water as being more valuable than oil or gold." As they walked into the empty, hollow chamber inside the monastery, Hannah pondered how many hours were needed to produce such a huge structure carved out of pure rock. "Did the Nabateans have slave labor, like the Egyptians?"

"Yes, there was slave labor in all of these ancient kingdoms. Fortunately for the Nabatean slaves, sandstone is reasonably easy to carve compared even to the limestone blocks of the Egyptian pyramids," answered Ibrahim

"I thought so," said Hannah. "When you realize how much slave labor was required and how many lives must have been lost, even the pyramids lose something of their aesthetic appeal, don't you think?"

"I suppose," mused Ibrahim. "That was so long ago, and today we are glad that all that hard work has left us these enduring treasures. It reminds us how great the ancient builders and carvers really were."

"Is Petra mentioned somewhere in other Jewish literature?" asked Kahlil.

"I'm glad you asked. Rekem is an ancient name for Petra and appears in the Dead Sea Scrolls associated with Mount Seir. Additionally, the Christian writers Eusebius and Jerome confirm that Rekem was the native name of Petra, supposedly on the authority of Josephus. Regardless, Pliny the Elder, a Roman, identifies Petra as the capital of the Nabataeans. It is still not completely clear to me what the relationship between the Idumean/Edomites and Nabateans was."

"But if they could have made their capital in ancient Damascus, why would they put their capital here?" wondered Kahlil.

"Aha! Another excellent question! Because Petra is on the direct north-south trade route from the Gulf of Aqabah to the Dead Sea and beyond! It was known as the Spice Road and later the Silk Road, and for sure many of the spices were stored and sold here. I like to imagine that the Wise Men passed through and bought gifts for Joseph and Mary and the baby. A nice image, yes?"

They all paused to picture this in their minds. Hannah remembered, "There's also an east-west trade route that crosses the north-south one not terribly far north of here. I believe it was called the King's Highway. It even connects to the Jericho Road. These were no cart paths! I'll bet the traffic got pretty heavy at times!"

Ibrahim agreed. "Sadly, the Nabateans didn't last long. They were wedged in between the Hellenistic or Greek kings who came before them and the Romans who took over in AD 106 or so. That's less than two hundred years. The dynasty of Aretas came to an end. But they sure left their mark! Even the Romans couldn't keep up the city. It was over. In the time of Alexander Severus, the issue of coinage comes to an end. No more building of sumptuous tombs!"

Kahlil was very surprised. "How could the city die so quickly?"

Ibrahim sighed. "Some sudden catastrophe. Maybe an invasion. Maybe a loss of trade—other cities were on the rise, after all, and sea-based trade routes were more popular. Earthquakes in the late fourth century didn't help either! At best, Petra held on as a religious site. Even the Christians were here in the fourth century. And here we are today, still wandering around the ancient city of Petra! Apparently we are now one of the New Seven Wonders of the Ancient World!"

Ibrahim smiled a toothy grin. His wizened, weather-beaten tan face, which had endured long hours in the relentless Jordanian sun, shone in the early morning light. And so it was that he and the el Saids spent a pleasant morning wandering around the more southern part of the Petran site.

"Of course if you are game, there are twenty-some miles of further tombs if you care to see them," suggested Ibrahim with a flourish of his hand across the landscape.

"The mind is willing," sighed Kahlil, "but the body cannot manage such a trek. So it will be best for us to return to the hotel before it gets any hotter. This old body has endured enough walking for one day!"

"As you wish. I am sure I can find a camel vender to carry you back," laughed Ibrahim, beginning to think of the handsome tip he could anticipate from this nice couple. In the Middle East tipping was very important to the guides, and certainly the best way to show appreciation for their hard work. The tour of Jordan had come to a happy ending, and in the morning the el Saids would head back across the Allenby Bridge by car on their way home to Jerusalem.

31

Evidence and Explanation

ART WAS FRANKLY A very worried man. What had he gotten himself involved in? Marissa had admitted to having an abortion. Was she also a dishonest scholar? Over his quiet breakfast he was praying through the matter. He remembered Marissa saying that she had been a nominal Christian at best for most of her adult life. For fear of reprisal, she certainly wasn't practicing her faith openly.

The heat was going to be considerable on this day, and Art was already feeling it at the breakfast table in more than one sense. Art was not a confrontational person and so he had little practice dealing with sticky situations of this sort. He decided that the smart move would be to talk about the local archaeological stuff first and then move to the conversation with Bill Arnold. Hopefully Marissa would not have any reason to be defensive.

The bang on the door was the lady herself, and in bounced Marissa, looking ready for work with the Red Sox cap Art had given her already in place. Art was weighing whether or not he wanted the buffer of Mrs. Demetrios in the middle of this conversation. He decided not.

"Good morning, sunshine! Or not—you look more cloudy," Marissa said to Art.

"Well, I do have a couple of things I want to run by you, but let's have breakfast first," said Art as Mrs. Demetrios brought in more dishes.

"Yes," intruded Mrs. Demetrios, "You no mess up my good breakfast with heavy talk. Digest first."

"Yes, ma'am!" Art and Marissa sang out in tandem.

The muesli and fruit and coffee slid down rather easily. As the couple rose to go to the site, Mrs. Demetrios cautioned, "Will be very hot today, so take it easy."

Art nodded as he closed the door behind him and the two began the trek up the hill. "Marissa you will not guess what I found in one of the crevices up there early this morning."

"I'm all out of guesses—what?"

"It looks like some sort of metallic rack. I can't figure it out yet."

"Even ancient people had to do laundry you know."

"I suppose. I can see the headline in the Athenian paper: 'Ancient laundry rack found at Corinth. Archaeologists all lathered up about it.'" Art made no attempt to laugh at his own joke, and fell very silent. Marissa patiently walked along. Finally, he said, "But we will look at my weird find more closely in a few minutes. Right now, we need to talk about something more important, apparently. I got a call very early this morning from a friend of mine in biblical studies, William Arnold. He forgot to check the time difference! Anyway, he did try to get in touch with you but your e-mail bounced back with an out-of-office reply. I've already asked the museum staff if we can use their wireless connection on occasion."

"Oops, I forgot about that! You're right. I so need to check my e-mails! Anyway, yes, I know of Dr. Arnold's work in ancient epigraphy and coins. So?"

"He's been working on some ancient Hittite inscriptions found at Hattusha, including the translation you recently published."

"And . . ." encouraged Marissa.

"Well, to put it directly, he thinks there's a mistranslation of the Kadesh part of the inscription. In fact, he even suggested it was deliberate," said Art scrunching his face in anticipation of the response he knew was about to explode from Marissa.

"What are you saying, Arthur James West!? Am I being accused of cheating!? Is this going public right away!? Is my career on the line here!? Are you sure he's even right about this!?" Marissa was visibly shaking, creating her own version of a personal earthquake!

Art sighed. Perhaps he had not been tactful enough. He would try again, but clearly Marissa's defenses were already up.

"Take a deep breath, Marissa, and hear me out. Bill claims that the inscription plainly indicates that the *Egyptians* won the battle at Kadesh and the *Hittites* sued for peace. The translated article says the opposite, and he thinks the translation is not a matter of interpretation but rather a deliberate change—in short, revisionist history, favoring the Hittites!"

At this point Marissa burst into tears and said, "But I clearly remember translating the inscription exactly as Dr. Arnold suggests! The Hittites did sue for peace though they tried to hide this in the inscription. Are you telling me that the English translation of my Turkish article reads the opposite of what I meant to say?"

"Yup, that's what I'm telling you. And are you telling me you never saw the English version?"

"No, I didn't. I just trusted Hakan Ertegun, my associate in Hattusha, and the people he commissioned to do the translation. I guess I should have double-checked. I swear to you I did not rig that translation to favor the Hittites. I wouldn't do that! But now I am going to call Hakan Ertegun and find out what happened and who did the translating into English!"

"Please do and do it quickly. Then you can contact Bill and hopefully work out something before he has to publish a reply to the article in the journal. Hopefully, no one else has sent letters to the editor yet!" Art was in some ways relieved by this revelation, but at the same time worried. If this hit the Turkish media, Marissa's reputation could be blackened whether or not she was responsible. It would be guilt by association. Just then the phone rang.

"Art, this is Bill Arnold again! Sorry to trouble you, but I contacted the journal and found out who translated that article into English. Thought that might be useful information. His name is a Turkish one I don't recognize—Mehmet Ertegun. Do you know him?"

"Mehmet Ertegun! Oh, yes, I know him well. He's the man who tried to seal me up in the plutonium in Hierapolis last year! And Bill, I'm with Marissa now. She entrusted that translation to her associate, Hakan Ertegun. She's devastated by the changes. I suspect they were deliberately done—by Mehmet—not so much to distort history but to ruin Marissa!"[1]

---

1. A tale told in the third Art West adventure, *Papias and the Mysterious Menorah.*

Marissa mouth was hanging open. "I never thought of there being a connection between Hakan Ertegun and Mehmet Ertegun. The name is an extremely common Turkish one. I can't believe Hakan had anything to do with this, but we all know what Mehmet can be like! I had better get to the bottom of this and quick!"

"Double quick," agreed Art.

"Bill, I must ask you to hold your fire a bit longer while Marissa tracks down the info on the translation," begged Art.

"I certainly will. I can't vouch for others who have read the article and may react a lot quicker. If letters start pouring into the editor, there will be repercussions."

"Let's hope we can get to him first, and clear up this mess before things gets entirely out of control," said Art hopefully before ringing off. Art did not know whether to be more or less alarmed at the situation. A scholar's integrity was his or her lifeline. Cut the lifeline, and no one would believe you again. Suddenly Art realized he was sweating profusely. And as for Marissa, she was running to get her cell phone. Time was a-wasting.

_32_

Games and Gals

GAME SIX OF THE first round NBA playoff series between the Celtics and the Bobcats commenced with an atmosphere as charged as any Carolina-Duke college basketball game. The good folk of Charlotte, basketball fans to the core, turned out in droves in burnt orange to support their home town team's first attempt to win a playoff series. The Cat's popularity had skyrocketed since the coach put him back into play. Kiosks were selling T-shirts featuring:

YOU'RE OUR BEST HOPE KOBY-ONE
PIXIES ARE ALLERGIC TO CAT FUR

Girls were flocking to buy shirts with Jake's handsome face on the back and "I LOVE CATS" on the front.

But game six was an elimination game for the Bobcats, and the Celtics were poised to win and move on to the second round of the playoffs. Something remarkable would need to happen to prevent that outcome, but in basketball remarkable things happen all the time.

After North Carolinian James Taylor sung the national anthem with aid from his son Ben, the usual revved-up version of line-up announcements was made, with the Bobcats being introduced over the blasting of Pat Benatar's "Hit me with your best shot . . . fire away." Behind the Bobcat bench in the diamond seats was a remarkable looking young woman, tall and leggy, wearing a black skirt and orange blouse to good effect. She was constantly flipping her blonde mane

106

to one side or the other, all the while keeping her eye on Jake Arafat. Higher up in the box seats was Joyce West, wearing her Bobcat sweatshirt. Caught up in the newfound craze for the Bobcats, she found herself as excited as she used to be about Carolina games when she and her husband attended them many years before. And for the first time, Jake was noticing the girls of all ages waving cards that said, "I LOVE YOU, JAKE!"

There are some basketball games that are instant classics even exceeding all the hype, and this was one of them. There was back and forth with the lead changing hands over and over again; there were few turnovers; there were spectacular plays; and there was drama and melodrama, tragedy and triumph. Jake Arafat demonstrated to one and all that he was the quickest, most athletic player on the floor, as he constantly beat his man down the court for alley-oop dunks, layups, and short jump shots. The Celtics tried a myriad of players to guard Jake, all to no avail. He was a man not to be denied on this day.

Entering the fourth quarter, the Bobcats were up by three points, the score being 85–82, and Jake had an amazing thirty-two of those points, including eight for eight from the free throw line. Sometimes a close game turns on a single play, and this was just such a game. Rajon Rondo, the Celtic point guard, was in foul trouble from guarding Jake most of the time, and he was getting frustrated. With four minutes left, he decided to drive the lane and dunk the ball over Arafat. The problem was, Arafat had as much "hops" as Rondo, maybe more, and so he went up with Rondo, met him at the peak of his leap, and cleanly blocked the dunk attempt, with Jake coming down with the ball in his hand. Rondo screamed for a foul, but none was forthcoming, and his lament went on a bit too long and with a bit too much color—he was called for a technical foul. When Arafat went to the line to shoot the free throw, Rondo was seething on his side of the court. Jake calmly made the shot, giving the Bobcats a five-point lead. Thereafter the Celtics got no closer than three points and the Bobcats won 111–101. The series would go back to Boston for a game seven, something the Celtics never expected when playing the number-eight seed in the Eastern Conference.

During the post-game interviews, one reporter asked Jake if he was dating anyone. For a split second he couldn't decide whether to say, "Absolutely not!" or "Not yet" or "I haven't had time," but he settled for a short and sweet "No." The coach looked amused. It was obvious that the reporters were hoping for something a little more exciting to report. When he finally escaped and headed for the locker he was approached by the tall blond from the diamond seats who quickly said, "Hey, big boy. Can you stop and talk for a moment?"

"Sure," said Jake anticipating another autograph. "Anything for a lady."

"My name is Sherry. How about meeting me across the street afterwards for a drink?"

"No can do," said Jake. "I have to take my aunt home after I shower and change."

"That's too bad," pouted Sherry. "How about a rain check?"

"Well, maybe after I get back from Boston," said Jake. And with that Sherry smiled and handed Jake her business card. "Call or text me. But don't play hard to get."

"Right now all I have to play is more basketball, but blessings on you and thanks for your interest." His self-conscious smile showed he was a little embarrassed by this conversation. The girls he knew, Middle Eastern girls, were not usually so forward.

Joyce West met Jake outside the stadium in the guarded lot where the players parked. Jake smiled and said, "Well, what did you think?"

"I think that was your best game ever, but don't get a big head. Ya'll haven't won anything yet."

"My b-ball game was on tonight. Sometimes it just feels right. But my social life isn't going anywhere. So far I've just ignored the screamers—specially the girls. But these American women sure are different from the ones I knew in Israel. What do you think about that!?"

"Lord have mercy!" exclaimed Joyce. "What prompted that question?"

"There was this blonde that came up to me after the game and asked me out. Here's her business card."

"It would have to be a blonde, wouldn't it?" said Joyce, musing over the card claiming that Sherry Berry was a freelance writer.

As the two were getting into the car, Joyce had to admit she didn't know much about today's dating scene. The whole girl-asks-boy-out routine was apparently common today but not in her dating days. Jake was about to enter the gene pool in which swam as many sharks as goldfish. Things were about to get more complicated.

33

A Herd of Nerds

GOING TO A TECH show is a head-trip. You will not only run into more gadgets and gimmicks than you knew existed, you will also run into more nerds than you see on CBS's *Big Bang Theory*. Manny and Grace were having fun tooling around the convention floor and checking out all the available hardware and software. Right in the middle of the center aisle was a huge booth with an equally huge neon sign that read "COHEN CHIPS AND GRAPHICS" in blinking red letters. Grace looked up at the sign and said, "Nicely understated. Subtle and yet compelling."

"Quite a remark by the woman known as the Velvet Sledgehammer," retorted Manny.

"So what's the objective at this show? Are you just trying to sell more microchips, or is there a bigger fish you are trolling for?"

"Let me show you something we have come up with. Undoubtedly you've heard of Twitter and tweeting?"

"Actually, no. I haven't been to a bird-watching convention lately."

Tactfully ignoring her comment, Manny explained, "It's a way of instantly communicating, and in any case, we have the patent on the chip that makes it go. But here is the really cool thing. We've come up with a state-of-the-art specialty processor that handles just the tweeting, making it super fast . . . indeed nearly instantaneous."

"It's all about the speed isn't it, kind of like with your Testarossa?" added Grace, rather wishing they were out cruising the countryside at this very moment.

"Reliability is big as well, but yes, speed is crucial. We came up with a chip that's not just a modest speed processor, but houses the electronics for everything a third party needs to put it in a small device with a screen and keyboard. Bingo—portable Twitter! Our product, being very cheap, would be key to marketing it as a fast solution for when you want to tweet but do not have a computer around. That's my angle on a Twitter chip—a full computer included, designed for running a little Web browser for reading Twitter text, and input for sending Twitter text, all in a chip the size of the end of your pinky. Online storage, or any off-site storage, is crucial for any business interested in having its data safe from worst-case-scenario losses on-site. Did I mention how cheap storage is now? Every individual in the future will likely keep their 'life data' in a secure place that's easily retrieved over the Internet."

"No dear, this is all new to me. In fact, most of what you just mentioned is way above my pay grade," said Grace in total confusion.

Suddenly a young man wearing a tie-dyed T-shirt said, "Cool, the famous Cohens in person. Hi, my name's Taylor. Come check out my new widget. Here's a couple you can compare it to, proving mine is way better."

Manny turned to the young man and said, "We are full up and fed up with widgets just now, but show me what you got."

"What in the world is a widget?" queried Grace.

Before Manny could answer, Taylor leapt in and said, "Well, Wikipedia describes a web widget as 'a portable chunk of code that can be installed and executed within any separate HTML-based Web page by an end user without requiring additional compilation. They are derived from the idea of code reuse. Other terms used to describe Web widgets include gadget, badge, module, webjit, capsule, snippet, mini, and flake. Web widgets usually use DHTML, JavaScript, or Adobe Flash. Widgets often take the form of on-screen tools—clocks, event countdowns, auction-tickers, stock market tickers, flight arrival information, or daily weather.' My widget here provides you with instant accurate translations of small bits of foreign-language texts."

"Do tell," said Grace perking up. "So if I was working on a puzzling ancient Aramaic phrase I could just zap up your widget, insert the phrase, and get a translation?"

"Pretty much, although I must admit we haven't installed the ancient languages yet."

"Well, make that your next move. Then it can be marketed to ancient history and biblical scholars, plus epigraphers like me," suggested Grace as Manny listened in somewhat surprised by Grace's sudden computer-savvy idea.

"Awesome!" said Taylor. "I will put it on the to-do list."

A little further down the aisle was a man with enormously oversized muscles. He was lifting a barbell with huge weights on each end, each sporting a sign. One said, "Let us do the heavy lifting." The other advertised, "Appleton Web Storage Systems."

"Manny dear, explain to me why one would need Web storage? Isn't the storage on your own computer or jump drive enough?"

"Not for everyone, and so now you can get storage on the Web for your extra but vital files. Think of it as a virtual basement or pod system. I sort of explained this briefly a couple of minutes ago."

"What will they think of next?" asked Grace.

"In fact, it's all about next in this business. The early bird gets the accounts and the cash. You have to stay ahead of the curve." And so the happy couple wove their way through the exhibits picking out a few tips and proffering a few deals to small businesses. This was not quite Paul's visit to the agora in the center of Athens, but it involved encounters with equally curious and odd characters, to say the least. Grace was secretly glad this was only a brief visit to Manny's business world. It was an alien world to her. Fortunately they would head for home soon.[2]

---

2. A special thanks to our son David for help with all the techno-speak in this chapter.

34

The Allenby Bridge

THE RIDE BACK INTO Israel or Palestine is always interesting if you cross the Allenby Bridge. The Israelis are very cautious when visitors cross. Here the pious but feisty Mother Teresa was searched and asked the question, "Have you any weapons?" She famously replied, "Yes, I have my prayer books!"

Kahlil and Hannah always got apprehensive when they arrived at this crossing point because so many of their Palestinian friends from east Jerusalem, though lifelong residents of the Holy Land, had been denied re-entry into their native land on suspicion of being suspicious, perhaps collaborators with the radicals in Hamas. Kahlil once met a Christian Palestinian who had been forced to live in Jordan for twenty-two years even though he was just a tour guide. His wife and most of his children lived in Jerusalem. No wonder Palestinians like Kahlil and Hannah got a little queasy at the border.

Stepping up to the passport window, the Israeli guard asked, "So, was this trip to Jordan business or pleasure?"

"All pleasure," replied Kahlil. "We took the trip of a lifetime to Jerash and Petra. It was a blessing. But we are happy to be returning home now to Jerusalem."

"I see," said the guard, thumbing through the two passports. "Did any strangers give you anything while you were in Jordan?"

"No, but there were some at Petra who tried to take things from us—gypsy children—pickpockets."

The guard allowed himself a slight smile and said, "Yes, I've had dealings with those urchins as well. You are through Mr. el Said. You and your daughter are welcome to drive through once we do the bomb scan on the car."

Surprisingly, their passage went without a hitch and Kahlil and Hannah found themselves driving up the Jericho Road to Jerusalem. The one-week tour had stretched into a second week, but it was well worth it.

"We need to get back to work in the shop," said Kahlil. "I've got some coins and small papyri to study, and we need to call Art West and see how his dig is coming along."

"Yes, Father, it would be good to catch up with them. And I am wondering how that relationship with the Turkish girl is coming along." All was peaceful and blissfully uneventful until they arrived home in the early afternoon and sorted through their mail. A very official-looking document from the Israeli military was addressed to Hannah.

"How odd," noted Kahlil as Hannah carefully opened the letter with a knife. Then her face blanched and her body went rigid. Kahlil grabbed the note from his dazed daughter.

> Your husband has been found alive on the Lebanese border. Please report to Detective Sharansky of the Jerusalem Police for more details.

Memories of the funeral—twenty years ago—flooded back. The original report from the Israelis was clear. Her husband had been killed in action against Hamas in a small town near Nablus during the first Intifada. He had been burned to death when a house was torched with a flamethrower, and his charred remains were returned unrecognizable. How could he be turning up alive now?

Kahlil wrapped his daughter in his enormous arms. "It will be all right, my angel. Allah will protect us. The great archangel Michael will keep the cosmic balance." The relatively tranquil life of an antiquities dealer in retirement living with his widowed daughter was about to change dramatically.

35

Marissa, Don't Lose That Number

FRANTICALLY SEARCHING FOR THE phone number of Hakan Ertegun, Marissa dumped her pocketbook upside down on the bed looking for her little address book. "Where is it? Where is it?" she yelled, at no one but herself. Art stood in the doorway of her little flat pensively watching. Out of the corner of his eye he noticed a little notepad on the bedside table and he quietly went over and picked it up. "Is this what you're looking for, honey?" asked Art quietly.

"Yes, yes!" snapped Marissa frantically as she flipped open her cell phone and began dialing. The phone rang for what seemed an eternity, and then finally a deep voice at the other end said, "Efendi?"

"Hello, Professor Ertegun?" said Marissa trying hard to keep her voice from shaking.

"Yes, to whom am I speaking?" countered Ertegun.

"This is your former associate, Marissa Okur."

"Ah yes, Marissa, where are you keeping yourself these days?" replied Ergetun, sounding quite happy to hear from her.

"Actually, I'm in Corinth for the summer. But let me get right to the heart of the situation. I have just been informed about a problem that I must bring to your attention. But before I do, let me ask one important question. Is Mehmet Ertegun some relation to you?"

"Yes, he is my first cousin, and also in archaeology. He has some good skills, especially at English translation. That is not my forte," acknowledged Hakan.

"I'm glad you mentioned translation because as you may or may not remember we wrote an article in Turkish about the inscriptions at Hattusha, particularly about the one that recounts the battle of Kadesh between the Egyptians and the Hittites. Do you remember this?"

"I do remember the article. And I remember that the Ministry of Archaeology assigned my cousin the task of translating the article. However, I have not seen the translation," replied Ertegun cautiously.

"Dr. William Arnold, a colleague of Dr. Arthur West, has sound evidence of a mistranslation, possibly deliberate, of the inscription. The translation makes it sound as if the Hittites, not the Egyptians, won the victory!"

There was a long silence on the other end of the line after which Hakan said, "What are you telling me? Are you suggesting that Mehmet deliberately doctored the English translation in order to favor the Hittites? But why would he do that? It is pointless, not to mention dishonest."

"I have a possible explanation. As you probably know, he and I had a falling out over the dig at Hierapolis, after which he was reassigned to Antioch to a smaller, less important site," said Marissa with a deeply furrowed brow.

"Yes, I remember him grumbling about that at a family dinner. It was an unpleasant scene! So?"

"Well, what if Mehmet, in his anger with me and Dr. West, deliberately doctored the translation into English to discredit my scholarship?" suggested Marissa.

"I see where this line of thinking is going, and I don't like it, not least because he would also be discrediting me, his own cousin, who helped him get an archaeological job in the first place! What sense does that make?"

"Well, I guess it depends on how badly he wanted to hurt me after he was shamed at Hierapolis," suggested Marissa, beginning to feel sorry for her old friend Hakan. He certainly didn't deserve this news.

Hakan sighed deeply. "I will look into this, naturally. First, I will call Dr. Koroturk and ask if he has seen the translation of that article. And then I will pursue the matter with my cousin. Rest assured I will get to the bottom of this, but if it is as you have suggested, he will find himself totally out of work very soon, very quickly. My reputation is also at stake here."

Marissa was finally starting to relax. "Thank you. Please let me know how it goes as soon as you can. Dr. Arnold plans to publish at least a letter to the editor pointing out the mistranslation. If it can be cleared up before he submits that letter, then all the better for both of our reputations."

Art watched this animated Turkish conversation from the doorway. It was obvious from Marissa's body language and tone of voice that she was deeply upset and worried. Art was beginning to feel better about the relationship.

Marissa hung up and turned to Art. "Shall I translate all that for you," she said with a laugh.

"The fact that you're smiling translates quite well," joked Art. "I suggest we go for a walk up the hill. You can regale me with all the gory details. And then maybe we can also find out what our earthquake unearthed for us."

36

The Boston Massacre

THE BOSTON CELTICS WERE not expecting to play seven games in the first round of the playoffs. Like a hornet that has been swatted twice unsuccessfully, the Celtics were now really, really mad. Losing two road games to a team from Charlotte with a 42–40 record was bordering on humiliation. The rightfully proud Celtics had won the NBA championship the previous year, adding to their league-leading total. They vowed to leave it all on the floor in this seventh game.

It was one of those "no blood, no foul" games, since the refs decided to swallow their whistles. This in turn meant that driving the lane, unless you scored, was not going to accomplish much; the refs would not be calling blocking fouls on either team. This favored the team with the better outside shooting—the Celtics. Both Paul Pierce and Ray Allen were on form, as was the three-point specialist, Jeff Green, who came in at the end of the first quarter and hit his first four shorts from distance, helping the Celtics to a fifteen-point halftime lead.

Jake Arafat for his part was still reasonably effective, but none of his other teammates could throw it in the ocean if they tried, and so it became an increasingly frustrating game for the Bobcats. Finally in the fourth quarter Jake dunked over the Celtics center but with five minutes left and being down twenty points it was too little too late. There was no game-changing play. The Celtics marched on to a twenty-five-point victory, and immediately after the game began celebrating. A glum Bobcat team sat on the bench watching, their season over.

Coach Brown addressed his team before they returned to the locker: "Now I want you to take note of them. Notice the heart of a champion. They do not celebrate unless and until they have won something. So much of this game is 'will more than skill.' All teams have all-Star players. We have now experienced the playoffs, but we have not experienced winning a playoff series. I want you to remember this feeling of disappointment after a long and tiring but exciting season. It's May, and until this evening we were still playing when most of the league's players were at home watching. Don't forget what it took to get here. Next year, if we play better during the regular season, we won't have to play the champs in the first round. So I say, congratulations on a breakthrough season! Let's all stand up, stand tall, stand proud, and congratulate each other!"

As the players were rising from the bench, Paul 'the Truth' Pierce headed over to shake a few hands. "You boys surprised us. I'm sure you'll be back in the playoffs next year!"

"The Truth has spoken," said Raymond Felton. "To the Bobcats and a better year next year!"

And the team huddled, high-fived and cried, "To the Bobcats!"

As Jake was walking back into the locker he noticed a message on his cell phone. It was from an unknown number, but on a whim he decided to return the call. The phone rang but once.

"Hello, you called?" said Jake. "Who's this?"

"Sorry you got the beat-down from the Celtics tonight. This is Sherry, how about that rain check drink you promised."

Hesitating a minute, Jake said, "Okay, but where are you?"

The voice replied, "I'm right here in the Garden, and I'll meet you outside the player's exit in a bit. Let's go to the Cheers bar and drown our sorrows!"

Just when you think the season is over, a fan declares, "It's overtime!"

37

Racking His Brains

IT WAS NOT USUAL for Art to see his work as merely a diversion, but today that's exactly what it was because he was more concerned with Marissa's mess. He was hoping it could be resolved before she lost her reputation as an honest and careful scholar. Holding hands as they walked up the hill one more time, they both wondered what the other was thinking, but they remained silent. Deep down they didn't want to face the answers. Art led Marissa to the back of the site and pointed emphatically.

"Here is the crevice where I found something strange." Pulling out his flashlight, even though they were standing in broad daylight, Art and Marissa knelt down and peered into the deep crevice. Shining the pinpoint beam to the very bottom of the shallow pit, Art urged, "See, right there! It looks like some kind of rack protruding up out of the ground. A drying rack? I have no idea. I have never seen anything like that before."

Marissa walked over to the little locked shed on the site where they stored their tools, took out a key, and extracted a pick and a shovel. Art and Marissa then began to dig rapidly through the topsoil on either side of the crevice until they got within two feet of the object in question. "We need to go slower and easier now," cautioned Art. "We've been lucky not to strike any other foreign objects so far."

"Right," said Marissa, who had tied her hair up in a ponytail and was wiping her forehead with a green bandanna. "Of course since we

119

are in Greece, every object we find is foreign! Shall we get the smaller tools then?"

"In a minute, but let's see if we can first remove about another foot of dirt."

The further digging revealed that the object was about three to four feet wide and A-frame in shape. "What in the world is this thing? And is it even ancient, or just one of Mrs. Demetrios' old laundry racks?" asked Art, not expecting an answer.

On their hands and pad-covered knees, Art and Marissa progressed to hand trowels and whisk brooms. Finally, drenched in sweat, they could see the object more clearly, though some of it was still buried.

"Like I said, some kind of rack I suppose, though after racking my brains, I've come up empty for an ancient use for this gadget," said Art with his eyes closed trying to picture a world two-thousand years ago.

"What about a stretching rack—maybe stretching skins or animal hides?" suggested Marissa.

Art's eyes popped open! "Yes! Of course! But why would we find something like that in this expensive villa complex?" At this point Art had crawled into the hole and was closely examining the 'rack' with a magnifying glass. All of a sudden, his jaw dropped. There, right under the magnifying glass, was a tiny piece of rawhide. "Wow! I think I'm looking at a piece of animal skin. You could be dead on! Maybe this rack was some kind of stretching device, but why is it so symmetrical in shape? Hides were certainly irregular, but this thing is in the shape of . . . in the shape of . . ."

"A tent!" cried Marissa. "You told me Priscilla and Aquila and Paul were busy making and selling tents in a shop on Lechaion Road."

"No way!" shouted Art. "Look what we have literally fallen into! Maybe this was the home of Priscilla and Aquila!" And with that thought racing through their brains, both Art and Marissa managed to totally forget their worries over Marissa's article. The "distraction" had become the main preoccupation once more. The heat of the day finally slowed their progress and they returned quite early for dinner.

Once the evening meal was over, Art raced back to his laptop. Some new thoughts had come to him relating to his historical novel about Paul in Corinth, and so he began to compose once more.

38

Once Upon A Time IV

*T*ROUBLE HAD BEEN BREWING *in Corinth for some time, as both Paul and Apollos gradually made a significant number of converts to the following of the crucified Messiah Jesus, but Paul had not expected that any of the Jews still in the synagogue would try legal action against him, since he was a Roman citizen and this was indeed a Roman colony city run on the principles of Roman justice. Nevertheless, there was a new proconsul for the region of Achaia, one Gallio, and apparently some of the Corinthian Jews thought he would be more amenable to their complaints than previous governors.*

One morning, without warning, Paul was summoned from the house of Erastus, where he was currently staying, to a hearing before the new proconsul. Like most such hearings, it was a public meeting, and Gallio sat in his sella currulus *(curule chair) on the* bema

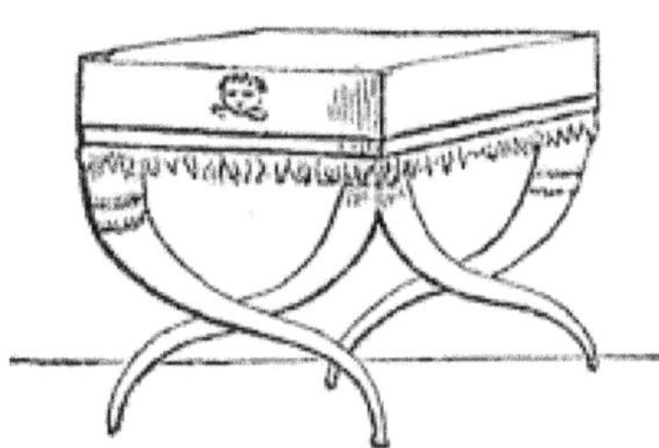

(raised platform) that faced the Lechaion Road. Paul was led before the bema *by one Sosthenes, a pugnacious man whom Paul had met previously in the synagogue. Unfortunately, Sosthenes had argued vigorously against Paul's views, and was responsible for getting Paul banned from speaking in the synagogue. "This man," Sosthenes charged when he was allowed to speak, "is persuading the people to worship God in ways contrary to the law!"*

Just as Paul was about to speak, Gallio curtly interrupted Sosthenes and those with him. "If you Jews were making a complaint about some misdemeanor or serious crime, it would be reasonable for me to listen to you. But since it involves questions about words and names and your own law, settle the matter yourselves. I will not be a judge of such things." So he had them ejected from his court. Then the Jews beat Sosthenes, not Paul! But Gallio showed no concern whatever, and told Paul he was free to go.

The experience had shaken Paul up a bit, but he realized a ploy like this would not likely be tried again while Gallio was around. But Paul also realized he needed to plan his next move. First, he would talk to Priscilla and Aquila about this matter.

Suddenly there was a loud knocking on his door, startling Art back into the present. "Hi Sunshine," said Marissa. "Are you up for a cup of tea and a chat about what we found today?"

"Sure," said Art, "And guess what? I think I'm beginning to make some progress on sketching out my Paul in Corinth novel."

"Which I will be reading and making suggestions on soon, I am sure," said Marissa in an authoritative tone of voice. "But for now, it's back to the future for you and me. How are we going to deal with our new find?"

39

A Chat at Cheers

Though it was only the façade of this bar that had actually been on the TV show *Cheers!* and though the TV show continued only in reruns, it was still a remarkably popular "meet and greet" place for the young and the restless. Jake certainly fit that category. Wearing jeans and a nondescript T-shirt, Jake mentally prepared himself to stay no more than thirty minutes with Sherry, find out what she wanted, and promptly leave. His gym bags were already on the team bus, which was heading to Logan airport in two hours.

Sitting at the bar, and drinking a small martini on the rocks, Sherry was being checked out by almost every available single male in the place. She was hot! Jake walked down the stairs into the bar and saw her immediately, the center of far too much attention. "Hi, Sherry. Let's sit in a quiet booth away from this traffic," said Jake to Sherry. "Soooo, why exactly did you want to see me?"

"As you may remember from my business card, I'm a freelance writer working on an independent piece—hopefully for *Sports Fanatics* if they're interested! Something outside the box—something quirky!"

"A reporter!" said Jake. "I've done my best to avoid the likes of you. I don't like reporters. Besides, all my official stuff is handled through the front office!"

"Well, that's understandable," cooed Sherry sweetly. "Some of us can be pretty obnoxious, but if you don't mind, I'd like to ask you a few questions, and you can be the judge of where this interview goes." Just then a waiter came by and Jake ordered a Coke Zero.

"You don't drink?" asked Sherry.

"No, not really. I'm an athlete, remember. I occasionally have a beer or a glass of wine, but no hard liquor."

"Wow" admired Sherry, "A true Spartan."

"Not exactly," replied Jake laughing. "I'm hardly Greek!"

"Right! You are Palestinian?"

"Yes, from Bethlehem, in fact."

"No wonder those folks in Charlotte think you are the Messiah come to town."

"I'm no savior, just a basketball player."

"How did you get interested in basketball as a Palestinian?"

"It's very popular over there. There are lots of teams, in fact, almost as many as there are soccer teams. And eventually someone noticed I could play and signed me on with a championship team from Tel Aviv."

"You played with Israelis?"

"Yes, and Americans as well. Michael Jordan himself came to Tel Aviv, saw me play, and recruited me for the Bobcats!"

"And how would you sum up your time with the Bobcats thus far?"

"I think we are a team on the rise, and I want to do anything I can to help Coach Brown and the team. We made the playoffs this year. Why not a championship next year?"

"Is that realistic?"

"Sure, but it will require lots of hard work and prayer. I'm a Christian you know, and wouldn't be here otherwise!" Jake was just about to launch into this new theme when Sherry jumped in.

"Let's pursue a different line of questioning, if you don't mind. Do you have a girlfriend?"

Jake blushed and then replied, "Sorry, I've been too busy for socializing."

"Ah, but you've just hit the off season. There must be a tiny amount of time in your schedule now for a date or two! How are you filling up your spare time?"

Jake suddenly perked up and got so excited he was nearly bouncing in his seat—and beginning to attract a crowd trying to listen in!

"I'm exploring food—all kinds of food—barbecue and soul food! Big surprise though—I can get all my favorite Middle Eastern foods, like *shawarma*, which is spiced meat, cooked on a spit, and shaved real thin. And *musakhan*, roasted chicken over taboon bread. And don't forget *maqluba*, which has everything from rice to eggplant, cauliflower, carrots, and lamb. My grandmother taught to me make that dish! And did I mention bread—all kinds of breads that we dip in *hummus, baba ghanoush, mutabbel,* and *labeneh.* And nuts and fruits—man, do I love apricots! Folks have been taking me out to eat local, like McCormick & Schmick's for seafood, and Spoon's for barbecue. Charlotte is a food capital!"

By now Sherry and even some patrons sitting nearby were laughing. Jake suddenly quieted down, feeling a bit sheepish.

"Okay, then, lots of food, but no dating! What else?" asked Sherry.

"I just discovered comic book shops—I'm into Ironman and Spiderman. Not so much into the video games—my teammates grew up with Nintendo and they are really quick, but I haven't figured it out yet! Some of the guys went to the PAX East video game convention here in Boston. Hey, I have a bus to catch soon!"

"I promise to wrap this up. How about a few stats, like, how tall are you really? And how high can you jump?"

"Well, I am 6′ 5″. And thanks to all that good food, I've grown another inch since I moved to Charlotte. The team stats guy tells me I have a 44″ vertical leap. You know I volunteer at the Bethlehem Center. We should talk about church too. Hey, this wasn't half bad!"

Sherry smiled sweetly, and thought, "This was too easy!" To Jake she said, "Well, that's all I need for now. Maybe we could hook up in Charlotte sometime."

"Well, maybe," said Jake grinning. "I think I'd like that." But as he was walking out the door, something began to nag at the back of his brain. He was puzzled by his mixed feelings about this so-called interview. She sure was pretty and easy to talk to, but why had the interview not been more about his basketball season? Jake figured he had not seen the last of Sherry.

40

Not Kissing Cousins

Hakan Ertegun did not like to be jerked around by his relatives, particularly his cousin Mehmet, who constantly wheedled him for favors over the years. One of those favors was suggesting to the ministry that Mehmet be allowed to translate such an important article. Hakan was very angry at himself for not checking the translation and promising Marissa that he would handle everything. Swamped with archaeological work at the time, he never gave the matter a second thought after that. Right now, if he had a gun and Mehmet was present he would probably use it. So he decided to wait until he cooled down to call Mehmet. Maybe, just maybe, there was a reasonable explanation. Or maybe not—maybe it was pure spite aimed at Marissa. But Hakan knew it could affect his own work as well.

Mehmet did not have a cell phone and so Hakan called the hotel where he was staying in Antioch. On the second ring the man at the front desk said, "Efendi?"

"I need to speak with Mehmet Ertegun immediately please."

"One moment please."

In fact it was a very long time before someone came back to the phone, and Hakan could hear an argument going on in the background. "How dare you interrupt me in the middle of shaving?"

"But there is a very insistent gentleman on the other end of the line, sir."

"If you say so. Hello, Mehmet Ertegun, to whom am I speaking?"

"Well, cousin, I am glad I tracked you down."

"Yes, and that would be because . . . ?"

"You remember that special article about the findings at Hattusha that you were asked to translate into English for me some time ago?"

"Yes, of course. And thanks for the assignment. I needed the lire, to say the least."

"Well, there is a problem with the translation, apparently."

"Really? What could be wrong?" responded Mehmet guardedly.

"What could be wrong, cousin, is a complete falsification of what the inscription actually says! Did you really produce a translation that claims the Egyptians lost to the Hittites at Kadesh and sued for peace?"

There was a long pause. "Well, I suppose you could read it that way. It was after all a piece of Hittite propaganda, was it not? Surely we would not want them to admit defeat at the hands of our rivals the Egyptians. It is a matter of national pride!"

"Let me see if I understand what you are saying—for the sake of national pride, or perhaps personal pride, you falsified a piece of historical evidence. Mehmet! What are you saying? That you agree with the notion of revisionist history? That we should rewrite the past the way it best suits us today? You numbskull, don't you realize you could ruin my reputation as a scholar! It's my name on that article, not yours. But I am thinking that it was not just national pride that motivated this deliberate altering of the text. I'm thinking it was your own pride, which got squashed by one Marissa Okur and you just couldn't tolerate that. So you thought you would sully her reputation!"

"How could you side with that despicable woman against your own cousin in this matter!" exploded Mehmet from the other end of the line. "Was it not enough that she got me sent to Antioch to do next to nothing, and put me under surveillance from Koroturk? Now when I try to extract a little revenge, you side with her? What happened to Turkish men sticking together, blood being thicker than scholarship!?"

"The only thing thick here is your head!" retorted Hakan. "You were willing to risk my reputation in order get her reputation tarnished. It was all about payback! That's hardly what I would call cousins sticking together! And let me tell you what is going to happen now. You are going to write a public apology to the journal that published the article. You are going to e-mail them today telling them it is coming. You are going to e-mail me today with the apology for my approval. And then, cousin, you are going to become an ostrich."

"What? What do you mean?" feared Mehmet.

"I mean you are going to stick your head in the sand of that tel at Antioch and not make a sound or come out until I say you can. Otherwise, you are going to be fired or go to jail or both! Am I perfectly clear? No problems of interpretation?"

"No," said a pathetic voice at the other end of the line. "No, I understand. Do me one favor and do not tell Koroturk."

"I can't do that. He needs to know, in order to do some damage control. And I have no idea what he will devise for your future after this stunt. I have no control over Koroturk."

At this point there was utter silence. "Mehmet, I have only one thing left to say. May God have mercy on your lying soul." And with that Hakan snapped his cell phone shut so hard that it fell out of his hand. "I must get back to Marissa now. What a mess!" Hakan seethed to himself.

41

Spin Cycle

NICK WAS SICK AND tired of doing his laundry at the local Corinthian laundromat, hauling his clothes back and forth from his apartment, but he had no choice since the earthquake caused electrical problems in his apartment which in turn fried his washing machine. He managed to get his cell phone up and running only to discover seven un-answered calls from Spiros urging him to get over to the archaeological site and see what was happening. He planned to do just that after he did his laundry. Spiros seemed to think there might be some new discoveries he would want to be notified about.

"Quite a mess this earthquake left us, do you not agree?" said an old lady doing laundry next to Nick.

"Ah, yes," replied Nick, "But we Greeks are tough and will recover."

"God willing," said the old lady dressed in electric blue.

"God really has nothing to do with it. If there really was a good God we wouldn't be suffering so much. A lot of good people died."

"You will do well not to mock God, son," said the wizened old woman. "It may come back to haunt you later."

Nick chuckled and said, "Thanks for your advice." Then he turned quickly and walked out the door.

~

Spiros was lost in thought about his latest column in The Owl on so-called "acts of God." He found it ironic that the insurance companies only dubbed disasters, never good things, as acts of God. Despite dozens of calls, he had heard nothing from Nick down in Corinth. Of course Corinth was closer to the epicenter of the quake, so perhaps there was a lot of clean up and power outages. Just then his cell phone started vibrating in his pocket.

"Hello, Spiros here."

"It's me, Nick, and I have finally dug out enough to get back on the job at the archaeological site. Sorry about not returning your calls, but my phone has been dead for awhile."

"Good. I was beginning to think you had dropped off the face of the earth. Don't trouble yourself with the old archaeological site. Rather, go up the hill behind it where the little school is, and see what is happening at the site assigned to West for digging this summer. If you run into him, just pretend you are a curious tourist. And, oh yes, take plenty of pictures for me."

"Will do. I'll get back to you soon."

"See that you do," said Spiros emphatically as he hung up the phone. "There is no telling what that earthquake uncovered."

∼

When Philippa's prophecy about the coming earthquake came true, overnight she became something of a sensation. All the major papers sought her out for interviews, and a debate swirled around whether she was a genuine living voice of prophecy in Greece. If so, was Philippa more like the ancient oracle at Delphi or like St. Philip the Evangelist's prophesying daughters? Philippa laid claim to the latter, not least because she was named after St. Philip.

In one surprising moment on an Athens morning show, Philippa let slip that she had a sense that the recent earthquake was but a preview of coming attractions. Naturally enough this produced a renewed sensation, and experts from Greece's Seismic Institute were brought in to comment. They could neither confirm nor deny that Philippa might be on to something.

"So, you are saying that more seismic judgments may be heading our way?" asked Lydia Nystra, the effervescent morning hostess of Good Morning, Greece!

"It would not be surprising, now would it?" asked Philippa, "After all, the Bible is full of earthquakes, and they are often attributed to God's anger with our sins, are they not? Just read the book of Revelation."

To this even the loquacious Lydia had no reply. She simply thanked Philippa for sharing and cut straight to a commercial. Spiros, on the other hand, swore loudly, nicked himself with his razor, marched to his TV, and kicked the off button with his right foot.

He took Philippa's comments as a rebuttal to his recent column in The Owl.

"That damn woman has no business being on national TV saying stupid things like that! She has no idea what she's talking about! There's no such thing as prophecy! It's all trickery and treachery," fumed Mr. Spandexikos.

42

"In My Mind I'm Gone to Carolina"

JAKE ARAFAT SAT ON the plane home pondering his conversation/ interview with Sherry. Listening to James Taylor's greatest hits on his iPod, he was glad to be getting back to Charlotte and his first off-season. Maybe he would head down to the beach in Wilmington for a few days. Aunt Joyce had a condo there in her hometown. Maybe he could actually go back to Israel and see his mother, who was living outside of Jericho safely tucked away in a monastery, far from the people who had killed her first-born son. Maybe he would spend more time at the Bethlehem Center and start a real basketball camp. Maybe . . .

The stewardess interrupted his train of thought with a beverage and a snack, which Jake inhaled in nothing flat. "Maybe I should remember to bring food on these flights!" His mind wandered back to life in Bethlehem and unbidden tears formed quickly when he saw his brother Issah in his mind's eye. It was still a nightmare that Issah had been murdered. He wondered how his mother and sister-in-law were getting on at St. George's monastery. Were they happy, healthy, fulfilled? Speaking of fulfilled, just how fulfilling was a career in the NBA? Did he want to get married? Have a family?

Part of Jake's problem was that he had been raised in a traditional Middle Eastern way, and women in that patriarchal world tended to be viewed in extreme ways—as saints or sirens. Arranged marriages were still common. Jake knew he did not want to go back to that world, but he hardly knew what to make of liberated American women like Sherry,

132

who seemed too forward, too direct, too strong. He hardly knew how to talk with such intimidating women, much less how to date them. Jake's jumbled thoughts kept him wide awake all the way to Charlotte, but very quiet in the car on the way home from Douglas Airport.

⁓

Art missed North Carolina like a soldier on a long tour of duty misses home. Getting engaged to Marissa had not taken away his homesickness. If anything it made him want to spend more time there, hence his thoughts just before he turned out the light in his little bedroom. He began to hum James Taylor's "In my mind I'm going to Carolina . . ." His mind drifted to his favorite haunts in Charlotte, football games in Chapel Hill, the condo in Wilmington, devouring the crab soup at the Sea Captain's in Myrtle Beach, watching the sunset at Linville Gorge.

⁓

Marissa was fretting about the translation mess. She worried about damaging her relationship with Art, though she cared about her reputation as a scholar as well. But these feelings told her much about where her heart was now—first with Art and then with her work. She must be in love, she concluded. And then her mind wandered back to her amazing trip last August to North Carolina with Art. The long flight! Meeting Art's mother. Meeting Jake. Eating barbecue and hush puppies. Seeing the Ben Long frescoes in downtown Charlotte. Riding the Blue Ridge Parkway up to Linville Gorge. And, of course, the Atlantic beaches. "Was it ever hot! I'll bet everyone is baking on the beach right now," she mused. Well, tomorrow promised to be another early summer scorcher here in Greece too.

43

Revelations at The Station

IT WAS AFTERNOON IN Jerusalem and the police station was incredibly busy with people coming and going in all directions. It took no little time for Hannah and Kahlil to find Detective Sharansky's upstairs office, but find it they did, and Hannah knocked on the door.

"Come in," said the deep baritone voice with the sound of some authority.

Hannah and Kahlil made their way through the door and there in front of them was as cluttered a desk as they had ever seen. Behind it sat the good detective, and he appeared to be very preoccupied. "I'll be with you in just a moment," he said without looking up as he scanned a report. Finally he raised his head and immediately recognized Kahlil el Said and his daughter Hannah. He jumped up and reached his hand out to shake Kahlil's hand.

"Please have a seat! It's been awhile since we worked that menorah case together. Now it is quite famous, is it not!? I actually went by the museum to see it recently. But enough about the past; we have a very real problem in the present." Holding up a large black and white photo of a man with a goatee, he asked, "Do you recognize this man?"

Trembling, Hannah replied, "Yes, it may be my husband Yassir, but I have not seen him in twenty years! Where is he?"

"Right now, he is being detained in a prison north of Tel Aviv. We found him crossing the border from Lebanon into Israel illegally. He seems to have been working undercover for Hezbollah, but he will

134

neither confirm nor deny this. Have you at any time in the last twenty years heard from him in any way?"

"No!" said Hannah rather angrily. "In fact, it was your people who told us he was dead and sent us the remains! We had a funeral!" And at this Hannah began to cry as all those horrible memories came back.

"I am truly sorry about that Miss el Said. This is a mess not of your making. As you will remember, Israeli troops found his ID bracelet and wallet in a little village near Mt. Gerizim where we had been fighting Hamas. The house was completely burned out. The story our soldiers told was horrible in every way. They looked into this house and saw women and children tied up inside. Suddenly, a bomb incinerated everything, slaughtered the family, and killed two of our men. Hamas had used their own people as human bait to lure our troops close to the house. I have to ask myself, what kind of people uses their own wives and children as bait in a trap?"

At this point Kahlil came into the conversation, "These horrible methods are things Hannah and I would repudiate instantly. We do not agree with the use of violence for such inhumane purposes, whatever one's political views."

"I am glad to hear this, and I agree with you. Miss el Said, do you want to see your husband? By law you have a right to see him. He is not likely going to be freed from prison, of that you can be sure. Indeed, he may be tried for war crimes some day. If you do not wish to go and see him, we have a waiver you need to sign which will mean you have renounced your right to visitation."

"Father, what should I do?" asked Hannah turning and looking directly into Kahlil's eyes. "Honestly, my feelings are all conflicted. I do not know what to think or do. Visiting may imply rekindling our relationship."

After a long pause, Kahlil responded, "I think you should pray about this for a while, if Detective Sharansky doesn't mind. Is there a time limit on making the decision?"

"There is no major rush," assured the Detective. "Yassir is not going anywhere! If you do choose to visit, you will have to wear a wire and the visit will be taped. Then you will be placed under surveillance. It will complicate your life a bit, but it is for your protection. But you need not be afraid."

"I see," said Kahlil raising his eyebrows. "We will take that into account in our deliberations."

As Kahlil and Hannah beat a fast retreat, Kahlil kept muttering to himself in a mocking tone what Sharansky had said: "'but you need not be afraid,' 'but you need not be afraid.' He can't be serious! Yassir is a dangerous man, all the more so since he is a trapped man, apparently back from the dead."

44

Racking Up Another Find

Tedious. Despite the glamour of movies like the Indiana Jones series, the day-to-day work of an archaeologist like Art West was tedious and meticulous. It required enormous patience and a high threshold for frustration. Art West had all of these qualities plus the sort of curiosity and persistence that led him to continue to pursue things others would have long since given up on. Marissa, having watched Art in action for most of an archaeological season, marveled at his quiet way of getting things done.

Take this morning, for instance. Art rose early, ate a little breakfast with Mrs. Demetrios, hiked up to the site, continued to dig out the rack, and then returned to the cottage. Mrs. Demetrios was already off to the market. Art woke Marissa by knocking gently on her door. Hearing "Come in," Art entered to find his fiancée sitting up in bed, her hair all askew but with a big smile on her face. Instinctively he went over and gave her a little kiss on the cheek and said, "Wait till you see what I accomplished on the site already!"

"Don't tell me you finished the job while I slept in!" retorted Marissa. "I have lots of questions. Will Nancy Bookides and her team be providing any assistance? Do we have to personally haul all the artifacts we find down to the museum? What about security? Which pieces will be studied? Which pieces will go on display? What happened to the items Grace found when she fell into a treasure pit?"

Finally there was silence. Art tentatively said, "Are you sure you're finished?" When he got a nod and a smile, he continued, "I already turned the glass bottle and amphora handle over to Nancy, so they are safe in the museum storage room. Obviously, we need to have another meeting with her to answer all these questions! But right now, I'm hungry enough for second breakfast, as Pippin would say. By the way, in Bavaria and Poland they really do eat 'second breakfast'—it's not a Lord of the Rings invention after all!"

After raiding the kitchen, Art strolled down the lane while watching the children rush into the little school. But there was someone else on the lane that morning, a man with jet-black hair in a tan suit heading up the hill. Art noticed he had a small camera in his hand.

"Not your usual tourist," thought Art to himself, but he gave the man no more thought for the time being.

Marissa joined him looking fresh as a daisy and every bit ready to conquer the archaeological world. The events of the previous day had not crushed her, though undoubtedly she would still worry until she heard from Hakan Ertegun.

"Did you eat breakfast?" queried Art.

"I am just going to chew on a power bar this morning." And so the two conspirators headed up the hill, eager to get to work. Upon arrival, they found the black-haired man had preceded them and was running around the site taking picture after picture, including, suddenly, a picture of Art and Marissa.

"Excuse me! This is not a public tourist area; it's a private dig site! I will have to ask you to leave. This site will not be open to the public for some time. There's still much work to be done."

The man smiled sheepishly and said, "Of course, you are right. I am just a native who is enthusiastic for archaeology, and I got excited when I found this new dig."

"But how did you find us?" asked Art. "There are no signs and it has not been announced to the press."

"Ah, but Corinth is a small town. Word travels fast when there is an American archaeologist and his Turkish helper in the area. I'll just be going now. Sorry to trouble you," and he began to leave.

"Wait a minute," said Art. "What is your name?"

"People call me Nick around here."

"And Nick, how exactly did you know we hail from the US and Turkey?"

"Oh, as I said, word gets out, word gets out," said Nick with a wave of a hand as he picked up the pace and headed rapidly down the hill. "Good luck with your dig. We will all be watching to see what you discover!"

"Who is we?" said Marissa to Art worriedly. "That man set off more alarms inside me than a burglar in a jewelry store."

"Me too," said Art with jaw clenched. "Let's see if Mrs. Demetrios knows anything about this character at lunch time."

"Right," replied Marissa, "And now, finally to work. Let's see what we left hanging on that rack."

The digging and cleaning went well that morning. Around noon, Art and Marissa turned over a piece of leather found near the rack to Nancy Bookides, and discussed some of Marissa's concerns. The leather fragment was instantly spirited off to the work room in the back of the museum. Art showed Nancy a number of pictures detailing the emerging rack.

"This ranks as the oddest find yet on this site. In my many years, I have never seen anything like it" said Nancy. "I mean it's clearly ancient. Art, you are quite right that it has bits of animal hide sticking to it in several places, so I guess the theory of it being a stretching rack for such hides is plausible. But for what?"

"Well, how about for making tents out of animal hide?" suggested Art. "We know that Paul and his coworkers made tents here. Why not tents for the pilgrims coming to the games?"

"I suppose that's possible." Just then a technician popped in and handed Nancy a note. "It's official already. The hide sample turns out to be goat or sheep skin. And not just any kind, but the sort called cilicium, originally from the dark hides of the goats of Cilicia."

"And this just bolsters my case, because we know that Paul came from Tarsus in Cilicia. He and his family made tents out of the goat's hair cloth. I'm not saying we found the house of Priscilla and Aquila where Paul stayed. We may never know. But it's possible. However, caution is in order since there must have been quite a few such tent makers in Corinth who then sold the tents in the shops just off the old Lechaion Road."

Nancy abruptly changed the conversation and asked, "Spiros Spandexikos from the Ministry is planning to make a visit soon, and I'd like to show him the rack. You should meet him."

"Actually, I have met him once before," said Art with no hint of pleasure on his face. "In fact, it was very uncomfortable. He insisted on showing me a lot of Greek erotic art, and he raved on about interference from the Greek Orthodox Church. I hardly knew what to say, it was such an outburst."

"You ran into the same buzz saw I've been dealing with for many years. He is a thoroughly unpleasant and, yes, sexist man."

The longer this conversation went on, the more Marissa liked Nancy and her moxy. She did not seem to be a woman likely to take a lot of nonsense from anyone, even her superior in the antiquities department. "It's been more a matter of working around Spiros than working with him," Nancy added ruefully.

"I face similar sexist issues with men in archaeology in Turkey," said Marissa sighing. "We should have lunch sometime and compare notes!"

"Yes, let's do!" smiled Nancy. Turning to Art, she laughed, "And forgive my own sexism, but this will be a girl's day out!"

"Fine by me," grinned Art. "But don't complain if I make another great discovery while you two are sipping tea!"

As Marissa and Art left the museum and headed back to Mrs. Demetrios' place for a late lunch Marissa asked, "What do you reckon Spandexikos will want?"

"You mean besides fame, fortune, and all the credit for whatever we find?"

"Yes, besides that," replied Marissa.

"Since the man is a repugnant egomaniac, most anything is possible. Let's be on our guard. I'm glad Nancy is on our side."

"She's first-rate," said Marissa with a grim look. "But she's going to have to be tough. It won't be just another day at the archaeological office."

45

Rendezvous at The Porch

G RACE LEVINE WAS SLOWLY sipping her latte and reading *Haaretz*, Israel's leading newspaper. Though she certainly enjoyed her brief trip to Greece, she was behind in her work. However, there was always time for a good coffee. Her friend Sarah's coffee shop, called Solomon's Porch, was now something of a mecca for upscale Jews in Jerusalem; indeed Sarah was so busy that she opened a second shop at the new mall on the west side of town. Grace's cell phone began to ring insistently. Extracting it from her big bag, she flipped it open and said, "Talk to me."

"Grace, this is Hannah. I need some friendly advice and was hoping to talk with you."

"Certainly! I'm sitting here at Solomon's Porch enjoying a latte and lots of ambiance. Care to join me?"

"Great! I'll be there in five minutes!"

Grace expected a conversation about some matter of antiquity. The paper had few stories of interest for her on this morning, except the notice that the Lazarus Museum was hosting so many visitors already that it was now turning a profit—the construction costs were paid off! This was good news.[1] But then Grace turned the page and read the following:

---

1 See the first and second Art West adventures, *The Lazarus Effect* and *Roman Numerals.*

> A New York man returned a marble fragment he took from an
> Israel Antiquities Authority archaeological excavation south of
> the Temple Mount twelve years ago in Jerusalem. The stone is
> from a column of the 1,200 year-old Umayyad buildings, which
> were being excavated when he was visiting Israel as an archae-
> ology student over a decade ago. He claims that the stone was
> handed to him by his tour guide and that he did not realize
> that it must have been taken without permission until he re-
> turned to New York, where he has felt guilty for all these years.
> He returned the artifact with an apology and a request for for-
> giveness. The Deputy Director of the Unit for the Prevention
> of Antiquities Robbery in the Israel Antiquities Authority, Shay
> Bar Tura, says that no legal actions will be taken due to the fact
> that it was returned, and that the man seemed sincere in his
> apology.[2]

"Well, I guess there are still a few people out there with a conscience," muttered Grace.

Minutes later, Hannah came running into Solomon's Porch, passing all those in line for their morning java, and heading right up the
stairs to Grace's usual spot in the window overlooking Ben Yehuda
Street. Breathless, she said, "I came as quickly as I could."

"Evidently! It must be something urgent," replied Grace.

"It is something potentially life-changing, and I don't know how
to respond."

"Sit down, catch your breath, and tell me about it," Grace said in a
maternal sort of way.

"Grace, do you remember that my husband was killed some twenty years ago. He was in the militant end of Hamas."

"Yes, of course, and I even went to the funeral. And . . . "

"Apparently . . . he is alive!" And Hannah began shaking once
again.

"Impossible! This is not another Lazarus tale, is it?"

"No, nothing like that! Apparently the charred remains were of
someone else. They found my husband's ID and wallet, but apparently
the body was not his after all."

"And you know this how?"

"I received word from the Israeli police. And my father and I had
to go down and identify the photo. He is in a maximum security prison

---

2   As reported on the BAR website on June 5, 2009.

north of Tel Aviv. And here is the hardest part: they want to know if I want to visit him, or if I want to renounce my right to visit him forever. They tell me he will either be in prison forever or executed. He will never be freed. I feel so many emotions about this—shock, fear, and even curiosity. I hardly know where to start. My head is saying, 'Let him go' since we can never go back to being a married couple. My father and I are doing fine without him, and if he found out we had money, who knows what Hamas would do. I'm sure you understand that. And the detective told us in addition that if we chose to visit him, we would be put under normal surveillance by Mossad, whatever that means."

"I would have all the same worries if it were me."

"My heart is saying, 'I'm still his wife.' So if I sign the paper, am I being a bad wife, a cold person? Maybe I'm supposed to forgive him before he dies! There are so many things I wish to ask him. Did he really love me? Maybe I just need closure. I don't know. I just don't know," said Hannah very quietly at this point.

"I haven't had much time to process this incredible news. But I do have one suggestion. Why not tell the officer that you wish to visit him once, and once only, to get the closure you need. Yes, you have things you want to say to him, and this may be your only chance to do so. You will never know his heart until you look straight into his eyes. If you see only the militant man, then walk away. Sign the paper."

"Yes, that sounds right. Father, of course, wants nothing to do with him. But, in my heart I know I must forgive him for all the horror he has caused our family. Then I can move on. I hope Detective Sharansky will agree to this."

"I know the man well; we have worked together on a number of cases since your episode with the menorah last year. With your permission I will speak to him—right now, if possible!"

"Oh, would you? I don't want to impose, but those Israeli police frighten me sometimes."

"No problem." Immediately, Grace dialed up the station where Sharansky had his office.

"Hello, please put me through to Detective Sharansky. Tell him Dr. Grace Levine is calling. . . . Hello, Detective. I am with my friend Hannah el Said. I have a question for you. Would she and her father be able to visit her husband just once and then sign the papers? She needs to get closure on that chapter of her life, and this would help." For some time the detective explained all the possibilities. Finally, Grace said, "Then it's not a problem? In that case, I am going to hand the phone to Hannah. You two can work out when she can visit him for that one time."

After only a brief conversation, it had been arranged for Hannah and Kahlil to make the trip to the prison the following Monday. Turning to Grace, Hannah sighed and said, "What would I do without you?"

"I'm thinking you would have tried far less Jewish food!" And at this Hannah just laughed, which broke the tension and strain she was under.

"Now, girlfriend, let me order you a cup of courage. What are you having?" asked Grace.

In almost childlike glee she said with a smile, "I'm having a white chocolate mocha grande!" And so Grace called the waitress over to fetch the elixir. Hannah and Grace continued to catch up for the next hour, with Hannah telling fascinating stories about their adventures in Jordan at Jerash and Petra.

46

A Date with Destiny

WHEN JAKE GOT HOME, life began to return to off-season normal, until one day, about a week after his season ended, the phone rang. Aunt Joyce picked it up and said, "West residence," and almost immediately she handed the phone to Jake.

"Hello, it's Sherry again. I promised I'd call when I was back in Charlotte. How about we get together for dinner tonight?"

"Okay. Anyway, I have some questions to ask you, so where did you have in mind?"

"How about the Red Rocks Restaurant, say about seven thirty?"

"That sounds fine. I'll meet you there," said Jake and hung up.

"That was Sherry, the beautiful blonde who claims to be writing a story for *Sports Fanatics*. So far she's only asked questions about my personal life."

"Doesn't sound like a sports article to me. Have you checked with your PR people? Do you really know anything about her? Are you sure this won't show up in the tabloids?"

"I understand your concern, and I'll be careful about what I say."

"Remember the old rule, 'When in doubt, don't.'"

"Right!" said Jake as he flashed his million-dollar smile. "Where would I be without you?"

"In a tacky but overly expensive man-cave apartment somewhere in Charlotte where there are no home-cooked meals!"

～

"Sherry," as she called herself, was hardly a dumb blonde. At 5' 9', she immediately demanded attention, and she used it to her considerable advantage. In fact, she was something of a collector of sports stars. Jake was next up on her sampler plan. Her real name was Monica Matson, but that did not suit the persona she assumed with regularity, and in any case her pen name, Sherry Berry, was certainly memorable enough. And while it was true she was doing an article for *Sports Fanatics*, it wasn't the sort of article that Jake might really want to be starring in. "Beefcake of the NBA" was to appear in an issue later in the summer! The magazine hoped to parody the swimsuit issue made famous by *Sports Illustrated*. Tonight she planned to get Jake to agree to the necessary photos.

Staring at Sherry's business card on his dresser while getting ready for his dinner out, Jake kept thinking about what he should talk about over dinner. He was now in his early twenties and he had never once dated a girl before. In Palestine he had been too busy with basketball and Hamas and his family. Girls just got in the way of his political obsessions. This was new and different. He knew better than to overcommit too quickly, but still his heart was aflutter with the possibilities. He figured he would just have to reconcile himself to being a little awkward and nervous.

As he walked into the den Aunt Joyce said, "Come over here and let me look at you!" She smiled and continued, "You definitely pass inspection as a lady's man."

"Thanks, Aunt Joyce," he said and gave her a little kiss on the cheek. "I'll be back after a while."

The drive to the Red Rocks Restaurant took only ten minutes as the traffic was light on Providence Road. It was a hot and muggy evening, and Jake parked his Highlander near the entrance to the restaurant, right next to a little red Ferrari, which was being ogled by the restaurant doorman. The license plate on the Ferrari said "SHRY TOY," and Jake figured this meant that the blonde was in the house.

The restaurant was crowded but Jake found Sherry at the bar, the center of all kinds of attention as usual. And then she announced, "Everyone, the Cat is in the house. Meet Jake Arafat." This was met with a general and genuine round of applause. One young man at the bar said, "You are the best thing that has ever happened to Bobcat basketball. Now if we can just draft some studs to give you some help.

"Drafting is up to Mr. Jordan and the front office."

"Before we get into a lengthy debate about draft picks, let's go order something," said Sherry as she snagged Jake's arm and escorted him off to a booth just outside the bar area. Sherry was wearing a low-cut top, and Jake was having a hard time keeping his gaze from dropping, but then this was the effect she was trying to have. She liked her men drooling and compliant.

After ordering drinks (sweet tea for Jake) Sherry said, "Let's talk business first and get that out of the way. We want to do a shoot with you at the Bobcat court first of next week, and some casual shots around town in downtown Charlotte, like maybe at your favorite hot dog place, Greens. Does that sound doable?"

"Sure, Sherry," replied Jake with an embarrassed smile. "I'm just not used to all this attention."

"Well, get used to it, because once you are in *Sports Fanatics*, there will be a lot more of it."

"I guess about now would be a good time to have a chat with my agent wouldn't it?"

"You think?" And then Sherry smiled broadly showing two rows of perfectly white teeth. "So tell me a bit more about yourself, and your family."

"Sorry, no! First I have a few questions for you. Can I see your credentials please?"

Sherry frowned. "You don't trust me now, do you? But no matter." And she dragged out of her purse a laminated plastic badge complete with her picture and the capital letters SF. But then Jake noticed something unexpected—the name on the badge wasn't Sherry, it was Monica Matson.

"It seems you have two names," marveled Jake.

"That's right, Sugar. In my business it pays to have a pen name, a name under which you write, especially if you are a girl like me. That way you don't have people tracking you down and banging on your door. But I'm so used to being called Sherry now, it's just second nature."

"Maybe I should get a pen name if I am going to become famous pretty soon!" said Jake with a smile. "So where do you come from, and how did you get into this business?"

"Good question. I majored in journalism at a little school down the road from here that you may have heard of—Wake Forest. Then I worked at a Winston-Salem newspaper doing sports. I tried a brief stint on local TV as a sports anchor. Didn't much like that. I did a piece on steroids that appeared in the *Washington Post* which got the attention of SF and I have been freelancing for them ever since. Now it's your turn. Tell me about your family."

"One more question. I reckon you are from around here, but do you have any brothers or sisters or parents? What do they think of what you do?"

"My father was my big supporter. He passed away several years ago."

"I'm sorry. I have the same story on that score."

"And I'm an only child," said Sherry matter-of-factly.

"Well, I am now," replied Jake. "I lost my brother. He was murdered in Bethlehem." Unexpectedly, Jake teared up.

Sherry did not know what to think, so she handed him a tissue.

Composing himself, Jake added, "My mother and sister-in-law live near Jericho. They cook and clean for a monastery down there in exchange for a safe place to live."

"For real?" said Sherry, who had turned on her little tape recorder in the front pocket of her purse.

"Yes. I call them regularly and send them things through channels. But I miss them. If it weren't for Aunt Joyce, I would be lost over here."

"Tell me more about Aunt Joyce. Is she really your aunt?"

"She's actually the mother of the famous scholar and archaeologist Art West. West was involved with my family in Palestine and helped me relocate to Charlotte. I live with his mom!"

"Do tell. And how has that worked out?"

"Surprisingly well! Aunt Joyce has been a help getting me acclimated to life in Charlotte and keeping me grounded."

"I'll bet she even takes you to church," hinted Sherry, realizing she had a genuine wet-behind-the-ears man sitting across from her.

"How did you know? We go to Myers Park Methodist Church, which is her home church."

"I see," said Sherry, beginning to feel a little shabby about what she was doing with Jake. "Let's stop the chat and order our meal. But first a question: can you call the team office and set up a time for a shoot in uniform at the court on Monday?"

"Sure. That's easy. I will call Mrs. Monroe in the morning and we can work that out for, say, ten a.m. Is that good?"

"Yes, that will work fine." Having obtained what she really wanted, Sherry then steered the evening through dinner and some more chit-chat. When the check arrived, she said, "Your money is no good here. The least I can do is pay the bill since you have been so kind as to give me this interview."

"Okay, but Aunt Joyce told me I had to get the check."

"You really haven't done this before have you?"

"No" said Jake, "But there is a first time for everything."

Sherry just sat for a minute and marveled. Jake was a genuine ingénue and she was becoming more uncomfortable with taking advantage of him, but not so much that it would derail her plans. As they walked out the door together, the doorman winked that knowing wink, and Jake opened the car door for Sherry. She suddenly turned and gave him a little kiss on the cheek. "That's for being such a big help," she said in her sultry voice. "I will see you on Monday at the Bobcat center at ten. Don't forget to tell them to let me in! And wear your home uniform. It will set off your olive-colored skin quite nicely!"

Jake blushed and said, "As you wish." As Sherry drove off in her little red ragtop, Jake just stood there in the parking lot staring for a while until the doorman interrupted his reverie. "She has that effect on a lot of guys I imagine," said the doorman.

"You're probably right," said Jake coming back to earth, and then as he got in his car he thought to himself, "I'm probably nobody special to her. Just another interview."

47

And The Answer Is . . . ?

Promptly at eight a.m. Marissa's cell phone rang. Running from the bathroom into the bedroom, she stubbed her toe on the foot of the bed and ended up hopping around to the night table to grab the phone. Checking the caller ID, she quickly opened the phone. It was Hakan Eretegun.

"Marissa, I have some good news and some bad news for you. Which do you want first?"

"Let's go with the good news."

"My worthless cousin did indeed doctor the translation of our article. And, I have forced him to send a retraction to the journal in question, and to copy it to me. I have it here, and it is clear enough. It states that the translation should have said that in the battle at Kadesh the Egyptians seem to have won, and in any case there was a peace treaty drawn up between them and the Hittites as witnessed by the treaty stone that has been found at Hattusha. It also says that this was an error of the translator, not those who composed the original article in Turkish."

"That's all fine. But what is the bad news?"

"Well, this is a quarterly journal. So the retraction will not be out for a while. Meanwhile there will be careful scholars like Dr. William Arnold buzzing around, critiquing the thing, and thinking we are responsible. So we will be answering questions we would rather not bother with just now. But it's the best we can do."

"It could be worse. Thank you so much for taking quick action. So what will happen to Mehmet as a result of this?"

"He was already on Koroturk's bad side, and now I have told him he has to be an ostrich in Antioch, sticking his head in the sand of the tel."

"I think it's pretty merciful he hasn't been fired already."

"If you are an employee of the government, it's hard to get fired, frankly."

"Ah yes, our tax dollars at work."

"Take care Marissa, and find something remarkable in Greece if at all possible."

"I already have, and he sitting right in front of me," Marissa said, as she found Art devouring a stack of pancakes in Mrs. Demetrios' kitchen and closed her phone.

"Some kind of gentleman you are, eating up all the food and not waiting for me," scolded Marissa.

"Is my fault," said Elena. "I told him eat cakes while hot, which is why they are called hotcakes!"

"I have news!" said Marissa. "Hakan Ertegun called and said Mehmet was made to recant, and the retraction will be published in the next issue of the journal, which unfortunately is not for three more months."

"Now I will call my friend, the good Dr. Arnold, and let him know. All's well that ends well."

"I am apt to say, 'It ain't over until it's over', because I will be doing damage control for the next three months," warned Marissa.

"True enough, but at least you know the correction is in motion. And now we need to get to work!" said Art, "Right after you have some of these scrumptious pancakes. Mrs. Demetrios, these are as good as my mother makes, and that's the best compliment I could give."

"I am your mother while you are here!" said Mrs. Demtrios, and then the wrinkles on her face turned upwards when she smiled.

"Ain't it the truth," said Art. "But in a few minutes we need to be checking out what Mother Earth can reveal to us."

"But first a phone call to Dr. Arnold, please," requested Marissa. The phone call to Bill went well. He agreed to wait for the retraction that would appear in the journal before commenting. Marissa arranged for Koroturk to send him a personal copy.

Bill said it was time for an article on poor and even unethical translations!

"I think Bill will be our ally. So in the short term there will be some damage control, but in the long term I'm convinced everything will be okay. So let's dig!"

48

Grounds for Investigation

Spiros Spandexikos had contacts—lots of contacts. He even had contacts in Turkey with communists there. And they most certainly had heard of Marissa Okur. She had been splashed all over the news as a result of the finds at Hierapolis during the previous year. But the most recent revelation that found its way to Spiros's desk, thanks to an underling, was an English translation about the finds at the Hittite site of Hattusha. The clerk pointed out that the translation differed from the original article written in Turkish with Hakan Ertegun. Spiros realized the significance of the differences. It was beginning to look like one could claim that Marissa Okur was either a careless, headline grabbing archaeologist, or an ideologue bound to reinterpret the data in a certain direction favoring a Turkish way of reading the evidence, at the expense of Egypt in this case.

Spiros had already dispatched Nick to take pictures of what was going on at the site in Corinth. One picture in particular fascinated him. The object protruding from the ground looked like something made of metal. Yes, it was time to head down to Corinth and check things out himself.

It was an incredibly hot day in Athens, and the smog was so bad that the air quite literally stank. After only five minutes of walking to his black Mercedes from an air-conditioned building, Spiros was wringing wet. It did not help that the seats were made of leather and the front of

153

the car had been sitting in the sun for several hours now. While waiting for the car to cool off, he decided to call Nick.

Nick was excited by the surprise call. "Where are you? I need you to come down here. Something big is going down, but I can't quite figure it out. I got to the site early and hid out. West and Okur arrived about thirty minutes ago. And then, Nancy Bookides showed up. They are all talking excitedly. Is there any way you can get down here?"

"I have a surprise for you. I'm spending the next few days on the road, visiting various sites, including Corinth. Meanwhile keep your eyes on things. Don't go wandering off too far. And alert our friend Andros who runs the ticket booth at the entrance to the old site. We may need to call a quick meeting of all our local friends. I'd like to talk to our party members in Corinth."

"Will do boss. See you soon."

～

Nick continued to watch the trio talk and gesture around a metal object now nearly unearthed on the site.

"Nancy, you are so right that this rack is a significant find, and the sooner we get it out of the ground, the less danger of looting," said Marissa with a worried look.

"Looting is a constant problem on all our sites," warned Nancy. "And this could be big. I agree we need to post some guards at this point. Fortunately, we have about fifty good photographs, and the pieces of leather you have already sent to our lab. We are going to need some kind of wench-and-pulley system to gently extricate this frame from the ground without damaging it." Nancy quickly grabbed her phone to put the wheels in motion.

49

A Heart of Darkness

THE TRIP TO HADERA, north of both Tel Aviv and the popular beach spot at Netanya, took much longer than expected due to construction around Tel Aviv. And the longer the trip took, the more Hannah felt dread building up inside her. While she didn't want the visit to be a confrontation with her husband, she figured it might well go that way, and she was not a confrontational person. In fact, she had despised her husband's life with Hamas, but she was powerless to stop him. Now that he had returned, almost from the dead, she really did not know how to respond. In some ways she was not glad he was back, but then it would be a violation of her own beliefs to wish the man dead.

When Kahlil passed Netanya he decided to break the silence rather than leave his daughter brooding in her thoughts. "Have you decided what you will say to Yassir?"

"My thoughts and feelings are all jumbled. I hardly know what to think or do. I do know that I cannot condone his behavior. Art West once talked about 'loving the sinner, but hating the sin.' I guess that's where I am."

"You realize that the Israelis will be listening in on whatever conversation you have anyway, so please choose your words very carefully. Make clear that neither of us supports his cause."

Finally, the uncomfortable couple arrived at the front gate to the maximum security prison in Hadera. "Stand and identify," said the guard at the gate. Kahlil quietly handed over the paperwork provided by the detective. Looking up, he could see the fifteen-foot-high walls, on top of which were bits of broken glass and barbed wire as far as the eye could see. There was a tall conning tower in the middle of the compound that reached another fifteen feet up into the air. Kahlil could just make out guards patrolling the parapets of the tower, watching everything that was happening below.

Once inside the front gate, Kahlil and Hannah were ushered into a little building where they were both searched completely. Sergeant Levi ushered the couple straight into the compound, past the exercise yard, through three locked doors and into an interrogation room.

There would be no direct contact between Yassir and Hannah, and this gave Hannah a certain amount of relief. The interrogation room had a glass partition down the center with desks and chairs on each side equipped with two-way push-to-talk microphones.

There was a somewhat muffled sound of a buzzer, and just as Hannah sat down a man walked through a door to the right wearing prison clothes and sporting a long beard. At first Hannah did not think this could possibly be Yassir, but the more she looked at his facial features and eyes, the more convinced she became that indeed it was him. Her right leg began to jiggle under the table as she became more and more nervous about what was about to ensue.

"So woman, I see you have finally come to see me," said Yassir abruptly.

"I could hardly get here sooner, since I was only notified last week you were even alive. I have not seen you in twenty years. Have you no concern for me?"

"I have followed your so-called career. You work in the antique shop with your father. You never remarried, which is interesting. I heard you came into some money. I will be needing money for my defense."

"There is not going to be any trial. Did you not hear? There are no more appeals. They will decide whether execution or life in prison is your fate, and apparently that issue depends on your behavior while you are here."

"You are just a woman, and do not know what you are talking about. I have an excellent lawyer, and so you may well expect to see me outside these walls, at which point I will come your way."

"No, Yassir, that is not going to happen! In just these few minutes, I can see there is no change in you, and no concern for my well-being.

I was a widow, but now apparently I am legally married. I am here to tell you I have made up my mind to quickly get a legal divorce, and a restraining order if you ever do get out of jail!"

At this announcement, Yassir swore in Arabic, and then spat on the glass. "You will do no such thing! I am your husband and you will obey me!"

Hannah was shaking at this point but she maintained her composure and retorted, "You stopped being a faithful husband twenty years ago. In your heart, you divorced me and married Hamas. I believed you were dead. I mourned. I gather you were in Lebanon?"

"Yes and no. But why should I tell you. You sided with the infidels from the very beginning. You were a traitor to the Intifadah as well!"

"I don't believe in your politics, Yassir. I never did, as you know. And now I will say goodbye. I will never see you again. What a bitter and terrible person you have become! May Allah have mercy on your soul!"

"You will see me again woman, and when you do, it will not be pleasant. I will claim the money as your husband. Mark my words." Hannah was already beginning to walk away, but Yassir was screaming now through the microphone, "You cannot escape me! I have returned and you will see me again! I will not forget how you behaved on this day and dishonored your husband! I will not forget and you will pay dearly!"

The tears streamed down Hannah's face as she left the interrogation room and was met by her father in the antechamber. Suddenly her emotions overcame her, and she felt a huge wave of nausea. The next thing she knew she was on her knees throwing up, and a female guard was racing over to give her some water and clean up the mess with a mop and a bucket.

"Do not feel badly about this. It often happens. The shock of seeing one's relative in such a place is great," explained the woman guard.

"Thank you for your kindness," said Hannah, as she wiped her face with the cold washrag. Kahlil then helped her to her feet and supported her as they left the room and began the return journey back out to the heat and the car.

"So did he say anything worthwhile, daughter?" asked Kahlil quietly.

"He was full of hate and false hopes of getting out. He claimed I must give him money for his defense. He said I would see him again outside this prison. He said he would come for me. I know it is not rational, but that is what shook me up the most."

"Understandably. I presume you will file for the formal divorce as quickly as possible?" suggested Kahlil.

"Yes. I have enough evidence now that he is dangerous still, and that he has no respect for me or concern for my well-being, but only for himself and his cause. I believe the mullah will understand if you present him the evidence with me."

"Of course, and then perhaps we can finally close the book on this sad and sordid chapter in our lives," sighed Kahlil.

"I hope so, ensh' Allah," said Hannah looking grim and determined. "But he still frightens me; his heart of darkness is still beating and his hatreds still drive him." And by then they had once more reached the car, having passed through all the security except the outer gate, and were finally heading for home. But that haunting angry voice kept echoing in Hannah's mind the entire ride home.

50

The Great Escape

As so often happens in life, the low man on the totem pole gets the most unpleasant jobs. Yassir's job was cleaning the latrines and showers in the prison. There was a central stall where the inmates were allowed to shower, under supervision, but what Yassir had learned from his shower duty is that the guards did not pay much, if any, attention to him when he was doing his dirty work. His detail was scheduled for early evening, after supper, so that everything would be clean for the next day.

The shower stalls all fed into a central drain where the floor was a little more concave. Covering the hole in the floor was a perforated manhole cover about the width of a small man. This sluice went somewhere, and since the prison was not two hundred yards from the sea, Yassir was betting it emptied through a drainage pipe into the Mediterranean. The prison was far enough removed from the town of Hadera that he doubted that the drain was connected to some city water system.

Ever since "that wretched bitch," as he now called Hannah, came to visit him in prison, Yassir became more and more determined to escape. He decided, since he did not yet know or trust any of the other incarcerated Palestinians, that he would chance going it alone. Yassir hoped for a maximum of ten minutes alone to get the manhole cover open, get into the pipe, pull the manhole cover back into position, and then start inching his way out of the pipe and back into the world. For three days he planned his escape, and each of those three days he took out a single bolt holding the manhole cover down to the floor. There were a total of four bolts. He managed to pilfer a small wrench from the janitor's closet where his mop and pail were kept. He did his best not to draw any attention to himself.

If he escaped, Yassir planned to flee on foot to nearby Nablus. If he saw a car with a Palestinian plate he would flag it down and try for a ride. He carefully thought out everything, or so he imagined.

Friday evening rolled around and he found himself in the showers alone as usual. This would be the night. Just then, a guard wandered in to urinate, but after finishing, he hung around watching Yassir mop and mop and mop and mop. He wouldn't leave. Yassir managed to go into the shower stall behind the guard. With wrench in hand Yassir came up silently behind the guard and clubbed him three times on the head with violent downward swings of his right arm. The man let out a small yelp but fell quickly to the ground. Groping around the man's waist, Yassir found the guard's pistol—a real bonus. After dragging the body out of sight, Yassir ran to the manhole cover, pulled it up, lowered himself into the pipe, pulled the cover closed, and then began the arduous task of wriggling down through the vertical pipe to the more horizontal one he had seen just below.

In his haste, Yassir had not thought to take the guard's flashlight, a haste borne of fear since he knew the guard would soon be found and the alarm sounded. His escape could have gone unnoticed for a longer period of time, if not for the stupid guard choosing this night to watch him mop. Finally, Yassir emerged from the smaller pipe into the bigger one below. Yassir found himself suddenly swept along with the current of gray water, and the end of this tunnel-like pipe was so far away that Yassir could not see it. Had he been able to do so, he would have seen that there was yet another cover on the end of the sewer to prevent escapes exactly of the sort he was attempting. After about fifteen minutes, Yassir found himself impaled by the current up against the outer cover. Through the few drainage holes, he could only see freedom.

Feeling in the dark for where the bolts were, he managed to get his wrench to loosen the top three located in the north, east, and west positions on the cover, but the bottom bolt was under water, and would

require him holding his breath, submerging and then frantically loos-
ening to get it off. There was no escaping this trap otherwise. The first
two attempts failed to loosen the rusty bolt on the bottom of the cover.
On the third attempt Yassir, already exhausted, finally got the bolt to
budge a little. Coming up for air, he submerged once more, and this
time he finally got the last bolt off, but the cover had rusted into place.
He still was not free. Kicking and kicking at the cover, he finally dis-
lodged it at the top, the middle, and finally the bottom, and there was
a great rush of water around him when it fell down. He was free! But
where was he?

Crawling out from the drain he looked up to see stars in the sky,
and he heard the rush of the ocean tide in front of him. He was on
a beach, somewhere near Hadera. He heard no voices, only a seagull
or two. He raced down to the shoreline, took off his shoes, and dove
into the salty sea. Yassir had been a good swimmer as a boy, and this
skill came in handy now. He thoroughly washed himself, took off his
prison overalls, and buried them in the sand. He had remembered to
wear a pair of shorts under his overalls. Wet, but refreshed, he put his
shoes back on. He had left the gun with his shoes on the shore, but the
wrench he took with him out into the sea and dropped it to the bottom.

Lacing up his shoes again, and sticking the gun in the back of his
pants but under his shirt, he decided the smart move was to walk down
the beach to the lights he saw a good ways away. This would give him
time to dry off in the shore breeze blowing on this hot night. Finally,
emerging onto a lit street in Hadera, Yassir saw a few signs of life. It
must be well after midnight. Suddenly a yellow taxi came around the
corner, a taxi with a Palestinian plate, and Yassir hailed it.

"Need a ride?" said the driver with the big handlebar moustache.

"Can you take me as far as Nablus?"

"Well, perhaps not all the way, but we can make a good start. Hop
in."

Yassir could hardly believe his luck. He was going to get away with
this. He was going to escape. Wait until Hannah and Kahlil saw him
coming into the shop! He could hardly wait to see the look of horror on
their faces. He could be reunited with his Hamas friends.

Freedom can make a person giddy, even reckless. What Yassir had
not noticed is that the taxi driver also had a gun, which he kept by
his side on the seat. And as the taxi was leaving the lighted streets of

Hadera, the taxi cab driver turned to Yassir, and Yassir suddenly found a gun pointing in his face.

"And now, welcome to your worst nightmare," said the taxi driver. "I work for Mossad, and was sent to recover you and return you to the prison. No trial for you! You will be executed for attacking a guard and trying to escape! You made a mistake coming to a town down the beach from the prison." Suddenly two shots rang out in the small confines of the car, and the car lurched sideways, skidded off the desolate road, and turned over in a ditch, swallowed up by darkness.

51

Wachovia Will Watch Over Ya

T HE TRUST FUND SET up for Art West's archaeological exploits and expeditions had been rolling along nicely until of course the economic crash in the fall of 2008. Art still did not know who set up this fund, though he had his suspicions. At ten p.m. Joyce went on line to check the monthly statement, but this month there was an odd warning at the top of the statement.

TRADING SUSPENDED; HEDGE FUND CLOSED.

The account still posted a substantial amount of money, but there had been a significant loss of funds, and the way the account was set up, if the amount went below a certain level then trading on the stock market would cease. In short, the account would be dead in the water. Art would be unable to take anything out of it until the stock market recovered. This was a protective strategy so that Art wouldn't suffer catastrophic loss if the market truly crashed. But it also meant that suddenly Art had a cash flow problem.

"Better call Arthur at once," said Joyce, muttering out loud. The phone rang for a while and finally Art picked up.

"Hullo? Who's calling?" said a sleepy voice.

"Arthur, this is your mom. What time is it there anyways?"

"It's five a.m. This is the second time I've gotten a call at five a.m.! Mom, this better be urgent!"

"You're broke!" she said matter-of-factly.

"What!?" said Art suddenly awake.

"Not exactly, but I knew that would get your attention. Your hedge fund has been suspended due to the downturn in the stock market, so you can't draw on your account until the market recovers. You still have a bundle of dough in the account, but it's not accessible now. Trading has been suspended. You may thank Wachovia's automated system set up to protect your fund from dwindling down to nothing."

"Yikes! This is not good news! I may have to borrow some money! Do you think the bank might be in a lending mood?"

"I doubt it son, since Wachovia was just taken over by Wells Fargo, but you can always call Dick Character."

"Will do. Guess what?"

"I'm not good at guessing."

"We may have found St. Paul's drying rack."

"You must be pulling my leg. I doubt Paul had a drying rack. How many togas did he have?" countered Joyce.

"Not for togas, for tents!" explained Art.

"Well, you just write a nice article in some archaeology journal, and I promise to read it. Meanwhile, how's that dark-skinned beauty of yours?" said Joyce changing the subject.

"She's fine. A little frazzled, but fine. We do want to talk about a possible wedding date at some point." There was silence on the other end of the line. "Mom, did I lose you? Hello!"

"No, son, you didn't lose me. I just never thought I'd hear those words—you being about fifty and a confirmed bachelor to date."

"Love is love at any age. Marissa and I don't want to waste too much time with a long engagement. As you hinted, I'm not getting any younger, which is why I need my beauty sleep. I'm going back to bed. I'll call Dick sometime tomorrow."

Joyce hung up the phone and sat there with little tears rolling down her face. Both her children had chosen career paths—Art in Archaeology and Laura in the mission field. Planning a wedding would be a whole new ballgame for this family. Morning, afternoon, or evening? Sit-down dinner or buffet? Jazz ensemble or deejay?

～

Art couldn't sleep so he decided to write a bit more on his novel. Opening up his laptop and waiting for it to boot up, he went and washed his face and combed his hair, making a start on the new day. He had an idea about what to write next . . .

52

Once Upon A Time V

*P*AUL HAD MONEY TROUBLES. *On the one hand, he studiously avoided patronage in Corinth because with it came reciprocity expectations and Paul didn't want to be anybody's paid in-house philosopher. On the other hand, he certainly believed in the saying of Jesus that "a workman was worthy of their hire" and that a minister of Jesus deserved to be paid. This whole sticky situation was made more difficult by the fact that he received support money from his congregation up north in Philippi, and the problem was further exacerbated by the fact that he was actually asking the Corinthians to contribute to the fund for famine relief in Jerusalem. Why was money always a problem, even for those "in Christ." Truth be told, Paul was a bit short on personal money at the moment despite what he earned for his leather goods. The Isthmian games were fast approaching and sales were holding on that front, but the locals were not buying leather goods at the usual level.*

The Romans, especially soldiers, wore leather coats to protect them from the cold, but those assigned to Corinth rarely needed such garments. Footwear and wide belts were still in demand, but the Romans rarely used goatskins—pig, sheep, and cattle skin were their top choices. Aquila and Priscilla were constantly thinking of ways to expand their line. Prisca, Priscilla's formal name, was gaining a good reputation as a smart businesswoman.

Prisca and Aquila were both out on business and the two young apprentices were helping at home this week. Paul had the shop to himself.

He took advantage of this by talking to the four walls. "Priscilla says they need me, but I hate imposing on their hospitality too long. Staying with Erastos is causing him some problems with the city government. His position is already in jeopardy. I can't really afford to have a home of my own – and besides I don't own anything to put in a home! I could always move on to another town that needs evangelizing, but that might look like I'm running away after the trial before Gallio." Paul stopped long enough to scratch his balding head, which was peeling due to sunburn.

Just then a rather dour-looking Erastos entered the shop. He took one look at Paul and said, "Did you know that the rent is due?"

"Blessings in the name of the Lord to you too!" smiled Paul. "Prisca is not here at the moment to solve this problem. Maybe you would like to sit down and share a bit of your day's troubles! Have some wine with me!"

"I have been fretting over treasuries all day—mine and the city's. Neither one is looking healthy. Rumor has it that less and less people will be coming to Corinth for the games and the locals fear the loss of revenue. Some wish the games would be held right here in Corinth rather than out of town in Isthmia. At home, my family begs for the latest fashions—my wife expects to be as elegant as my station allows. And now, I have converts asking for alms. Meanwhile, you are collecting funds for our brethren in Jerusalem. It is hard to convince anyone to support your fund when our people are only looking to their own wants and needs. Finally, thanks to you, I'm no longer skimming city funds. Being a follower is proving to be anything but lucrative!"

Paul listened patiently to Erastos' litany. He decided against a lecture in favor of simple support.

"I agree with you. Although my overhead is very low, thanks to your hospitality and my position here, I too have been pondering money problems. Truly this is a subject for prayer. I suggest we pray about this at our next meeting at your home."

"I am a man of action. Praying requires patience. I never really prayed to the

gods before I was converted. So praying for me does not come easy," admitted Erastos.

"Which is all the more reason why we will pray about our finances. Practice makes perfect," smiled Paul

53

Amir and The Night Visitor

YASSIR FIRED DIRECTLY THROUGH the seat, twice, into the exposed midsection of the taxi driver/Mossad agent. The car rolled completely over and righted itself. Yassir pushed the profusely bleeding and unconscious driver out the door, climbed into the driver's seat, and after a couple of false starts, drove off to Nablus. Wouldn't his old compatriots there be surprised to see him! It had been years since he operated out of Nablus for Hamas, but he still knew a couple of the ardent supporters there who would hide him in a heartbeat. He was exhilarated, but vowed to be cautious.

In these early hours, Nablus revealed no life other than stray dogs and feral cats wandering the streets looking for a morsel of food. Due to cutbacks, the city lights were mostly out, but Yassir could see his way along with the aid of his headlights. His plans were to go to Amir's house, wait until dawn, knock on the door, and take it from there. Nablus, near the base of Mt. Gerizim, had long been a hotbed of ferment and fervor when it came to things revolutionary. The Israelis had put down squabbles and protests more than once in the region. As a result, Palestinian Christians had fled the city and it was almost entirely in the hands of Muslims, some more, some less, radical. There were as well a few Samaritans, but they were never any trouble, and the locals hardly even considered them Jews. Nablus was a place Yassir could feel right at home and hopefully be welcomed.

Yassir waited until seven thirty before he got out of his car and went up the apartment steps to bang on Amir's door. It was already a hot morning, and figured to be blisteringly hot by midday. Such was life in the summertime in Nablus. After knocking rather vigorously once, Yassir heard sounds of scrambling inside the house, and finally someone came and opened the door a crack and peeped out. "Who is there?"

"It is me, your old friend Yassir. Is Amir there?" The door closed again but Yassir could hear a female voice holler, "Someone get my useless husband out of bed."

Yassir just chuckled. Life was much the same now as it was years ago. People were still poor. Wives still got up early, did chores, and got the children off to school. Husbands arose later and either went to work, or went downtown to talk politics with their friends and play boardgames like backgammon. Finally, Yassir heard heavy feet plodding towards the door. Amir had always been a big man, but now he was huge.

The door opened dramatically and a very sleepy man with uncombed hair and unshaved face said, "And who are you supposed to be?"

"*Salam aleichum* to you, Amir," said Yassir. "Long time, no see."

Then Amir's eyes went wide open and his mouth agape. "Is that really you Yassir? I was sure you were dead. In fact, I attended your funeral. Allah be praised, you have arisen from the dead!"

"My death was greatly exaggerated. But I did just escape from an Israeli prison and I need help. I have been in Lebanon for many years, working with Hezbollah for some time. But then I was caught by some renegades, traded for another prisoner and ended up in the hands of the Israelis in the Hadera prison. Can I please come in?"

"Of course, of course, and Amir opened the door wide. We are glad to see you. I must call Kamil and tell him you are here. He will want all the news." Kamil was the local Hamas contact, and Yassir did not know him.

"I have not eaten now in more than a day. Would it be possible for me to have a little breakfast before we meet Kamil?"

"Certainly," and then hollering into the back of the flat he said, "Wife, set another place at the breakfast table for our long-lost friend Yassir."

"Won't Kamil be shocked! It will be the talk of the town."

"Well, it would be best if it was kept very quiet Amir," stressed Yassir. "Remember, I am now a wanted man and an escapee from Hadera Prison."

"I see your point, but Kamil at least must be notified."

"Yes, that makes sense. I must get back into the Hamas network again."

After a light breakfast and some brief conversation, Amir and Yassir decided to go straight to Kamil's office and have a chat. By now the sun was halfway up the sky, and people were doing their best to stay on the shady side of the street. Kamil's office was in an old limestone building that could be easily missed, it was so small and unobtrusive. Amir had called ahead, and Kamil said he would see them as soon as they could get there.

The office was not air-conditioned; all the windows were open and an old fan was running. "Come in, come in," said Kamil in a short, clipped way. He did not look happy to see them.

"We will skip the preliminaries since I know who you are. I must ask you a direct question and I expect a straight answer. Did you by any chance shoot a Mossad agent near Hadera yesterday and leave him for dead?"

Yassir had already been sweating but now he was really sweating. "Yes, he held me at gunpoint and was going to take me back to prison. I couldn't let that happen."

"You realize of course the penalty for shooting a Mossad agent. It's open season on you now, without due process of law even. And worst of all the man survived the gunshot wounds. He can identify you. He has the license plate number of the taxi, which is now sitting in front of my office!"

"Oh no," was all that would come out of Yassir's mouth.

"So you cannot stay here. The Israelis will be snooping around here soon, looking for that taxi and you. So here is what we are going to do. We are putting you on a Palestinian bus to east Jerusalem immediately! As for the taxi, Amir, you know exactly what to do with it. Yassir, when you get to east Jerusalem you are going to have to go underground to Bethlehem or Jericho. Do you understand me? You must disappear."

"I understand," said a glum Yassir. "It seems no one wants to hear the tales of my heroic escape or courageous deeds in Lebanon."

"Maybe later, much later," said Kamil. "For now you are too hot to handle, much less to hide. The bus leaves very soon and you must be on it. In the back you will find a change of clothes, a bag, and a few shekels. We will shave your head, and give you a mustache."

And as Yassir got on the old black and white bus to a destination where he would probably not be any better received than in Nablus, he looked out the back window just in time to see two Israeli Jeeps pull up outside the office of Kamil. He hoped he had not caused too much trouble, but it had managed to sink in to his rather thick head that from now on he would be a fugitive. Escape from prison did not mean life going back to normal. It meant life on the run, always looking over his shoulder.

54

Courting Disaster

BOBCAT ARENA WAS RIGHT downtown in Charlotte near the intersection of the two major streets, Tryon and Trade, just off the new tramline. Jake decided to take the tram for a change, and so he parked at the station on South Boulevard and enjoyed the ride into town avoiding all traffic. With his iPod on and his ear buds in, listening to Bob Marley's greatest hits, he was oblivious to all those around him, and truth be told, they didn't recognize him in his tracksuit either. Jake had not yet attained instant-recognition status in Charlotte, and he enjoyed his anonymity. Occasionally someone would ask for an autograph but that was usually after a game, when he was still in uniform, and he gladly obliged.

Like most NBA sites, Bobcat Arena was state of the art with the usual luxury boxes and amenities. When Jake arrived, Sherry and her cameraman were already there waiting in the concourse for him. Larry, the security guard, immediately lit up when he saw Jake. "The Cat is in the house! To what do we owe the pleasure?"

"We need to do a photo shoot down on the court, and the front office says fine."

"Come right this way. Let me unlock this door and turn on the lights, and ya'll can go to work."

"Thanks so much," said Sherry, who was wearing a black and white polka-dot outfit with a wide-brimmed white hat. She cut quite a figure, and frankly Jake was feeling increasingly like he was way out of his league, budding NBA star or not.

"You run along and change, and we will get things set up down near the goal. We want some action shots of you shooting and dunking, plus some stills. And one more thing. Do you mind if we do a couple of shots of you taking your top off and throwing it to an imagined fan in the stands?"

"Well," said Jake with some hesitation, "I guess that will be alright. All in good fun."

"Absolutely," said Sherry with a disarming smile.

After changing into the road uniform, which Sherry preferred since it had more color, Jake laced up his Nikes, grabbed a ball, and headed back to the court, thinking this might be fun.

Jake, with his height and dark skin set off against an orange and dark-blue jersey, would immediately stand out in a crowd. When Sherry saw him dribbling the ball she instructed the cameraman to start taking multiple shots from a floor-level camera angle—shooting up had become fashionable. This was followed by shots of Jake doing monster dunks, turn-around jump shots, free throws, or just posing with the ball under his arm and a big smile on his face.

Finally Sherry said, "Jake, now pretend you've just hit a game winning shot, and the fans are all going wild. You are heading for the tunnel and you see a fan screaming for your jersey, so instinctively you take it off and throw it into the stands."

Jake was trying hard to please, so he endured this routine three separate times until Sherry and the cameraman were satisfied. And Sherry was satisfied, because they snagged some great closes ups, action shots, and more importantly, those never-seen-before shots of Jake without a jersey!

"Lunch is on me!" said Sherry when Charlie the cameraman was packing up. "We are going to Greens, of course, and Charlie will get a couple of shots of us having lunch. Then we are done! Now wasn't that easy?"

"And when does this spread come out?" asked Jake.

Sherry replied vaguely, "In the near future when we do a feature on rising rookies of the NBA."

Greens was packed during the lunch hour as usual, and two of the businessmen recognized Jake, came over, shook his hand, and nodded in Sherry's direction. Green's Lunch had been a Charlotte institution since 1926. Jake ordered their signature dish—hotdogs all-the-way with mustard, ketchup, the secret-recipe chili, onions, and slaw.

Once Jake finished consuming no less than three dogs, Sherry tilted her head, leaned closer, and asked, "How about a real date Jake? We've done the business, how about some pleasure. Say dinner and a movie, home before eleven? You can drive the Ferrari, and I'll navigate to my favorite restaurant—a surprise I think you'll love. I know Charlotte pretty well."

"You know a lot of things pretty well," said Jake, trying not to act too giddy. He was in over his head, but he liked the rush of adrenaline that coursed through his veins when he was with Sherry. He had instantly agreed to the date without even checking with Aunt Joyce. Life was looking up, he thought, as he walked the four blocks to the tram. Sherry and the cameraman had gone back to the arena to pick up their car.

Jake sat in silence as the tram pulled away from Bobcat Arena. Conflicting emotions piled one on top of the other and he was feeling confused. On the one hand he definitely liked being with Sherry, and he definitely wondered what it would be like to really kiss her. But the comfort level wasn't there—her take-charge attitude bordered on manipulation. He was not sure what was next, but he would not have to wait long to find out. He'd better get home and get his act together for the big date.

55

An Exercise in Patience

Art was not at all looking forward to his little meeting with Spiros Spandexikos, nor was Marissa, who was convinced the man was the proverbial male chauvinist pig. Fortunately Nancy Bookides would be present during the whole discussion, so Art figured things couldn't get too out of hand. Mrs. Demetrios had warned Art to be on his guard, as she had heard some cautionary tales told about this man in the tabloids. Her main advice: "Be patient. Don't take the bait if he tries to provoke you."

By the time Art and Marissa arrived at the Corinth Museum and walked through to the workshop, there was Spiros Spandexikos sprawled out in a chair smoking a big cigar while Nancy was busy opening a window. "So you have finally showed up," said Spiros looking askance at Art.

"I believe our appointment was for ten a.m. and it is just now ten. I would like to introduce you to my colleague, Dr. Marissa Okur," replied Art calmly.

"Ah, yes, the Turkish archaeologist. What's the matter, couldn't you find someone here in Greece to work with?"

"We are working closely with Dr. Bookides, whose work is well-known here in Greece. I will add that Dr. Okur is my fiancée so I think you will see the logic of our working together," countered Art with a pleasant smile.

"I suppose," said Spiros, blowing a smoke ring in the general direction of Art and Marissa. "So what's this about finding some kind of rack? I would hardly call a laundry rack a great find. Now maybe a rack on which they stretched people . . ."

Marissa entered the conversation and confidently replied, "It is not a laundry rack. We are suggesting that this rack was for stretching animal skins, not human beings."

"And *why* would that be of any great significance?" retorted Spiros.

"Because, of course, the New Testament tells us that Paul, Aquila, and Priscilla plied their trade of tent-making here in Corinth. It is premature to say who exactly is the owner of the villa with its workshop at the back, but we are dealing with a first-century villa, so anything is possible," explained Marissa.

"Come, come. You have no hard evidence to connect this find with those early Christian folks," argued Spiros.

"Not yet, but we *will* keep looking," said Art. He clenched his jaw.

Eyes narrowing, Spiros leaned forward. "You do that, but let me make something perfectly clear, Mr. West. All finds at this site belong to Greece, and they will be turned over promptly to Dr. Bookides and then to me. Further, I will not allow you to call the media or notify the press about a find without clearing it with me first. And I do not think this find is yet newsworthy. If I discover you going behind my back to publish results prematurely, I will have you deported. Am I clear?"

It was all Art could do to be civil at this point. "We know the laws *very* well. We have a good relationship with Dr. Bookides and all finds will be turned over to her. As for publishing the results, we have permission to do so from the government who employs you!" Art now produced his trump card, a memo from the Ministry of Culture, from Spiros's immediate superior, Petros Thanatopsis. "As a courtesy we will let you know if we choose to do so, and will send you a full copy of the report."

Spiros's face reddened, and he sputtered, "Do not think you can go over my head to get approval to do your usual American publicity-seeking tricks. I will not allow it! Am I clear?"

"I believe we get the picture," said Art leaning back and smiling calmly again. "And now if you don't mind, we will get back to work."

"By all means, but bear in mind I will be checking up on things from time to time." Spiros blew two more smoke rings at the departing couple.

When they were out of hearing range, Art said to Marissa "He wins the award for most obnoxious Greek of the year. I will cast him as a villain in my novel about Paul!"

Marissa nodded. "At least he's not hanging around the site today. There goes his Mercedes back to the highway. How in the world does Nancy put up with that man? I couldn't bear having him around me for more than five minutes." And the couple breathed a collective sigh of relief as they headed back to the site.

56

The New Acropolis Museum

THE LAST PORT OF call for Grace and Manny before they left Athens was a visit to the new, gleaming Acropolis Museum, opened in 2009. Art and Marissa decided to pay the new museum a visit after Grace sent Art an e-mail raving about the place and its four thousand displayed artifacts.

While nothing could be more breathtaking than seeing the Parthenon lit up on a clear night, it is fair to say that as far as modern structures go, the new Acropolis Museum is almost equally stunning and eye-catching. Costing some $200 million, and sitting at the base of the Acropolis, this 226,000-square-foot masterpiece is an essential part of the long struggle by Greeks to recover their antiquities. For instance, since the early 1800s the British Museum has been home to much of the original Parthenon frieze, the marble structure created to adorn the upper part of the Parthenon between the pillars and the roof.

The section of the frieze housed in London is part of the Elgin marbles, named after Thomas Bruce, Earl of Elgin and British ambassador to the Ottoman Empire, who engineered the removal of priceless antiquities specifically from the Acropolis. For many years the British government refused to return its portion (about fifty percent) of the Parthenon frieze saying that there was no proper, climate-controlled museum for them in Athens. The British Museum claimed, with some justification, that it was protecting the Parthenon frieze from the pollution even now destroying monuments in Athens. Needless to say, most Greeks found this whole attitude demeaning and insulting, and now with the new museum in Athens, the pressure mounts for the return of the Elgin marbles, especially the frieze.

Though Marissa was thrilled to finally get to see the Parthenon and its new museum, there was also some trepidation involved, for she knew her Osmanli (i.e., Ottoman) history too well. When the Ottomans ruled in Greece they managed to turn the Erectheion, a temple dedicated to the Greek hero Erichthonius, into a harem, and the Parthenon, dedicated to the goddess Athena, into a mosque! And it was the Ottomans with whom Lord Elgin "struck a bargain" to remove so many Acropolis antiquities. No wonder so many Greeks felt such animus for Turks, even today.

Art, ever the collector of museum catalogues and guidebooks, was reading out loud to Marissa as they walked past the Parthenon section of the museum. "It says here, that the architect Phidias designed the frieze to represent the Pan-Athenaia festival, the celebration of the goddess Athena who protected the city. It's too bad we can't follow the whole story—maybe someday all the parts will be in one place. Meanwhile, the Parthenon frieze seems to be in as many different cities as Tasty-Freeze back home," joked Art.

"It's no joking matter to the Greeks, unfortunately. I'm paranoid enough to think they are mad at me personally for what they consider the theft of their antiquities. Let me read some more," as Marissa snagged the guidebook and took up the oration.

The frieze consisted of 115 blocks. It had a total length of 160 meters [525 feet] and was 1.02 meters [~3 feet] high. Some 378 human figures and deities and more than 200 animals, mainly horses, are presented in the process. Groups of horses and chariots occupy most of the space on the frieze. The sacrificial procession follows next, with animals and groups of men and women carrying ceremonial vessels and offerings. The procession concludes with the giving of the *peplos*, the gift of the Athenian people to the cult statue of the goddess. . . . Left and right of the *peplos* scene sit the twelve gods of Mount Olympos. From the entire frieze that survives today, 50 meters are in the Acropolis Museum, 80 meters in the British Museum, one block in the Louvre, and several fragments are scattered in the museums of Palermo, the Vatican, Würzburg, Vienna and Munich.

Walking along, Marissa and Art suddenly stopped together to look at a particularly beautiful block. "I love how the frieze, even in marble, is able to convey the sense of the motion of the horses in the processional parade," marveled Marissa.

Moving on to the exhibit on the Erectheion, Art and Marissa were rendered speechless by the elegant Caryatids, which once graced the Porch of the Maidens on the south side of this temple. Instead of columns, six graceful maidens, looking very feminine despite the weight they bear, once upheld the roof of the porch.

Perhaps most stunning of all was the hall of the Archaic figures from the seventh century BC. Art and Marissa found themselves mesmerized by all the beauty and careful arrangement of the exhibits in the museum.

Both of them appreciated the glass flooring on the first level, which revealed the archaeological dig still ongoing under the museum!

"Now you see what real funding of an archaeological project can achieve," said Art. "If only we had some more funding for Corinth now," he added wistfully.

Giving Art a comforting hug, Marissa said, "We have enough money for the moment, and I've got a paycheck coming in from Turkey in about a week. We will get by. Do you worry that Spiros will interfere and steal our thunder?" asked Marissa.

"Yes, but I think I made clear to him that I could go over his head if I need to. But we will have to watch our step."

"Tell me about it," said Marissa. "Being a Turk, I feel like I've been walking on eggshells the whole time we've been here."

"The British Museum has been put on notice that Athens is now ready to have its frieze back, to say nothing of the other Elgin marbles." Art looked at his watch and was stunned to discover they had been wandering around the new museum for almost three hours already. "Time flies when you are in the presence of something timeless like all this," mused Art.

"It's true. What is that old Latin saying?" asked Marissa. "*Ars longa, vita brevis*. Art is long, but life is brief."

"Well, this Art is long overdue for some supper. How about we walk over to the Plaka and visit my favorite restaurant and my friend Christos who runs it."

"You don't have to persuade me," replied Marissa, "I'm famished." And so they left, silently marveling at the marbles they had just seen.

"The Greeks may have lost their marbles, but what they've done with what they have left is marvelous," quipped Art with a smile.

57

Darkness on The Edge of Town

THE BLACK AND WHITE bus that left Nablus in the morning meandered all over the map, dropping passengers here and there in small Palestinian towns and villages before finally passing through Jericho, then Bethlehem, then east Jerusalem. By the time the bus reached the Jerusalem bus station, it was already eight in the evening, and rapidly getting dark. With no air-conditioning, it had been a long, hot ride, complete with flies, sweaty passengers, and two live, constantly-cackling chickens. Yassir, completely frazzled, managed to get himself dropped off across from the Damascus gate and the Muslim quarter of the old city—not two hundred yards from the shop of Kahlil and Hannah el Said.

Yassir spent his last shekels in Jericho when the bus stopped there for an early evening meal. The only thing he now had was a gun, stuffed in the back of his pants under his shirt, and a burning hatred for what his wife said she was going to do. Wouldn't she be surprised to see him tonight! But Yassir had no plans to kill his "disobedient" wife; he planned to extract two things—payment and punishment—before going underground again with Hamas.

The shadows were lengthening in the Cardo, and most of the shops were closed with shopkeepers hustling off to their homes if they did not live in the old city, and no one took any notice of the disheveled and dirty Palestinian coming in through the Damascus Gate and heading down the right side of the Cardo. As luck would have it, Hannah had not yet locked the door to the shop, as she was expecting her father back anytime from his shopping trip. Cleaning up in the center aisle of the shop with her back to the door, she did not see anyone approach nor did she hear the door open.

Stepping quietly up behind Hannah, Yassir suddenly put his strong hand over her mouth and his gun into her back and said, "Get down on the floor woman, and do not make a sound. First you will tell me where you hide the money."

Hannah was so shocked by this turn of events she just froze. She mumbled something about the cash register on the counter, and Yassir, already seeing it, opened it and took every bit of money he could carry out of it, concentrating on the bills.

"I want you to lie face down on the floor, NOW!" shouted Yassir, and Hannah obediently turned over. Suddenly she felt Yassir pulling up her dress and then his hand grabbed her underwear and ripped it off of her. "This is for shaming me with your threats of divorce," said Yassir in a low growl full of venom, and he thrust himself inside Hannah for the first time in twenty years. Hannah screamed when she was penetrated and it seemed like the rapid-fire rhythmic motion went on forever as Yassir worked himself up to the climax. Just as his orgasm was finishing with his outcry of satisfaction, from out of nowhere a shot rang out, and Hannah felt the dead weight of Yassir fall upon her back. And there was sudden darkness on the edge of town.

58

Beefcake

SO PLEASED WAS _SPORTS Fanatics_ with the article and pictures Sherry Berry had come up with, they decided that it deserved to be rushed into print as the lead story for the Fourth of July. And the cover boy was one Jake the Cat Arafat tossing his jersey to an imaginary fan, muscles rippling, with a big smile on his face. Below the picture in red, white, and blue bold letters was the heading "BEEFCAKE OF THE NBA." When Charlotte distributors, news agents, and bookstores saw who and what was on the cover, they ordered enormous quantities of the magazine.

Jake, oblivious to what was happening, had slept in on the morning of the magazine's release, but Aunt Joyce had gone down to Harris Teater to do some grocery shopping first thing that morning. All had gone well and she was making her way through the checkout lane when her eye glanced over at the magazines, mostly tabloids, on the right hand side of the aisle. There for the entire world to see was Jake Arafat in the flesh, so to speak. Joyce's eyes got big; she dropped her purse; and then she said in a loud voice, "Lord Have Mercy!" Picking up a copy of the magazine, she turned it over and threw it on the conveyor—she was too embarrassed to have it staring at her face up.

The checkout girl had other ideas, turning the magazine over and saying, "Wow! He's hot!"

"Not nearly as hot as he's going to be when I get home," said Joyce with a determined look on her face.

"Why? Do you know Jake the Cat Arafat?"

"Know him! I'm practically raising him, and clearly I'm not doing a good enough job." Grabbing her two bags of groceries, she stormed out of Harris Teater, a woman on a mission. Gunning the engine of her Toyota, Joyce floored it and headed straight for home, smoke coming out of her ears.

Jake was barely awake when he heard what sounded like a herd of elephants storming through the house and coming down the hall. Then he heard Aunt Joyce yelling, "Jacob Arafat, you get up and get dressed ASAP! You have some serious explaining to do!"

Not at all sure what could have so frosted Aunt Joyce's cake, Jake got up out of bed, threw on a Bobcat T-shirt and some shorts, and muttered to himself while stifling a yawn, "What in the world have I done this time?"

When Jake opened the door there was Joyce standing in the hall fuming and holding up the magazine so he would see its cover immediately.

"Oh, oh," were the only words that came out of Jake's mouth, and then he saw the header, BEEFCAKE OF THE NBA. "Aunt Joyce, you may not believe this, but I had no idea this was what Sherry had in mind when she interviewed me and took some pictures."

"Didn't I warn you to be careful?" raved Aunt Joyce. "Didn't it occur to you something was amiss when that blonde bombshell asked you to take your jersey off and throw it to the fake crowd? Now you will become nothing but a sex symbol. Just you wait until the mail and calls roll in! All the wrong sort of people will be after you!" wailed Joyce with great emphasis. "What were you thinking, or was it that pretty blonde who did all the thinking?"

Jake, now fully on the defensive, said, "I thought she was interested in me and basketball, not in just using me to sell magazines. She seemed nice enough, and she did not throw herself at me. I'm not naked for heaven's sakes, just shirtless! Calm down! I am not going over to the Dark Side, and I'm certainly not making porno movies! I may be a rookie, but I'm not totally stupid!"

Joyce began more softly this time. "I guess I can see that. Well, Jacob, I still think you got taken for a ride. So you need to get your head on straight now. How about talking to your coach?" Just then Jake's cellphone went off, and looking at the number and name, he smiled and said, "I'd better take this, it's Sherry."

Aunt Joyce just groaned. "Before you hang up, I would love to give that woman a piece of my mind!"

The fallout from the *Sports Fanatics* cover had begun and Jake the "Beefcake" was nurturing an enormous beef against one Sherry Berry. Her recent phone call was succinct and to the point. She congratulated him on his newfound fame and expected Jake to thank her. Instead Jake exploded. Sherry quickly said, "Adios amigo!" and abruptly hung up the phone. Jake had been taken for a ride in a car he wasn't driving; going in a direction he wasn't willing. And now, some of that old "angry with the world" attitude he had nurtured as a member of Hamas was raising its ugly head again. Jake wanted to hit someone or something. He wanted to quit basketball and sue *Sports Fanatics.*

Sitting at the breakfast table, aimlessly stirring the spoon in his cereal bowl, Jake was scowling. Even at this hour, he was wearing sunglasses. The darkness suited his mood. Aunt Joyce, of course, had an opinion on this.

"Take off those silly sunglasses! Who are you hiding from? If you ask me, the best way to fight fire is with fire. I would suggest you call Ron Green, the sports guy on our favorite Charlotte TV station, and do an exclusive interview with him. Tell him about Sherry the reporter. Now bear in mind that sports figures are always claiming to have been misquoted or taken out of context when they don't like the outcome of an interview, but from reading the article, I don't think that's the problem here. You were misled not misquoted. And there are some nice pictures of you dunking the basketball as well in that spread. It's not all terrible."

Jake slid his shades down his nose and looked at Aunt Joyce. For the first time in two days he stopped simmering. "You know Aunt Joyce, that's not a bad idea. I will call that reporter this morning and we will see if we can mount a counter attack. Won't Sherry be surprised!"

59

The Smoking Gun

HANNAH DID NOT MOVE when the shot fired. She did not move when Yassir fell with his full wait upon her. She did not move when Detective Sharansky, holding his smoking revolver, called her name. He checked her pulse—Hannah was alive but probably in shock. He rolled the dead man away, covered Hannah's limp body with his jacket, and called for the ambulance, police backup, and the coroner. Locals heard the shot. Sharansky was blocking the doorway when Kahlil arrived, pushing his way through the crowd. When he saw Sharansky, Kahlil yelled in a voice full of pain, "What has happened here? Where's Hannah?" Sharansky ushered him into the shop; closed the door behind him; and briefly shook Kahlil to get his full attention.

"Be calm, Mr. el Said! We received a tip from our operatives in Nablus that Yassir might well be coming this way by bus, and so I have been waiting around at the bus station across the way. I did not recognize a shaven Yassir when he got off the suspected bus. When the bus was empty, I decided to come straight to the shop. Unfortunately, Yassir came directly here. Your daughter appears to have been raped by her former husband. Yes, I shot him. He is dead! The medics are on their way to help Hannah."

Kahlil was speechless as Sharansky led him to Hannah. "She has a good pulse, but she is unconscious. And here are the medics!" sighed Sharansky with some relief. The coroner and forensics team followed behind.

In very short order, Detective Sharansky and his team began their inspection of the crime scene. Kahlil held Hannah's hand as she was strapped to the stretcher and taken off to the ambulance waiting at the gate. Sinai Hospital was close by—a familiar place to the el Said family. "Mr. el Said, would you like an officer to drive you over to the hospital?"

"Yes, thank you, and could you please call my friends, the Cohens? They will want to know about this at once."

"Gladly," said Sharansky, reaching for his cellphone.

"*Shalom*, Mrs. Cohen?"

"*Alechum shalom*. Yes, this is Grace, who is calling?"

"This is Detective Sharansky at Kahlil el Said's shop. Hannah has been assaulted by her former husband. She is alive but we are taking her to Sinai Hospital. Kahlil asked me to call. Our officer will bring him there very soon."

"Oh, no! I'm here in Jerusalem at Hebrew University so I will be there as soon as possible!" promised Grace.

And with this the detective helped Kahlil, weeping profusely, to close up his shop and make the walk to a waiting police car.

60

The Owl Hoots

Though his initial idea of blaming Art and Marissa for stealing antiquities from Corinth had been thwarted by Nancy Bookides, Spiros figured out just exactly how to get his devoted readers to help him shove Art West and Marissa Okur toward the deportation counter sooner rather than later. The opening of the Athens Museum had prompted a new resurgence of Greek pride, and there could not be a better time to dish the dirt on Americans and Turks always trying to steal the limelight from the Greeks. Spiros eyed his gossip column for *The Owl* and smiled.

Plastered to the right of the column was a picture of Art kissing Marissa at the Athens airport, and the banner headline over the column read, "HAS GREECE LOST ITS MARBLES AGAIN? WHO IS REALLY DIGGING AT CORINTH?"

William Arnold wasn't the only one who spotted the discrepancies in the Hittite article. A vigilant clerk recently pointed out the problems in the original and translated articles, knowing Spiros's interest in all things going on in Corinth. As a result, his expose led with a paragraph on Marissa, detailing in full the story about her article about the Hittites and how the English translation had been doctored to favor the Hittites. That paragraph finished with, "Why exactly then should we trust Okur when it comes to handling our heritage in Corinth?"

The next paragraph explained how, despite objections from Spiros, West had been given full rein to dig in Corinth, even though everywhere he went controversy seemed to follow. Art was painted as a headline grabber, based on the recent showing on Greek TV of the news conference in Istanbul where he had spoken about the Papias findings. The paragraph ended with, "And as anyone can see from the picture above, West is at least figuratively if not literally in bed with his fiancée Okur when it comes to this Corinth project and what he intends there!"

Spiros figured this would raise enough stink that maybe even the Minister of Culture would be forced to see things his way and send these two foreigners packing. At the very least West and Okur would end up spending endless time doing damage control.

~

The fallout from the gossip column in the *The Owl* blanketed the local communist party. A protest was organized by the party at the US embassy in Athens for Saturday morning, and reporters from various Athens papers were sent to Corinth to interview: 1) Nancy Bookides, 2) Art West, and 3) Marissa Okur, the really big prize. It looked like Art and Marissa would not get back to real digging any time soon. Instead they would be digging themselves out from under the ashes that Spiros Spandexikos had just dumped on them. Marissa, who had more of a temper than Art, was furious, as was Mrs. Demetrios, who secretly dreamed of interrupting the interview and giving the reporters a piece of her mind in a string of choice Greek phrases. She was a woman not to be messed with. Art and Marissa realized they needed to do this interview in order to have some ability to steer a story careening out of control.

The interview was scheduled for ten a.m. in front of the main gate of the Corinthian archaeological site. Various cameras, microphones, and reporters were milling around waiting for their prey to emerge from the museum. The sun was sifting through the tall fir trees surrounding the entrance to ancient Corinth, as Nancy, Art, and Marissa stood behind the battery of microphones. Fortunately, English was the chosen language of the day.

"I have a prepared statement to read first," said Nancy Bookides. "Then I will take questions. First of all, Professor Art West was invited here by the Greek government to complete an archaeological dig begun some time ago, but for which the government did not have sufficient funds to bring the matter to a satisfactory completion. He is backed by his own personal funding. All artifacts thus far discovered have been turned over to me, as the author of that column in the *The Owl*, Spiros Spandexikos, knows perfectly well. He recently had a meeting with us to discuss the latest findings. I am afraid a gossip column, which has now smeared the reputations of two professional archaeologists who are guests in our country, is not a source of reliable information in this matter."

"This brings me to my second point. The journal article referred to in the Spandexikos column was deliberately mistranslated by a disgruntled colleague with the intention of discrediting Dr. Okur. She had neither knowledge of, nor anything to do with, the English translation of her article. The antiquities authorities in Istanbul have corrected the matter, the perpetrator will be disciplined, and a retraction will be printed in the next edition of the journal. I suggest that you interview Dr. Spandexikos, who obviously did not know that the problem is being resolved. I will take questions now."

A small man with an Errol Flynn moustache raised his hand, was recognized, and asked, "Are you saying that Spiros's article is a deliberate attempt to smear the work of Drs. West and Okur and stir up racial hatred against foreigners?"

"All I can say is that Dr. Spandexikos does not support archaeological programs having to do with early Christianity. He is on record with his opinion. The claims in his column are simply false. You can draw your own conclusions from his article and his associations with certain political organizations."

Another hand went up from a female reporter in the back of the pack. "Is it true that Spiros Spandexikos is a member of the communist party? Is that public knowledge?"

"I know it to be a fact; I don't know whether it has been made public. I suggest that his ideology explains his actions and motivations," replied Nancy curtly.

After several more questions on less crucial points, Art moved to the microphone. "I think Dr. Bookides has adequately covered the basics. Let me just add that Dr. Okur and I look forward to getting back to work, and hopefully uncovering more of Greece's rich heritage, including its Christian heritage, for the people of Greece."

"Dr. Okur," yelled another member of the press, "Is this your first visit here? What's your impression of the state of archaeology here in Greece?"

Marissa was pleased to reply to these questions! "Yes, this is my first, and long overdue, visit to this remarkable country. If Dr. Bookides is any indication, then archaeology here in Greece is in good hands for the most part. We all wish for more funding, of course! But the state of the Corinth site and the beautiful museum here are remarkable. We recently visited the new museum at the Acropolis—absolutely stunning! As a country, you can be very proud!"

"Professor West," said a small voice from a tall man, "I am a reporter from the Greek Orthodox paper, and wondered if you could comment on the innuendo that you are here in Corinth living in sin with your fiancée."

Art was so shocked at this personal question that he simply said, "No!" Fortunately, he didn't continue with "and it's none of your business!"

Seizing the moment, Mrs. Demetrios jumped up and loudly proclaimed in her best English: "I am Mrs. Demetrios, good Greek Orthodox believer. I take care of these good people Dr. West and Dr. Okur. She live in my very own house—with me. The good Dr. West— he live in little bungalow that I own. They are good people. But Mr. Spandexikos! He insults us; he insults our Greek Christian heritage. I could say more. He not a nice man! Lots of scandal! I read in your papers about his problems. And some of you reporters know all that. Admit it!"

The press knew when it had a sensational story. It would not be long before Spiros would find himself under the white-hot spotlights of the press. And as the three compatriots walked away from the site and up to their houses, Art said to Mrs. Demetrios, "Way to go! I gather you set the hounds on the trail of Spiros himself."

Mrs. Demetrios smiled triumphantly and said, "It could not have happened to fatter rabbit. We see how he hops now!"

"Only thing is, that hare is hairless and harebrained too," replied Art, and for the first time all morning they all had a good laugh.

61

Crime and Consequences

WHOEVER FIRST SAID THAT for every action there is an equal and opposite reaction did not have it quite right when it comes to human behavior and events. It would be better to say for every action there is a consequence. Yassir was dead due to his own foolish and criminal behavior, and no one was mourning his passing. Unfortunately, there were consequences for the innocent as well. Kahlil had been reduced not merely to tears as a result of discovering his daughter raped and comatose, but also to self-recriminations, blaming himself for not getting home fast enough. In truth, he had stopped for coffee at Solomon's Porch on the way back from buying a handgun in new Jerusalem.

"If only I had gotten here sooner," was his constant refrain. Grace tried to console Kahlil but with no success. He was inconsolable as he sat in the emergency waiting room in Sinai Hospital.

Looking up, Kahlil saw Nurse Rosencrantz coming his way, a thin elderly woman on staff for many years. "Mr. el Said, we have cleaned up your daughter and ministered to her bruises. There was some vaginal bruising which will take time to heal. Other test results will not be back until later. The police are talking to the doctors. Our plan is to move her into a semi-private room in the next hour. Then you can visit. She seems to be drifting in and out of consciousness, however, and has not spoken directly to the doctors or the police."

"When I was here some time ago with a wound, you were angels of mercy to me,[1] and I have friends like Grace to stand by me, so God be praised."

"Yes, and may you know his shalom soon," said the nurse as she walked away.

"You see, things are beginning to turn in the right direction," said Grace. "All is not lost, and for sure Yassir will never again plague your family."

The time passed quickly as Grace distracted Kahlil by asking him a multitude of questions about antiquities in his shop. "I trust you have been up to the museum to see how nice the menorah looks on the display there. And to think I could have had that menorah as a wedding gift!"[2] said Grace sighing.

Kahlil laughed at the memory. "Yes, in fact Hannah and I went to see it again just last month before we took our holiday to Jordan. I must tell you that Jordan was an embarrassment of riches. I was totally entranced with both Jerash and Petra, and would gladly go to those places again. Have you ever visited Jordan?"

"Sadly no," replied Grace with a smile, "but I am hoping to persuade Manny to go there in the next year. We did get to Greece recently! Art and Marissa seem to be doing well enough."

"It's hard to picture Art domesticated and married," smiled Kahlil.

"You would have said the same about me a few years back, but it happens!" said Grace with a chuckle. "Love happens—unbidden and surprising!"

"As does tragedy," and Kahlil, voice cracking.

"Hannah will survive this Kahlil," reassured Grace, "She is a strong woman."

"I'm sure you are right," said Kahlil, but deep in his heart he was not absolutely certain of this. Rape is a woman's worst nightmare. Fortunately, at this point the nurse returned and Kahlil rose to meet her.

"We have Hannah all safely moved to her room. But we are concerned about one possibility. It appears that Hannah was ovulating at the time she was assaulted. It is possible that she is pregnant, but it is

---

1. A story told in the first Art West adventure, *The Lazarus Effect*.
2. A story told in the third Art West adventure, *Papias and the Mysterious Menorah*.

much too soon to have a positive test." Grace's eyes widened; Kahlil collapsed back into his chair.

"One problem at a time, but if you are wondering if we would want to do something about the baby, I can tell you now, Hannah will insist on keeping it. It is unfair to the unborn child to judge it for the sins of one or the other of its parent. I know my daughter," Kahlil stressed.

❧

Hannah slept through the night and on into mid-morning. Her social network was beginning to arrive at the hospital in the hopes of visiting. Sarah was one of the first to arrive, and relieved Kahlil at Hannah's bedside while Kahlil ate a late breakfast. His food was eaten in silence, and he returned to Hannah's room still deep in his own thoughts. When he entered the room Sarah said, "Guess what? Hannah seems to be waking up!"

Kahlil looked at his daughter's face, all pale and pacific, and then she opened her eyes and saw her father. There was a long pause before she whispered, "Where am I?"

"You are in the hospital but are going to be just fine," assured Kahlil.

And then finally the shock of recognition came and she said, "But where is Yassir!"

"Gone, my little one, gone forever. He is dead!" said Kahlil emphatically.

Releasing her grip on her father's hand, she relaxed and said, "As Allah wills."

"Yes, I thought you would see it that way," said Kahlil assuring her.

"How did Yassir die? Did *you* kill him?"

"No, Hannah, no. Detective Sharansky saved you. When I returned it was all over! I am sorry I was not there for you!" said Kahlil beginning to tear up.

But Hannah was beginning to get drowsy again. "Well, you must thank him for me. I am so tired." With this she turned over and went back to sleep.

"She seemed coherent, but I doubt she really understands all that happened, and she probably won't remember this conversation so you may need to break the news to her again," said Sarah. "I will go speak to her friends in the waiting room."

"I just hope another, maybe bigger shock, is not yet to come. But it can wait for another day." Sarah left. Kahlil prayed.

62

Getting It Right This Time

THE SHORT INTERVIEW WITH Ron Green would be taped and aired for five minutes on the six o'clock and eleven o'clock evening news. Jake made up his mind to come out swinging but fight fair. An hour-long special was in the works that promised to feature the real rookies and how they were coping with today's sports world.

Ron Green was a savvy reporter who knew how to dish it out as well as take it. For years he reported the Duke-Carolina border wars in basketball. Ron was a no-nonsense guy, although on camera he seemed to be all sweetness and light. At the opening of the newscast, a teaser of Jake slam-dunking would hopefully keep the viewers waiting until the segment ran at the end of the newscast.

Jake, wearing his best sport's coat, tie, and khaki pants, looked every inch the young gentleman. Joyce had taken him to a local hair stylist she frequented to get his locks shorn. He wanted to look his best. He might not be comfortable being a sex symbol, but he didn't want to appear to be a slob either. On the set at WBT, a full-board picture of the *SF* spread had been arranged behind the camera as the backdrop for the shoot. Ron Green came waltzing into the studio wearing a turtleneck and a blue blazer. After makeup he looked like the well-known sports reporter he was. Shaking Jake's hand he said, "Well, sport, let's get down to business."

"Certainly," replied Jake sitting up straight in the easy chair they had provided for him. The props included a little table with coffee mugs saying WBT and the aforementioned backdrop, which caused Jake to scowl again.

"I'm here speaking with Jake Arafat, known to his fans as Jake the Cat, who recently made the cover of *Sports Fanatics* magazine. And an interesting cover it is, don't you think Jake? How do you feel about the story?" said Ron right off the top.

"I was not pleased, Mr. Green. There is no doubt about it. Ms. Sherry Berry, whose real name is Monica, led me to believe she was doing a feature on NBA rookies, as a freelance writer for *Sports Fanatics* magazine. I did not expect the male equivalent of the swimsuit issue!"

"And yet there you are, shirt off, throwing your jersey to the crowd," replied Green.

"Indeed. Perhaps you will remember the famous Coke ad, recently redone for Coke Zero, where the Pittsburgh football player throws a jersey to the young fan. This was the precise image Sherry said they were striving for, and there was nothing sexy at all about that commercial, now was there?"

"Good point. But the question going forward is, what will you do about your newfound celebrity, or maybe I should say notoriety. I'll bet your cellphone is ringing off the hook for interviews, never mind dates."

"Tell me about it. I'm tellin' folks, don't bother to call! I'm only interested in dating Christian girls like some I meet at church! Don't expect to see The Cat in the alleys at night!"

"Whoa, sport. You're saying the beefcake image doesn't suit you? I'm guessing the box office doesn't mind. Ticket sales are probably up!"

"Maybe so, but for all the wrong reasons. I play basketball, that's it. I love the game. As for everything else, I'm saying publicly here and now, media and businesses that don't promote values consistent with my Christian faith should just keep their distance!"

"You just lost some serious coin in endorsements!" cautioned Ron.

"I really don't care," said Jake. "You may remember what Jesus said about gaining the whole world and losing your soul. I am not going down that road, even a short ways."

With this Green looked at the camera and said, "And that is but a foretaste of the interview you'll be seeing in the upcoming special that will feature the outspoken superstar of our Charlotte Bobcats, Jake the Cat Arafat!"

"Cut," said Green. "We got it in one take."

"That was a gutsy statement. I wonder how your teammates and coaches will react," said Green to Jake. "You stick by your guns and we'll get on with that hour special. We want the first part to be dedicated to the remarkable story of how you got here, your connection with Jordan, your living situation, and your recent performance in the NBA playoffs. And we can pursue other things, like your charity work at the Bethlehem Center. How does that sound?"

"Fine by me, but this time I want all that in writing. I've learned a few things from my mistakes!"

"Would you like to join me at my uncle's place for supper? We've got a lot of planning to do."

"No lie, your uncle owns Green's? That's cool!" Jake was smiling. "That's the way an interview should end!"

63

Writing on The Stone

IT WAS WITH MORE than just a little relief that Art and Marissa got back to the primary task of their summer, namely digging the site where the house with the mosaics and the tent rack had been found. The first job was to uncover once more the mosaic, which had been found when the first excavation was done some years before, find out its full extent if possible, and then take detailed pictures, before covering it up again. The problem with ancient mosaics left out in the sun is that they quickly bleach out and are ruined. The mosaics in this particular house were located in part between two existing Greek houses, so it was difficult to determine how far they went in the east–west direction.

These mosaics were not notably different from the ones found in the Corinth museum depicting cavorting Dionysius and his nymphs, or Poseidon, or the usual geometric designs in multiple pastel colors. In the course of uncovering these mosaics Marissa discovered something not previously noted in the archaeological records. There was some writing at the very edge of the mosaic. It read:

DEMETRIOSTECHNOSPROSERASTOS

Art squinted his eyes and stared long and hard. "I think this is the signature of the artist. It says his name was Demetrios and he calls himself a *technos*, which usually refers to a carpenter or a stonemason. The last part certainly means 'for Erastos.' It could be the Erastus mentioned in Romans 16 and in the field over in front of the theater! Of course,

'Erastos's is the Greek spelling of Erastus. That was a fairly common name, but not for a rich person. Maybe Erastus is another one of those famous freed men climbing up the social ladder. Maybe Paul ended up working out of Erastus' house? Now that would be exciting news!"

"Slow down! We have much more work to do before we draw such a dramatic connection and conclusion."

"You're right, of course, but it sure is fun to speculate don't you think?" asked Art.

"Yes, but too many scholars publish mere speculations. And you know what happens. It starts as speculation, then it's called a good possibility, then, presto, it becomes a virtual certainty, and then it's the well-assured results of scholarly labor, then a consensus opinion! Sometimes, Art, your enthusiasm not merely propels you into the subject, it affects your objectivity, if you don't mind me saying so in a sweet kind of way," and Marissa gave him a kiss on his dirty cheek.

Art sighed and responded, "Right again! I think you will have a good tempering effect on me when it comes to these sorts of things. I need it. I guess I tend to overinterpret sometimes, or jump to conclusions."

The couple worked through the morning and into the afternoon, heading in the direction where the rack was found. Suddenly they looked up to see Mrs. Demetrios staring at them.

"And when were you coming for my lunch?" she said, "I have been on my hands and knees cleaning kitchen, but you are on your hands and knees getting dirty."

"Yes, Mrs. Demetrios, but look here at this inscription we uncovered this morning." Pouring a little water on the mosaic, Art was able to point out the word DEMETRIOS. Mrs. Demetrios' eyes got big and she said, "Is ancient relative! I wish my husband here to see this!"

"Slow down! Demetrios is a first name. But it *is* the same name," noted Art smiling at Mrs. Demetrios.

"Time to eat," said Mrs. Demetrios. "All working and no eating no good!" And the three of them rose, dusted themselves off, and headed down the hill.

64

American Woman

THE PRIMETIME SPECIAL WITH Ron Green made all the other TV stations in Charlotte green with envy. Jake was just happy it was all over and it was now the off-season. He was in no mood to face the fans or his teammates anytime soon.

On this morning Jake was going to see his pastor James Howell to talk about American women. The new wing of Myers Park UMC was fairly gleaming, and James's office was up a marble staircase and to the left. Jake always felt a little overwhelmed in such a beautiful place. No church in Palestine, except perhaps the new one next to the Church of the Nativity, looked like this at all. Walking down the hall, Jake found the door to Dr. Howell's study wide open, and there was James safely ensconced in his comfortable chair, awaiting Jake's arrival.

"Come in, come in. Its good to see you!" said James, standing up, shaking Jake's hand, and pointing Jake to the chair opposite his own.

"Thank you for seeing me on short notice. I've just had a rather bad experience with a woman, and I feel used and manipulated, and don't want it to happen again."

"Well, 'once bitten twice shy' as they say, so your instincts are good. But tell me about you. I've seen you at the games and in church with Mrs. West, of course. You're quite a star now. What do you think about that?"

"Therein lies the problem," said Jake looking down at the floor. "I'm not really all that comfortable with being a so-called star on the rise, and I'm even less comfortable with the kind of crowd and attention it appears to be bringing me, especially the women."

"Understandable. But what is your dating history or track record with women, if you don't mind me asking?" said James.

"Apart from a couple of recent dinner dates with that reporter, I don't have one."

"Come again?!" said James raising his eyebrows.

"I've never really dated before now. We didn't do that in our little Palestinian Christian enclave in Bethlehem. In fact, in my family we still hold to the tradition of arranged marriages. I escaped all that by coming here at a reasonably early age."

"You must be the only NBA player with no track record with women!"

"I expect so, which leaves me at a decided disadvantage, not least because, as Aunt Joyce claims, I'm naïve about people."

"I'm guessing women would be very, very eager for the money and attention that surrounds a player with NBA mystique, but I'm also guessing they are after the jersey, not the guy who wears the jersey."

Jake looked dismayed and replied, "Probably, and lots of the guys drift off with the groupies after the games. I just go home. I can't control other people's actions and desires to get close to so-called famous people. And I don't want to become a hermit. I would actually like to have a normal dating relationship, if such a thing is possible for me. I have to admit to being frustrated that I haven't learned how to relate to American women. I heard that old song 'American Woman' that Lenny Kravitz redid, and boy could I relate to that! The women I see in America seem much too forward, too assertive, and too demanding compared to women where I came from."

James sat quietly for a moment rubbing his forehead before saying, "You could use a friend, almost a bodyguard, to warn you, to whisk you away from trouble, to keep you out of bars and nightclubs. That's the downside of things. But here is the upside. What an opportunity you have to be the rarity, the astonishing witness for Christ—a Christian and a Palestinian who is clean, who isn't part of the 'bar chick' scene!"

"That would be nice but I'm not ready for that! Aunt Joyce is good to me and all, but . . ." Jake's voice drifted off but it was obvious that James understood the problem with the age difference. "Would you help me find some guys to hang out with that I can trust?" Then Jake started laughing, "And while you're at it, could you find me the perfect girl who's crazy about sports but not sports stars? . . . I realize that last part is a tall order!"

"I must admit," replied James laughing, "I don't get requests like that every day! Look on the bright side. You've not made any fatal mistakes yet. You obviously have your head on straight. My suggestion, of course, is that you get more involved here for starters. We do have a young-adult group, you know. It won't take long before they just accept you as Jake, not Jake the Cat Arafat. I'll keep my eyes open, but I really think you will make your own friends—just give it time."

With a big sigh, Jake finally looked relieved and said, "You give me some hope of living a somewhat normal life even after my stupid mistake with Ms. Sherry Berry."

"With a name like that, you should have known she was a fruit," said James matter-of-factly. "But not to worry, you stumbled, but you did not fall. Come see me again soon and give me a progress report," said James as he rose to shake Jake's huge hand again.

"I will, and by the way, I really enjoy your sermons—most of them! They often speak to me," said Jake with some earnestness. "Thank goodness my mother knew Art West and helped me find a good Christian home here in Charlotte, and a church to go to."

"Thank goodness indeed," replied James. After Jake left, James muttered to himself, "He must be the last remaining virgin in the whole of the NBA!"

65

Spiros Hits The Downward Spiral

SOMETIMES THE SNAKE YOU let lose on someone else's trail comes back to bite you instead, and this is exactly what happened to Spiros. It wasn't so much the testimony of Nancy Bookides as the outburst of Mrs. Demetrios that got the Greek public riled up over Spiros. The phones at various TV stations in Athens rang and rang complaining about Spiros and lauding Mrs. Demetrios. The calls were going a hundred to one against Spiros. And even worse, he had been outed as a communist and womanizer. The Minister of Culture was not amused when he first saw the press conference, and then went back and read the article in *The Owl*. He summoned Spiros to a long meeting.

Spiros figured he had better tidy himself up, so he had put on his best gray suit, tucked in his shirt over his rotund belly, and combed back the few remaining strands of his jet-black hair. He stoically prepared himself for an ugly session, knowing full well that the minister was not sympathetic to the Party line.

Petros Thanatopsis was a no nonsense guy. In fact, some called him Dr. Death, based in part on his last name. He had not climbed up the ladder of governmental success by suffering fools gladly, and he was very glad on this morning that he finally had an excuse to do something about Spiros Spandexikos.

The gleaming marble hall of the Ministry of Culture building was flanked on either side with replica statues of the gods of the Greek pantheon. Spiros felt rather like he was taking a walk through the halls of

Mt. Olympus as his stubby little legs propelled him towards his rendezvous. Sweat broke out on his brow just as he arrived at the appropriate door and knocked vigorously. Even the secretary frowned as she pointed him to the director's inner sanctum.

Dr. Thanatopsis pointed to a chair left of a small table full of brochures about the new Acropolis Museum and just stared at Spiros for an uncomfortable few moments. The Minister of Culture was a thin man with graying hair, in his late fifties. "Well, you've really done it this time Spiros," said Petros.

All apologetic and clasping his hands together, Spiros said, "I guess I went a little over the line this time."

"You think!" was the instant reply. "As much as I'm eager to lecture you about your unfair treatment of scholars, especially the ones I personally endorsed, it is my first duty to inform you that you have broken the law!"

"What law?" said a trembling Spiros.

"All government employees are required by law to disclose membership in a political party, and perhaps most especially the KKE! You can't really expect me to believe you didn't know about this regulation. This alone is grounds for your dismissal. However, I have here on my desk a file that has been filling over the years with complaints about your lack of professionalism from just about every corner of this country. The majority are from women, I might add. Many times we have spoken about this, but I see no improvements. The whole problem is greater than the sum of all the parts. You've had too many chances to clean up your act. So as of this morning, you may clean out your office. You are fired. I'll let the human services department figure out your severance package, but I doubt it will be generous.

"Oh, and one more thing, I have spoken to the editors at *The Owl*. We had a chat about freedom of speech, freedom of the press, and all that, but they agreed that you will write a column apologizing to Drs. West and Okur. You were trying to ruin their reputations, and since your insinuations were false, you and the paper could be liable. So the editors are now genuinely concerned about the possible lawsuits should either of them want to pursue the matter, and I might personally encourage them to do so if I were so inclined," smiled Petros. The threat was thinly veiled.

Spiros was struck speechless by this whole salvo from Petros. He had expected a warning, not a tongue-lashing. And he certainly did not anticipate that a long-time employee of the Ministry of Culture such as himself might actually be fired!

Sweating and trembling, he was about to open his mouth when Petros added, "I don't want to hear any more of your excuses. Just get out of my office and don't ever ask for a recommendation." Petros rose and pointed to the door.

Like a whipped dog, Spiros rose, turned and walked out the door, tail between his legs. His posture said it all. The secretary wouldn't even look at him. Like most bullies, Spiros Spandexikos could dish it out, but he really couldn't take it.

66

The Villa of Erastos

MODERN CHRISTIANS SELDOM HAVE any idea what "church" life was like in the first century AD. Christianity was not legal; in fact it was a belief system branded by many as a *superstitio*. It was a life without church buildings. The faithful assembled in homes, which had to be large enough to accommodate all the faithful! Art carried with him a mental image of what an ancient villa would have looked like in Paul's day, and this guided him in his explorations at Corinth. He constantly imagined events like early Christian worship, fellowship, and the Lord's Supper, all of which transpired in homes.

The problem with archaeology is that too much of the time the excavations only uncover the foundations—a bare outline of what a house would look like. There were exceptions however. At Pompeii whole houses, which had been covered in ash from the eruption of Mt. Vesuvius in AD 79, had been preserved. These homes were elaborately decorated in a riot of colors. Art remembered a particular home in

Pompeii where the painter had created lavish scenes on the wall of an even grander building, grander statues, and grander entranceways.

Of course there were the usual images of gods and goddesses, nature and family members, painted on the walls as well.

The house he was excavating was situated on a little hill on the edge of ancient Corinth. He tried to imagine the layout of the rooms. Maybe this house was similar to the drawings he had often seen of Roman villas, which featured beautiful courtyards (atria) and even shops for the owner's business. The entranceway usually lead directly into the atrium where there would be a fountain (*impluvium*) to catch the water coming through the intentional hole in the roof. There was also indoor plumbing in many of the villas of the wealthy, which explains why bronze pipes have been found in the excavations but seldom any outhouses. Could early Christians have held their meetings in homes like this?

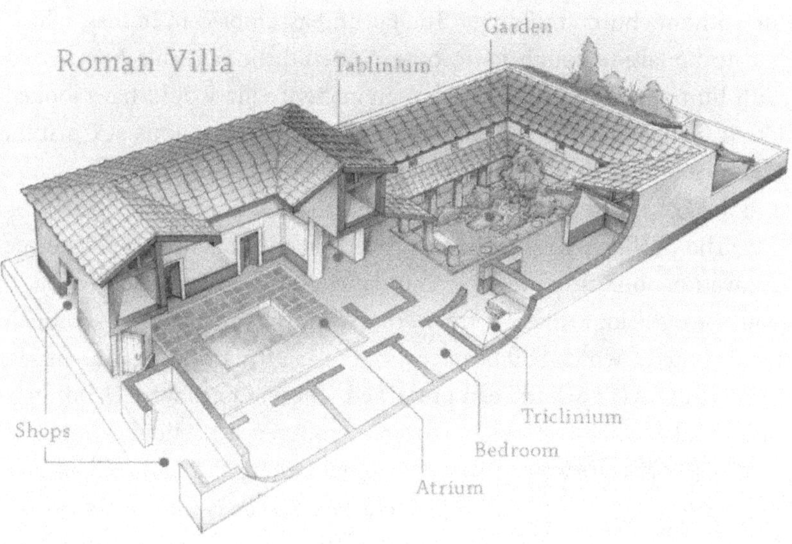

In Art's estimation, the meetings probably took place in the garden because most of the rooms were too small for a large crowd. Perhaps fifty to a hundred persons could be in such a villa, but not all in one place at one time. But if a *synposion*, a meal followed by an after-dinner speaker, was held, then reclining couches would be needed in the dining room (*triclinium*) so that the patrons could sip their wine while listening to the evening's lecture. Art stared anew at the villa's mosaics, which tended to be in special rooms, like the *triclinium* or perhaps the library. More than likely, there were lots of little meetings in several different houses when it came to Christian worship and fellowship. However, Paul does speak of events where all the Christians came together in one place, like in Erastos's villa.

Art moved on to a section beyond the mosaic floor. "Marissa, this looks like a piece of some giant vase or amphora."

Marissa stopped her careful work of uncovering more and more of the mosaics. "Well, the handle is certainly large enough to be from a wine or olive oil amphora, but we need to uncover more to find out. I suggest we take a break from sweeping mosaics and dig around for awhile. Besides, for the last half hour you've done nothing but stand around daydreaming!" she chided.

"Sorry! I'm having trouble multitasking these days. My brain starts churning, but my hands stop working. I was just imagining life in the villa. Actually, the folks were ecologically ahead of their time—catching the rain water, tending indoor gardens, working at home. . . . I've got an idea! Let's build a Roman villa after we get married!" said Art laughing.

"Hey, I could really get into that! We can use this one as a model— if we ever get the work done!" hinted Marissa.

The afternoon was entirely spent meticulously removing the dirt from around a shattered pottery object. Both Art and Marissa had often excavated such objects, which usually end up in museums. The Roman amphoras tended to be much less ornate or colorful than the Greek ones. As the afternoon wore on, it became clear that this amphora, shattered into over a hundred pieces, was simply clay-colored, with no ornate glaze at all. It was rather like the two now being exhibited in the Corinth museum, complete with metal holder to keep the amphora upright after it had been opened.

"*Now* we know that the residents of Erastos's villa were not teetotalers," joked Art. "I wonder if they even had teetotalers in those days!"

"I doubt it," replied Marissa. "I mean it was either wine or water for the most part for everyone in antiquity, and the water was usually nasty tasting from what I've read. Even children drank wine on a regular basis. Personally, I'm not a fan of retsina, but I hear it goes back to the first century when wine jugs were lined with Aleppo pine resin. I love white wine, but retsina is too strong for me!"

"I occasionally try a glass!" admitted Art. "There were probably some true ascetics, like John the Baptizer, who abstained. It's clear that Jesus knew the difference between good wine and bad wine, and there's no hint that he abstained!"

"The story of Jesus' first miracle is one of my favorites," commented Marissa. "And isn't it true that the Corinthian Christians drank real wine even during their Christian meetings, because Paul criticizes some of them for getting drunk during the fellowship meal! Those Corinthians caused Paul no end of heartache, and you don't even have to read between the lines in 1 Corinthians to come to that conclusion!"

"Sad but true," agreed Art.

By four thirty in the afternoon Art and Marissa had the makings of a good jigsaw puzzle lying before them. It was an amphora alright, but they would have to clean and then lay out all the pieces before they could reassemble it.

"Looks like we will be glued to this project for a while," quipped Art.

The relaxed conversation reflected the fact that Nancy Bookides had been informed, and had relayed the good news that Spiros Spandexikos would not be troubling them again. Art's reply was, "Let's go out and celebrate this divine intervention!" The three, joined by Mrs. Demetrios after some arm-twisting, planned a nice evening meal by the Isthmus. Finally, these friends had turned the soap opera channel off and the history channel back on in their lives.

67

Once Upon A Time VI

Pulling up his toga so he could sit and then recline on the couch, *Paul found himself directly opposite Camilla and Alexia. In front of him was a table filled wih fruit, chicken, and leeks, along with his goblet of delicious red wine.*

"You have really gone all out tonight, Camilla," he said raising his goblet to her.

"And with every reason. My sister is here; Erastos will get re-elected aedile; and winter will soon be over."

The meal went through several more courses, but towards the end, Paul sat up on his couch and announced, "Everyone, it is time to share together in the Lord's Supper with this last cup of wine and this unleavened woven bread that Camilla has baked for us. It is time for us to turn our attentions to our Lord."

Raising the bread first, and then the cup, Paul said, "For I received from the Lord what I also passed on to you: The Lord Jesus, on the night he was betrayed, took bread, and when he had given thanks, he broke it and said, 'This is my body, which is for you; do this in remembrance of me.'

"In the same way, after supper he took the cup, saying, 'This cup is the new covenant in my blood; do this, whenever you drink it, in remembrance of me.' For whenever you eat this bread and drink this cup, you proclaim the Lord's death until he comes.

"So then, whoever eats the bread or drinks the cup of the Lord in an unworthy manner will be guilty of sinning against the body and blood of the Lord. Everyone ought to examine themselves before they eat of the bread and drink from the cup. For those who eat and drink without discerning the body of Christ eat and drink judgment on themselves. That is why some among you are weak and sick, and a number of you have fallen asleep.

"But if we were more discerning with regard to ourselves, we would not come under such judgment. Nevertheless, when we are judged in this way by the Lord, we are being disciplined so that we will not be finally condemned with the world. So then, my brothers and sisters, when you gather to eat, you should all eat together as we have done on this night, with all waiting for one another to dine together."

This last instruction was a reminder that some of the slaves from the other house churches usually came a bit late, after they had finished their work. Paul wanted them to be treated as equals at this meal, sharing the first fruits not the leftovers.

At this point Paul broke the large woven bread, and told each person to take a piece and hold it until all had the bread. Once this transpired, he then passed around the cup, telling each person to dip their bread in the cup, and partake of it together. He then said, holding his stained morsel up high, "Because we are all one body, we all partake of one and the same loaf, and drink from one and the same cup."

With this, all consumed the little bit of wine-soaked bread, including Nicanor. He was not about to break the religious protocols. Growing up with Greek religion, he had been taught that if the ritual was not observed perfectly by all, it had to be done all over again. Sacrilege had been committed. Nicanor had taken Paul to be warning against such sacrilege. But he really did not understand why the bread and wine were called the body and blood of Jesus. Perhaps that would be explained later.

Just at that moment, two of the household servants entered with lyres in their hands, and began to play. Paul told the group, "We will now all sing together a hymn to Christ our God." With the leading of the two young slaves who had beautiful tenor voices one and all began to sing.

> Christ Who, being in very nature God,
> did not consider equality with God
> something to be taken advantage of;
> rather, he made himself nothing

> by taking the very nature of a servant,
> being made in human likeness.
> And being found in appearance as a man,
> he humbled himself
> by becoming obedient to death—
> even death on a cross!
>
> Therefore God exalted him to the highest place
> and gave him the name that is above every name,
> that at the name of Jesus every knee should bow,
> in heaven and on earth and under the earth,
> and every tongue acknowledge that Jesus Christ is Lord,
> to the glory of God the Father.

Nicanor was just along for the ride, or so he thought. Listening to the singing, with its various melodies and even some harmonies, was wonderful. This was not like the moaning and intoning he had heard in temples before, but rather the singing of songs with intelligible lyrics, though often he did not understand what they were talking about, especially the stuff about Jesus rising from the dead. Music had seldom moved him so much and when the last song was especially winsome, he found himself wiping his eyes with his sleeve.

Of course he knew the tales of gods coming to earth disguised as humans; Zeus and Hermes visited Lystra. But would a god really take on the form of a servant and then submit to a slave's death on a cross? This sounded like foolishness to Nicanor, and what was that second verse about? Would the most high god really exalt and praise this Jesus for dying on a cross? It was one thing to make a hero like Herakles a demi-god, but a Jewish carpenter? This totally inverted the normal notions about honor and shame and what the gods thought was praiseworthy behavior.

Nicanor was going to have to ask some questions about these things, but now his curiosity was peeked. The one question that presented itself immediately in his mind was, How could such loving and honest and kind people who otherwise seemed in their right minds and not prone to some religious mania, believe such a tale, unless there was some sort of compelling evidence? Nicanor was not sure he was prepared to believe in a literal resurrection of a crucified dead Jew, much less his ascension to the right hand of the most high god. That seemed to stretch credulity to the breaking point.

Camilla broke his reverie by announcing, "Let's adjourn to the courtyard. The braisers will keep us warm. We will continue our worship and will let the Spirit prompt the prophets and prophetesses to speak."

Paul stood in the middle of the courtyard with all those present circled around him, some holding torches so everyone could see. It was customary after the meal to enjoy wine, and listen to a speaker. The house wine amphoras were emptying one by one, and soon each person's goblet was brimming. The wine put everyone in a mellow mood, and indeed some had drunk too much once again. Nicanor really wasn't sure what to expect next and then all of sudden a prophet started exclaiming a message to his left."[3]

3. This is an edited excerpt from my forthcoming novella for InterVarsity Press entitled *Nicanor's Dilemma.*

68

The Resident Patient

HANNAH WAS PHYSICALLY FINE. After two days in the hospital she was discharged. But she was not recovering as fast as Kahlil would like. She was still sleeping most of the day; when she was awake she was listless and spoke in monotones. She had lost her appetite, and Kahlil realized for the first time how inept he was in the kitchen. She was all too aware of what happened to her in the very shop where she always felt so safe. However, she refused to talk about it even with her father. Kahlil decided not to tell Hannah she might be pregnant. What would be the point if it never became a reality?

The rape crisis unit visited Hannah a number of times while she was in the hospital, and they encouraged her to continue counseling. Kahlil was very old-school and didn't know what to think about psychologists and counselors. He was prayerfully mulling over this possibility. In her current state, Hannah had not said a word about counseling, so he didn't want to bring up a sore subject that would tax her emotionally while she was trying to heal physically. But maybe this was exactly the time she most needed a counselor. He didn't know what to do.

In his mind he relived Hannah's last day in the hospital. When the elderly nurse Rosencrantz came to the room, Kahlil, unshaven and groggy, was surprised to hear the nurse say, "You know, you look like death. You really need to go home, take a good bath, shave, get a nap, eat some of your own food, and then come back. Then, and only then, will I help you get Hannah ready to go home! I expect you to come back this afternoon looking like a new man!"

"I guess I have my orders!" said a surprised but compliant Kahlil. "But I will wait until Grace arrives and . . ."

No sooner had he said the name Grace than the woman herself walked in the door with a big smile on her face and said, "You called? 'Ask and you shall receive,' a famous Jew once said."

Nonplussed by the timing of her entrance, Kahlil stood up, gave Grace a hug, gathered his things and said as he was parting. "I have been told in no uncertain terms to go home and clean up. Only then will I be able to take my Hannah home!"

"I completely agree with that plan! Off you go! I'll stay and talk to Hannah, that is, if she ever wakes up," replied Grace with some concern as she looked at the ever-sleeping Hannah. Turning back to Kahlil, she shooed him out the door.

Kahlil mentally limped home. Why didn't he skip that coffee? Why couldn't he have gotten back to the shop before the disaster happened? Why does God let these things happen?

These thoughts still plagued Kahlil days later as he puttered around his shop wondering when Hannah would be up and flitting around like she always used to do. He sorely missed her cooking; now he also missed her chiding and fussing over dusty artifacts and overdue paperwork. Maybe straightening out the old bookshelves would brighten Hannah's day. He set to work.

69

Where's The Beefcake?

WRIGHTSVILLE BEACH WAS ONCE a quiet little barrier island. It was so no more. Aunt Joyce decided it would be wise for Jake to get out of Charlotte for a couple of weeks, and so she and Jake conspired to leave town under the cover of darkness to avoid prying reporters with fancy cameras wanting one more shot of the cover boy. When they headed east for Wilmington, no one knew the details except James Howell, who was sworn to secrecy. Jake volunteered to drive the four or so hours to Joyce's beach condo.

Late the previous evening, Jake enjoyed a long conversation with his mother in Jericho. She had been very glad that Jake had met with "Father" Howell, as she insisted on calling him, and she approved of his advice as well. This made Jake feel like he was at least beginning to get a grip on his own situation.

The drive to Wilmington was uneventful, but it was so hot that one could see the mirage of water appearing up ahead on the road. Jake had seen that before in the desert in Palestine and knew this meant high heat and humidity. Even his olive skin wouldn't protect him from the sun's killer rays.

"The beach will be really crowded," said Aunt Joyce with a warning note in her voice. "So I'm thinking you should lay low during the day, and wait until late afternoon to hit the beach. I never go until after four in the afternoon myself. Too many skin cancers have scared me off the hot beach! I look pretty silly all covered up hiding under an umbrella on a beautiful beach day! What's the point?"

Aunt Joyce babbled on most of the way, telling stories about Wilmington in the old days, and the rise of Wrightsville, or New Hanover Banks, as it was originally called. The first bridge from the mainland to the island was built in the late 1800s, followed by the railroad, followed by the electric beach trolley. That opened up the island to visitors year round. Even Joyce remembered the famous 12,500-square-foot Lumina complex that hosted the best of the big bands until it closed in 1973. Dancing under the stars and watching movies on a screen that was actually positioned over the ocean waters—that made Wrightsville Beach the place to be!

But Jake was getting so used to her chatter that he could tune her out on occasion without her ever knowing. No one was expecting Jake to turn up in either Wilmington or Wrightsville Beach. To be sure, there were basketball fans in Wilmington, but it wasn't so much for the Bobcats as it was for college teams like Carolina or Duke or even the local team, the UNC–Wilmington Seahawks. Jake shouldn't have to go incognito to have a quiet day at Wrightsville Beach.

The barrier islands just off the coast of North Carolina are reached by crossing the Inland Waterway. Whether one is at the Outer Banks or further south at Wrightsville Beach or Kure Beach, these little islands have become overrun with tourists and residents who covet the soft sand, warm waters, gentle waves, great seafood, fishing, golfing, etc., etc. Fortunately, Jake learned how to swim by going to the public pool in Bethlehem as a youth. He was very much looking forward to a week of Atlantic delights.

After settling into the two-bedroom condo on the east side of Wilmington, the most unlikely pair one could imagine headed off to Mallard Street at Wrightsville Beach to find a parking space, waddle over the sand dunes, and stake out a spot surfside. The tide was coming in and, it being late in the afternoon, the surfers were coming out. Fifteen minutes after their arrival, when Jake headed for the water to do a little body surfing, along came a blond-haired man in his early thirties who said, "Wait a minute! I think I know you. Aren't you Koby Arafat from the Bobcats? I'm Ralph Sorensen, a Bobcats season-ticket holder. Would you mind if my wife gets a picture of us, maybe with my two kids for the vacation photo album? The guys at the bank in Charlotte won't believe this!"

Jake groaned. "Well, alright, but let's make it quick, and do me a favor. Keep the picture to yourself. Don't sell it to the press or anything."

Ralph was running off to his beach chair, and over his shoulder said, "Don't worry! I'm one of your biggest fans!"

But Jake, with a weary look on his face, muttered to himself, "That's precisely what I'm worried about. So much for anonymity; the Beefcake has been found. Let's just hope I don't get grilled while I'm here."

70

Hannah Hovers

Hannah was not doing well at all. Kahlil discovered her soaking wet with a high fever. She was soon back in the hospital—in an ICU isolation room.

Dr. Jacobi had a private meeting with Kahlil and explained to him that it would be awhile before they discovered the cause of the fever. But he was sure she had contracted some type of flu. "Hannah seems to have a virus that her body is not fighting off very well. I suspect swine flu, H_1N_1, which the World Health Organization declared a pandemic in 2009. The officials recommend that only hospitalized patients' flu virus strains be sent to reference labs to be identified. I will do that. Meanwhile we will treat this as a viral infection, keeping in mind that she may be pregnant. I will contact the prison to see if they have new cases. I don't believe the coroner tested Yassir, but he could very well have been the carrier."

The tone of the doctor's voice had a more than sobering effect on Kahlil. "It's time for some serious praying," said Kahlil calmly knowing that all was in Allah's hands at this point.

Nodding his balding head, Dr. Jacobi replied, "Yes, it couldn't hurt."

Walking down the hall to the elevator, Kahlil resolved to go somewhere quiet to make his phone calls so he rode the elevator down to the main floor, where there was a chapel. His intuition was correct, for there was absolutely no one in this quiet room. He started down the cell phone list: Grace, Sarah, Art. Until now, he had not bothered Art with latest tales, but things were getting out of hand.

As luck would have it, Art was just getting out of the shower when the phone began to ring, and so he managed to pick it up before the call went to voicemail.

"Hello, this is Art West," said the soggy scholar. Discovering that it was Kahlil, he excitedly began to bring Kahlil up to date on the happenings in Corinth. But soon he realized that Kahlil was not responding. Finally, Art said, "Kahlil, something is wrong."

Kahlil sighed and began slowly. "Hannah is not at all well. And recently she suffered a terrible trauma. She was raped by her ex-husband!"

"But, but, he's been dead for twenty years!" sputtered Art.

"So we all thought, but in fact he had been working underground for Hamas and Hezbollah in Lebanon all these years. He resurfaced in Israel only to be taken prisoner by Mosad. We actually went to visit him in prison. And somehow, some way, he escaped and came after Hannah. She planned on getting an official divorce, and she refused to give him money. I got there too late—too late!" With this Art could hear Kahlil weeping and coughing. He then continued, "Fortunately, the police were after him. Detective Sharanky arrived at the shop and Yassir was shot dead on the spot. But only after Hannah had been raped! She stayed in Sinai Hospital for two days, then I took her home. But we are back. She is very ill with a flu of some sort. They must quickly find the cause! They may have to send her blood work to specialists, maybe even your CDC in Atlanta."

Art was speechless. He mumbled something about promising to pray for Hannah, and asking if he and Marissa should come to Jerusalem. "If you need anything, anything at all, please call me right away. I'll talk to Grace too." As the conversation was winding down, Kahlil heard his name being called over the intercom system in the hospital. He hung up and raced back to ICU. Coming out of the elevator he slammed right into Dr. Jacobi.

"Excellent! Mr. el Said, I was just coming to find you. One of the blood tests has come back. We've discovered at least one of the things wrong with Hannah. She has contracted a sexually-transmitted disease."

"Please tell me she does not have AIDS!" said a frantic Kahlil.

"No! She is infected with a bacterium called *Neisseria gonorrhoeae*. We need to treat this gonorrhea right away, not least because it can affect the unborn child, if there is one. If a pregnant woman has gonorrhea, she may give the infection to her baby as the baby passes through the birth canal during delivery. This can cause blindness, joint infection, or a life-threatening blood infection in the baby. Of course, pregnant women are usually tested for this disease."

"Praise Allah! But does this account for the fever also?"

"No! We are now treating this as a severe flu, probably swine flu. The tests have come back indicating as much. We are putting her immediately on a regimen of proven antivirals, in fairly strong doses. Pregnant woman are particularly at risk. I know we covered this when she came to the hospital earlier, but are you sure she is not allergic to any antibiotics?"

"Not to my knowledge," replied Kahlil confidently.

"We live in hope, we live in hope," said Dr. Jacob; and he smiled as he turned to go. Kahlil was left standing in the hall, pondering what might be next. "Sometimes hope in Allah is all we have to hang on to," said Kahlil reassuring himself.

71

Marissa Dreams

DREAMS ARE STRANGE THINGS, borne of memories, hopes, traumas, possibilities; things we've recently thought, read, feared, loved. After all that transpired—trouble getting into the country, telling Art about her abortion, having her reputation publicly questioned—it was not a surprise Marissa was showing signs of stress, even in her sleep patterns and dreams. Lately she was having a recurrent dream that Art had disappeared, leaving only a note on her door saying their relationship was over. Doubtless this was a dream version of one of her deepest fears, and Marissa found herself waking up in the middle of the night sweating and anxious. She lay in bed contemplating whether she should just ignore her problem or confide in Art. Maybe she could exorcise the fear through reassurance from Art. She decided on the latter course of action.

The knock came on the door of Art's cottage early in the morning just before they usually rendezvoused for breakfast. "Art, it's Marissa, can I come in?"

"Sure, the door's open, come on in."

Marissa walked in looking fresh as a daisy, except for the furrowed brow. Not what Art was expecting, so he gave her a longer than usual kiss, and ushered her into the easy chair next to his bed, while he sat on the bed itself.

"So what's on your mind, love of mine?" asked Art.

"I'll get right to the point. I've been having bad dreams of late, dreams about losing you."

"Sounds more like a nightmare to me! Have you been watching horror movies or eating spicy foods lately?"

"No, silly, but I think it does reflect my fears, which I need to take seriously. Art forgive me for having to ask, but do you really want to marry me? I'm not your typical American bride—I'm not even an American!"

At this question Art paused a moment. He needed to be very careful at this point. No more jokes. A silly dismissive comment would not satisfy this earnest enquiry. "Marissa, I confess I had some worries when you told me about the abortion, and then the translation of the article raised a doubt or two, but I have laid those things at the altar of the Lord and I am not only at peace with them, I am very much looking forward to our becoming more in love and closer as time goes on. We agreed that this year would be a trial period; little did we know it would be a trial by fire in some ways. But I believe our relationship has come through the fire without the passion being burned up and exhausted, and without feeling too much like toast to continue, to mix my metaphors. At least that's how I feel about things. That may not sound very romantic. I probably fall short in that department. You've caught me daydreaming in the field. Usually it's about the site, but lately I've been mentally making a trip to Charlotte and planning the wedding. I'm tired of daydreaming! Let's do it!"

Marissa smiled wanly and said, "Honestly, I don't feel I deserve to have someone like you in my life. It's a miracle, and a blessed surprise." And then Marissa surprised him by joining him on the bed.

Sitting close to each other, Art gently took Marissa's hand, and said to her quietly, "Now listen to me, pretty lady. I do love you and you need to let the Lord still that emotional storm within you." And with that he gave her a long and lingering kiss, which reminded them that the best was yet to come.

72

Once More with Feeling

SOMETIMES HISTORY REPEATS ITSELF simply from sheer human stupidity and failure to learn the lessons of the past. The problem with Wrightsville Beach was simple—too many young, good-looking, scantily-clad women on the beach. Jake found it necessary to repeatedly go into the water to "cool off" in more than one sense. But this time when he went into the water a brunette called to him saying, "Hey, are you new here? I know most of the regulars on this stretch of the beach, but you do look familiar. My name's Melody."

"My name is Jake, and you may have seen me on TV. I play pro basketball with the Charlotte Bobcats," said Jake already drawn to her dark-brown eyes.

"Sorry, I don't follow pro ball very often," replied Melody.

"Really? It's hard to imagine a North Carolina girl who doesn't watch basketball."

"I watch college games between the big four—Carolina, Duke, Wake, and State—but rarely the pros. I have to study sometime!" admitted Melody. "Oh dear, now I remember! Weren't you just on the cover of some magazine I saw in the checkout aisle at the grocery store?"

"You win the observant prize," said Jake, his expression souring.

"Hey, it was a great picture, but I can tell from your face you aren't very happy about it."

"No, I'm not! I got taken for a ride, and I didn't want to be turned into this month's beefcake poster boy. It brings a lot of unwanted attention, you know."

"Oops, I suppose I fall into that category. I'm sorry if I'm bothering you, but honestly, I'm no groupie!" said Melody as she turned to leave Jake.

"Slow down! I didn't mean to scare you off! Do you live here at the beach?"

"Yes, my folks live in the ancestral home on the waterway—four generations. Except for a few years on the mission field in Kenya, I've lived here all my life—so far anyway! My Dad's a local pastor at Grace Baptist. That makes me a PK and an MK. Do you know what that is?"

"That's pretty good credentials, that's what it is! Let me guess. PK is for pastor's kid, and MK is for missionary kid! How did I do?"

"Two points! The waves are too quiet today, but there's a storm kicking up offshore, so maybe I'll bring my board tomorrow. Will you be around for awhile?"

Jake was already thinking, not long enough! "I promise to be around at least for two weeks, but I don't have to be back in Charlotte for serious practice for quite awhile. I'm staying at a condo in Wilmington for now. Let me guess again. I'll bet you know the best restaurants in town. Am I right?" asked Jake, feeling very smooth and confident.

"Absolutely! I can honestly assess any restaurant within twenty-five miles of here!" claimed Melody equally confident.

"Well, then, are you free for dinner—say tomorrow night? Your choice!" promised Jake.

"Tomorrow is Wednesday and I promised my Dad I would help with Vacation Bible School. It's potluck night. Here's a long shot. How would *you* like to come to VBS—you being a basketball player and all! Would you believe our theme revolves around being a good sport as well as a good Christian?"

"You're kidding! You just nailed my two goals: to be a good sport and a good Christian. I'd be honored to come but I can tell you I haven't spent any time with really little kids except to sign autographs. Usually my height scares them off! I do help out at a teenage center in Charlotte sometimes, playing ball with the guys," said Jake, wondering how he would manage a pack of kids.

"I'll protect you! I usually come here late in the afternoons. Have you ever tried surfing?" asked Melody.

"Never! In fact, I've rarely been to any beach, at least not like this. There aren't too many beaches in Bethlehem."

"Bethlehem, Pennsylvania? Probably not," agreed Melody.

"No, I was referring to Bethlehem, Israel—my hometown."

"You're from the Holy Land!" gushed Melody, her eyes widening despite the sun.

"The one and only," replied Jake with his famous smile. "I would like to see you here, same time, same place, tomorrow for my first surfing lesson. Bring that board you talked about!"

From a distance, sitting in her chair, Joyce watched the conversation between Jake and Melody go on and on for nearly thirty minutes. "I wonder if I should have sprayed him with Off! before letting him go in the water?" muttered Joyce to herself as the sun sank behind the dunes.

73

Household Hints

Nancy Bookides and Art stood at the archaeological site surveying the results. Marissa, meanwhile, was in her cottage with her computer, recording results. Not as much had been accomplished as Art wished. He could blame this on the nature of digging or just the nature of life, with the problems and surprises that can sidetrack any endeavor.

"It seems clear to me that this was a major villa, with an industry attached to it, where they made leather goods. It seems equally clear to me that the owner was named Erastos, at least at some stage in the history of this house. I am inclined to think it was the Erastos of the NT period, because this house and the pottery bits and glass all suggest a first-century date for the home."

"I agree," replied Nancy. "But I think there's much more work to be done here. Would you like me to hire some laborers to speed the process along?" Nancy laughed a little devilishly. "I always hide away some money so we can finish off projects just like this one! How would you like to be crew boss over some of my favorite local characters! I guarantee they will provide you with some local color!"

"Sounds like fun! Maybe I'll have some good stories to bring back to my students in the fall!" replied Art laughing.

Art had been thinking more about the possibility of Christian meetings taking place in a house like this. He reckoned it could handle maybe fifty or so people in close proximity, and perhaps as many as a hundred if they were scattered around—but then, how could they all hear what the speaker was saying if he was in the dining room? These practical issues were seldom discussed in scholarly circles. There was certainly a need for many homes to accommodate all the Corinthian Christians who wanted to meet in small groups, but what did they do when they all wanted to meet together? Perhaps further excavation might provide clues to answer these questions.

Art also wondered how much hot water Erastos could have gotten into, as the city *aedile*, by hosting an illicit religious group. After all, he was well known in the city, maintaining the public buildings and over-seeing many of the public festivals. Paul arrived in Corinth in AD 50 or 51 and stayed about two years. Erastos was still a city official when he sent greetings to Paul's Roman Christian friends at the end of Romans 16, and that letter was probably written sometime around AD 57. He obviously managed to juggle his public and private lives. Erastos must have been one wealthy, smooth operator to remain in public office and remain a Christian as well.

Art also wondered if Erastos was one of the people Paul warned against going to meals in pagan temples in 1 Corinthians 8–11, since, as *aedile*, Erastus might have been obliged to participate. This would have really put Erastos in a tight spot. How could he maintain his public honor and office if he shunned various civic functions in temples and insulted his Roman superiors?

Suddenly his cellphone started buzzing in his pocket. At the other end of the line was Kahlil, breathing heavy.

"Art, I have never asked this before of anyone, but could you de-vote some serious time to pray in the next forty-eight hours? Hannah is critical. She has a potentially deadly form of flu, H1N1. They are putting her in ice baths to bring down the fever, filling her with antivirals, and they will probably put her on a ventilator. The next two days are critical, and her life may be hanging in the balance. Worst of all, she seems to have lost her will to live. My faith tells me Jesus is a great prophet. Your faith claims that Jesus is a healer. Pray with me."

Art could tell how frantic his friend was. Kahlil was an old man, groping for answers, and Art sought to reassure him. "Kahlil, dear friend, you can always count on me, and I will have Marissa pray with me because the Bible says where two agree together on anything it re-inforces the prayer. I will join Marissa, and we will get down on our knees just as you do when you pray. And please let me know what is happening. We are ready to fly to Jerusalem any time you want!"

"I will, I will. Thank you," said Kahlil, his voice cracking, with tears rolling down his dark cheeks. Hanging up, Art began running towards Mrs. Demetrios's house where Marissa was working. He decided he would ask Mrs. Demetrios to pray with them as well. The more the better since "the prayer of a righteous person availeth much." Time was a-wasting.

74

The Oracle Orates

THOUGH YOU MIGHT NOT guess it from her recent local celebrity, Philippa Philapousis was a rather shy woman in everyday life. She minded her own business, and as a widow did her own shopping and walked to church on Sunday. Her life was ordinary, except for the fact that she was a prophetess. This blue-sky morning she was on her knees weeding her garden, when all of a sudden a strong feeling overcame her, a compulsion to stand up and start walking towards the town square, or *plaka*. The sun beat down on the streets and sidewalks, but Philippa would not be deterred. There was a message coming, and she was God's messenger. Arriving at her usual spot across from her favorite icon shop, she shooed the pigeons off her park bench, climbed on it once more, cleared her throat, and made her pronouncement in a strong, clear voice.

HOW THE MIGHTY HAVE FALLEN,
THE WICKED FROM ON HIGH.
THEIR SECRET LIVES DISCOVERED,
THEIR RUIN LIES NEARBY.

INTO A PIT THEY FALL,
NEVER TO BE SEEN AGAIN.
THEY SLOWLY SINK INTO SHADOW,
THEIR SINS DO THEM IN.

BUT THE UPRIGHT SHALL SHINE
AND HEALING WILL COME.
RIGHTEOUS PRAYERS ARE HEARD.
GOD'S GOOD WILL BE DONE.

TAKE NOTE OF GOD'S JUSTICE,
HIS COMPASSION AS WELL.
CLING TO THE SAVIOR,
IN HEAVEN YOU WILL DWELL.

This oracle was longer than usual. Aristotle, as usual, was having his morning cup of coffee at his favorite café. He saw her coming, walking with determination toward her bench, and grabbed paper and pen. But he had trouble keeping up, writing down things as fast as he could. He knew soon enough the local reporter would soon come to him, wanting the full scoop. What could this prophecy be about? Another earthquake? The fall of a great politician? Who was ill? Philippa did not say, and if asked she would say she did not know. Aristotle knew this was true prophecy in a biblical sense. Philippa herself once told him, "God reveals enough about the future to give us hope and warning, but not so much that we do not need to continue to have faith and trust God."

Aristotle had hardly stopped taking notes when Philippa began walking once more out of the *plaka* in Naflion, heading home. The news spread quickly. And sure enough, the local newsman who missed the "news from above" was soon hurrying his way. Aristotle enjoyed the roll he played. At least it made for an interesting diversion from the usual tourist business and humdrum of daily life.

75

Beach Blankets

MELODY MORRIS WAS LIKE a breath of fresh air: a polite, Southern Christian girl who even passed muster after Aunt Joyce's thorough grilling. Indeed, it turned out that Aunt Joyce graduated from New Hanover High School in Wilmington along with Melody's grandmother. And Aunt Joyce was always interested in those family and friendship connections.

"So you are saying your grandmother Sarah, my classmate, passed away just last year?" asked Joyce.

Sitting on her little beach blanket and answering every question, Melody responded with a smile. "Yes, ma'am, and I miss her a lot. I really do. We used to play cards together and walk on the beach. She wore a big hat like yours, so you kind of remind me of her. She was so old-school."

"Old-school," repeated Joyce. "Yes! We both went to an old school, New Hanover High."

Melody just went on. "I graduated two years ago and now I'm at UNC–W. Can't decide between education and marine biology! By the way, you wouldn't happen to know Mr. Furr, my principal at New Hanover, would you?"

"Know him? I used to live three houses from where he was born and raised. His mama, Katherine, is my best friend. She still lives in the old house on Princess Street right across the street from the school. My house was on the corner. Would you believe it was used in a movie called *Dream a Little Dream*, starring Jason Robards? That was in 1989. Time sure passes. I've got to tell you that story!"

"Could I get a word in edgewise?" asked Jake. "The lemon ice lady with her cart is coming down the beach. I know I want a cone. How about you two?"

"Thank you Jacob. That's very thoughtful of you. Get three—my treat," smiled Joyce, who then turned her full attention back to Melody.

Jake loped off to catch the lady ringing her bell and pushing her heavy lemon ice cart. Joyce said to Melody, "Now Melody you seem like just the right kind of girl for Jake. He's hardly ever dated, and being so far from home, it's hard for him to fit in here. So promise me you will take things slowly, if you don't mind my asking you. I know I'm too protective, but I'm all he's got here in North Carolina."

"Thank you for the advice, Mrs. West. I think I catch your drift. Trust me, I'm no barracuda!"

"Well good, because Jake just escaped one in Charlotte, and she nearly had him for lunch," said Joyce.

"My life is a lot tamer than that! I'm sure Jake told you about his adventures yesterday at our VBS! I wish you had seen the faces of those kids when he walked in—all six feet five inches of him! A lot of the kids knew him. And so did the parents! Fortunately, no one mentioned the article in *Sports Fanatics*."

Just then, Jake came back with three ice-cold cups of ice shavings flavored with tart lemon syrup. He frowned when he heard the words *Sports Fanatics*. There was an awkward pause, before Aunt Joyce piped in with, "That was yesterday. Today we enjoy the beach!" Together they toasted each other with their little cups of pure refreshment.

"So Melody," said Jake. "I promised you a real dinner out at your restaurant of choice, not a church potluck! How about tonight! Joyce told me all about Lumina in the old days. Are you free to go dancing under the stars?"

"My dance card is not full! What time should I be ready?" replied Melody sweetly.

"How about six o'clock?" beamed Jake, a little overeager. And as this negotiation went on for a few more minutes, Joyce West had the good sense to keep her mouth shut. It looked to her like Jake was finally on the right track with women.

76

Touch and Go

LIVING OFF IV FLUIDS, Hannah had lost a good five pounds already. Kahlil tried to talk with her and explain to her what was happening, but she did not seem to care; indeed Kahlil feared she was losing her will to fight and to go on living. Parents, in his mind, should never live to see the death of their children, and Kahlil was seriously worried he might do so. There had been a lot of prayers offered up to God on behalf of Hannah by Muslims, Jews, and Christians—good people working together for a common cause.

Dr. Jacobi stopped by the room. "We are doing all we can to help Hannah, but she needs to fight this virus, which is spreading from person to person worldwide, probably in much the same way that regular seasonal influenza viruses spread. So, I am calling in a specialist in this matter." He leaned over and patted Kahlil on the shoulder as he rose to leave. He knew it was hard on Kahlil. Hannah was in the quarantine unit, and even Kahlil was not able to sit with her. For now he was relegated to watching from behind a glass window.

Dr. Jacobi was worried. It appeared that Hannah had a bad case of swine flu, and he had already lost patients this year to the disease, a fact he did not share with Kahlil. The gonorrhea was coming under control, but having nipped one problem in the bud, this second one was not responding to treatment. Hannah now had a fever of 103, and the IV fluids did not seem to be preventing her from losing more and more weight. Dr. Jacobi had been on the phone talking with both the CDC and the Mayo Clinic for treatment advice, since this strain of H1N1 began in the US. In his office, he dialed his contact in the US, Dr. Emily Arnot, for advice.

"You are doing everything you can," assured Dr. Arnot. "However, there is a report from Hong Kong that says the use of blood plasma donated by recovered H1N1 patients could reduce the death rate if the patient is severely ill. Apparently the treatment also reduces the inflammatory response. This is not a new idea. We have treated other infectious diseases with plasma from recovered patients because that plasma contains important antibodies. And I'm guessing your patient's immune system has been compromised. But, this is still very experimental."

"I understand," replied Dr. Jacobi. "Let's hope she responds to more conventional treatment. But, as I mentioned to you before, I have lost two patients already."

Dr. Jacobi then made another call to the prison, which confirmed other but much more mild cases of flu. Apparently Yassir left the prison with more than just a gun and a wrench.

77

Over The Edge

G REEK NIGHTLIFE CENTERS AROUND the bouzouki clubs. It's not cheap—a table and a compulsory bottle of whiskey can run well over a $100. But the clubs are filled every night with people of all classes moving to the sounds of pop music and maybe even the occasional bouzouki, the mandolin of Greece. Spiros spent way too many evenings in his favorite bouzouki club, especially since his finances were dwindling rapidly. He sampled his whiskey and then ordered a glass of ouzo, the anise-flavored Greek liqueur he favored. For a change, he was alone. Gone were the days when he had a platinum blonde on his arm and money to splash around. Tonight he was nursing an enormous grudge against anyone remotely connected to *The Owl* or the Ministry. Spiros was not the kind of person to take life's disasters lightly, especially when he believed he had been victimized. His sense of entitlement was strong. He stared into his glass, contemplated his state of affairs, and planed revenge.

By day, Spiros had taken to joyriding in his Mercedes all around Athens and up into the hills above the city. On this morning, nursing a hangover, he was thinking about creating a forged document on official Turkish government stationery in which some fictional government warned his superiors that West and Okur were subversives who stole small antiquities from the site in Hierapolis when they had worked there the previous summer. He would then leak this document to newspapers through indirect channels, and just wait for the fallout. Well, it was an idea at least, one of many, and not the worst he had concocted. If Nick was still speaking to him, maybe he could help put the plan into action. To that end Spiros was now dialing Nick on his cell phone while driving up a windy road above the west side of Athens. Naturally, he did not see the enormous overloaded truck coming his way, swaying over the midline of the narrow two-lane road. Having punched in the numbers, Spiros glanced up just in time to see the truck. He swerved towards the guardrail in plenty of time to avert disaster, but what happened next no one could have anticipated.

There was a huge noise, like dynamite exploding, and right before his eyes the road ahead cracked, split, crumbled, and tumbled down the hill, taking the guardrail with it! His car was heading toward the precipice! Spiros slammed on his brakes, but it was too late. The Mercedes—his pride and joy—slid sideways down and down the hill, landing finally in a gigantic hole left by an abandoned rock quarry. The pit was partially filled with water ten feet deep, and by now Spiros was barely conscious, but he still clutched his cell phone in his hand.

"*Nai* [yes], Hello, Hello! Is that you Spiros? I can't hear you, speak up?"

But Spiros could not speak up. He was full of panic as his car rapidly sank under the water. Just before he blacked out, his brain flashed back to the recent news article about Philippa the prophetess and what she had said:

> INTO A PIT THEY FALL,
> NEVER TO BE SEEN AGAIN.
> THEY SLOWLY SINK INTO SHADOW,
> THEIR SINS DO THEM IN.

78

Good News for Greeks and Jews

A RT HAD BEEN PONDERING for a long time the implications of what had been found thus far at Corinth. It was late in the evening, and Art still had his reading light on, reflecting on the meaning and nature of Paul's mission in this crossroads town. It seemed clear that Paul had worked primarily with Gentiles while he was in the city, though all of his initial contacts and converts had been out of the synagogue.

The notion that Paul would still be welcome in the synagogue after converting two of its leaders and winning a court case against some of the remaining leaders was a non-starter! No, he had probably retreated to places like Erastos's house, or, even further afield, to Phoebe's house in Cenchreae, not least because even his Gentile converts were inhospitable when he returned to the city a second time, as 2 Corinthians makes evident.

It could not have been easy for Paul to be rejected by his fellow Jews and yet accepted by many Gentiles, even high-status officials like Erastos. How was this Good News equally for Jews and Gentiles if the Jews rejected it? The pain Paul was later to admit to in Romans 9, about his fellow non-Christian Jews, was profound.

What *was* good news is that Art had uncovered yet more evidence that Christianity was meant for all kinds of people up and down the hierarchy of Corinthian society. The snobby patricians, of course, would have looked down on Paul for choosing to do manual labor to support himself, but Art doubted there were very many true patricians in the church. But some well-to-do citizens, elite Christians in Corinth, wanted to be Paul's patrons. Who were they? And why did he refuse their patronage? Was Erastos one of those that Paul snubbed?

Art could well imagine a dinner at the house of Erastos, where some Jewish Christians would come and then worry about whether they should eat this or that dish since it might violate the Jewish food rules. It seemed a wise word from Paul to tell them not to do anything they couldn't do in good conscience. Art was impressed with Paul's ability in 1 Corinthians to agree with the "strong" that no food was unclean, while at the same time siding with the more scrupulous Jewish Christians in saying that the "strong" should not cause them to stumble by violating their conscience on a mere food matter. It wasn't worth it. The body of Christ should not be divided over such matters.

But how would Erastos explain his sponsorship of Christian meetings and meals in his home? How would he explain to non-Christian Gentiles his endorsement of Paul's tent making? Would he play the Pauline trump card of Roman citizenship, as Paul occasionally did in extreme situations? And what about Priscilla and Aquila? How would Erastos defend them and their work in Corinth? The social dynamics in Corinth were difficult to puzzle out.

Art was tired. Finding that rack for stretching hides had proved that tent making went on in Corinth, and not just anywhere in Corinth but in the backyard of Erastos's villa. And finding the two things together made it very probable that this was indeed the household of the richest and most elite Christian in town, which was no small discovery. Art and Marissa would cowrite a report, run it by Nancy Bookides, and then submit it to the Ministry of Culture in Athens. He decided there was no need for fanfare about this particular find now. He would let Nancy publicize the summer finds as she saw fit.

He had plans, however, to hold a press conference in the US with plenty of pictures and PowerPoint slides. He would make sure that the world knew that Christianity had indeed spread far and wide, and up and down the social ladder, in Paul's day and through Paul's ministry. Having sorted these things out in his mind, he was able to put his work to bed and his mind to rest. Tomorrow would be a day off, and he was looking forward to it.

79

A Prophetess for Today

ART WAS IN THE shower, and since he had run out of his Head & Shoulders he had borrowed Marissa's herbal shampoo. Marissa knocked on the door of his cottage and poked her head in to say, "You about ready?"

"I'm using your shampoo at the moment," replied Art speaking loudly so his voice would carry over the sound of the water. "When I come out of here I will be smelling like a fruit smoothie!"

Marissa laughed. "That's you alright, both a fruit and a smoothie!" This caused Art to drop his bar of soap, he was laughing so hard. "Hurry up! We've got places to go and people to meet," reminded Marissa. "I'll meet you next door."

Today Art and Marissa were actually going to meet the famous Philippa, a meeting arranged by her friend Mrs. Demetrios. They would drive over to Nafplion and have lunch with the most famous, or infamous, resident of that town. Her last pronouncement made all the local papers, of course, and Art wanted to talk with her about the ancient Christian prophets and her own calling. Art and Marissa had been looking forward to this trip for a while, and this latest prophecy had prompted them to take action.

Nafplion, being southwest of Corinth, required navigating the E65 and then taking smaller roads. The two planned to stop at Argos and see the great theater with its amazingly large number of seats,

indicating a considerable population used to come to see dramas and other productions in this ancient Greek town.

Nafplion was the epitome of a beautiful Greek seaside village, with all the usual charm one would expect in such a place. The ancient castle ruins that overlook the city make it in some ways resemble Corinth with its Acrocorinth. Though it had taken some time, Marissa began to fall in love with Greece, especially its coastal towns and villages far away from the pollution and heat of Athens. When they drove into the city and began to look for the Ellene Café, they could hardly take their eyes off of the beautiful harbor, and the Castle of Bourtzi, which had been a fortress, a home for executioners, and a hotel. It was a favorite destination for tourists.

But just as many tourists were captivated by the icon shops around the *plaka*. Aristotle's little shop was one of the most popular because he had the original icons, not just the recent copies. While the originals tended to be more faded and worn, the detailing and quality of workmanship usually made up for the results of aging.

Art drifted into lecture mode as they strolled through the *plaka*. "Icons are viewed by the Orthodox as windows on heaven. They are seen as a reminder of the communion of saints—how the saints are alive and well in heaven and care about their fellow Christians on earth. They serve not as objects of veneration, but as facilitators to commune with the saints or even solicit their help. This is a rather different than the Catholic theology of veneration of Mary or praying the Stations of the Cross."

Marissa halfway listened to this mini-lecture, but her mind was elsewhere. She was simply taking in the beauty of the seaside on a perfect day—sunny but not too hot and with a light breeze off the harbor.

Art and Marissa arrived at the café a few minutes early, sat down at a little table, and ordered some coffee. "This coffee here is much the same as in Turkey, which is to say too thick and dark for me," moaned Art. Before he had time to attempt his first sip, in through the door came a small Greek lady with a lace scarf around her head, wearing an ornate gold, gem-studded cross.

Art stood up. "You must be Philippa!" And when she smiled and nodded he pulled out a chair and offered her a seat. "Thank you so much for taking time to see us."

"It is always good to see fellow devout Christians, is it not? What do the Scriptures say? 'How beautiful it is when brothers dwell together in unity.' Elena, my old friend, has already told me a lot about you both. She thinks highly of you as Christian persons. I see you try to drink our coffee. You must try honey pastry; it is wonderful and will make coffee not so bitter!" With this Philippa spoke in Greek to the waitress, who brought over another cup of coffee and a plate of small dainty honey-soaked pastries covered in confectionary sugar.

"So, if you don't mind me asking," began Art, "when did you first realize you had the gift of prophecy?"

"I was a little girl," replied Philippa. "A Word of God came to me about my Aunt Maria, who was ill. I told my mother she must see doctor because God said something was wrong in her female parts. My mother was so surprised to hear me say this! I was only twelve! But I kept saying it was from God. So Aunt Maria go to doctor, and sure enough she had a growing tumor. Not cancer, but it could be big problem. That was the first time. I had picture in my mind of a lump.

I did not hear God speak. But sometimes I hear Him—he talks to me in poems."

Art smiled. "Maybe you know that much of Hebrew prophecy in the Bible is poetry, particularly some of the material in Isaiah."

"I can't even make a rhyme if I try! I have no gift of poetry. This is one way I know it must be from God," replied Philippa nodding her head up and down in confidence of her belief.

Marissa gently asked, "Can you tell us about the most recent prophecy? It's really quite dramatic. Is it somehow different from the others?"

"You need to know I am just messenger. I cannot tell you what will happen in future. I not fortune-teller!" replied Philippa a bit vehemently. Then almost sadly, she continued. "Sometimes I wish I know meaning of God's words. Maybe then I could help people, like I did Aunt Mary. Do you know meaning?"

"Not really. But one part of the prophecy keeps coming into my head. You, or I should say God, spoke of the falling down of the wicked and mighty into a vast pit. Have you no idea what that is about?"

Philippa thought for a while. "Maybe I do. I feel prophecy is fulfilled. Let me ask you question. Has there been bad man in your life while you are here?"

Marissa and Art looked at each other in surprise. They were both thinking the same thing! Marissa ran with the idea. "Yes, Philippa, a man named Spiros Spandexikos from the Ministry of Culture was very mean to us!"

"No worry about him anymore. Earth swallowed him up! God rules!" said Elena triumphantly.

Art and Marissa barely knew how to react to such a statement. Could it be that Spiros was dead! Art pressed on. "But what about the righteous shining like the sun? What is that about?"

"Wait and see. Maybe good news will come into your life! Be patient with God," Elena smiled as she chided them.

Marissa was transfixed. "Philippa, when you think of yourself, do you compare yourself to the New Testament prophetesses?"

Philippa chuckled and said, "I am named for St. Philip the Evangelist. Did he not have daughters like me who prophesy? God still speaks to us!"

Art wrinkled his brow and leaned forward. "Philippa, I believe the prophecy in Corinth was not mainly about future events, or foretelling. I believe it was about God sending messages of encouragement and the like. Do you see the difference? Am I explaining myself clearly?"

Philippa thought for a moment. "Maybe so. Things do happen after the prophecy. But maybe also people are encouraged as you say. I do not question the heavenly message."

"Do you hear the message in your mind, before you speak it, or do you just open your mouth and see what comes out?" asked Marissa.

"I see in my mind, and then I just say it. That is why I close my eyes when I prophesy, so I can see God's word." And Philippa closed her eyes and just sat quietly for a while, smiling.

When she opened her eyes, Art continued, "It's like your mind is a message board where God posts something, and you then freely repeat it!"

"It is more than that. The word overpowers me! I cannot stop myself. I must come to *plaka*! I must share God's words! Nothing will stop me, I promise!" replied Philippa rather excitedly.

"I understand," said Art. "Sort of a fire in your bones that you must let out."

"And God help me if I do not! I would be in agony until I delivered His word!"

Art and Marissa talked with Philippa for a full two hours non-stop, and when they came up for air it was already lunchtime. "Would you care to be our guests for lunch?" asked Art.

"No! You are kind. I go back to house now," said Philippa sounding a bit tired. "My garden is calling me to tend it."

With this Art and Marissa rose. Marissa gave Philippa a hug. "God bless you and your ministry. Thank you so much for taking this time with us."

"My pleasure," said Philippa simply.

As the couple stood in the little café contemplating their next move, Art said to Marissa, "I wonder if anything happened to Spiros?"

"We may never know," said Marissa. "We may never know."

80

Hot Date

Wrightsville Beach is always blazing hot in mid-summer, but this particular day might well set a record. When Jake went to pick up Melody, he turned the air conditioning on high, especially since he was already sweating. Melody used an extra dose of deodorant. She decided they would go to Bluewater, a landmark restaurant on the Intracoastal Waterway. Jake picked the movie—*Iron Man*.

All day Aunt Joyce nagged Jake with specific instructions on how to treat Melody like a lady—in the old Southern sense of the word. There was a lot to remember. He would try. He really liked Melody.

As soon as he parked, Melody emerged wearing a flower-print blouse and white linen slacks. A flower beret held back her shock of dark brown hair. As she approached the car, Jake jumped out and opened the car door for her.

"Thank you, kind sir," said Melody. "I don't believe any boy has done that for me before!"

"You are so welcome, and if you don't mind me saying so you look fantastic!" replied Jake beaming.

"A girl tries to please," said Melody as she slid into the front seat. "Shall I navigate?"

The ride to Bluewater took a little longer than expected because they had to wait for the boats to pass while the drawbridge over the Waterway was open. But they were still early enough to get a quiet table at the far right end of the famous restaurant, their table overlooking all the activity along the Waterway. A massive hundred-foot yacht was tied up at the marina capturing everyone's attention. Even the seagulls seemed to be lined up on the pilings watching the activities on the spectacular boat. Dinner was, as usual, delicious, beginning with Bluewater's signature hot crab dip. Jake opted for scallops, a first for him. Melody admitted to being a shrimp lover.

"We have some extra time before the movie. This may sound a little strange, but I would really like to hear your testimony. How did you become a Christian? I'm more interested in that than in how you became a basketball player."

Jake looked a little surprised. "This will take awhile," he cautioned. When she gave him the go-ahead he took a deep breath and began. "I was born in Bethlehem in Palestine, and my mother was always a Christian. I was an altar boy in the Catholic Church before I got involved with Hamas. But at the same time I was pursuing my love for basketball and ended up on a professional team, the Maccabee Elite. Hamas approved—I had money! This next part is hard for me to tell, so bear with me. I had a twin brother named Issah, which is Arabic for Jesus."

"Wait a minute. You had a brother named Jesus?"

"That's right, and my birth name is not Jacob, it's Ishmael. In honor of my brother, I chose to be called by Jacob when I converted, because his is a story about transformation. He became Israel. Anyway, my brother was a freelance cameraman in Jerusalem and a devout Christian. He was upset, to say the least, when I got involved with Hamas, but I did it because the Israelis brutally killed some of my Palestinian friends. One of the missions I undertook for Hamas led to the kidnapping of Grace Levine and a hostage swap for Art West."

"Hold the fort for a minute! You mean Joyce West's son, the archaeologist?" said Melody looking truly shocked.

"The one and only! Anyway, after the hostage swap, Issah convinced me to rescue Art West from the Hamas leaders in Gaza. So we staged a rescue, which was successful. But our plan was for him to look like me and vice versa. It's complicated, but Issah was only trying to protect me. Being twins, this wasn't difficult and, long story short, Art West was freed, but at a great cost. An international bad guy named El Tigre, who provided Hamas with arms and money, figured out what had happened, and my brother was murdered." At this point Jake had to stop as the memories flooded back. Melody reached over and touched his hand.

"It took his murder to convict me. I've hurt so many people, and now my brother was dead because of my sins. I realized I wanted to be more like Issah, and the person he was named for. So I went and saw our priest, Father Abbas, and asked to be baptized, and have my name changed, and as they say the rest is history. I got to North Carolina because Michael Jordan recruited me off the Maccabee team, and the Bobcats signed me. And it was Art West who paved the way for me to live with his mother in Charlotte. I usually go to church with her at Myers Park. I guess you can see why she's so protective. I've only been here about a year. I miss my brother. I miss my mom; she had to leave Bethlehem with Issah's wife, but they are safe from Hamas now."

"That's an amazing testimony to God's grace," said Melody. "My life is far less dramatic. I already told you I was an MK and a PK. Basically I grew up in Grace Baptist Church here in Wilmington but was pretty rebellious in my senior high years, and came back to the church and the Lord a couple of years ago through InterVarsity Fellowship on the campus of UNC–W. I've been a happier person ever since. I've dated a few boys along the way, none all that seriously or for that long."

"I've been hoping to find a girl, but I couldn't figure out how to go about it."

"God figured it out for us, without a lot of effort on our part. You know what the Bible says?" asked Melody.

"Not as well as I would like," admitted Jake.

"It says God works together all things for the good of those who love Him."

"Right. I do believe that's true. On a lighter note, we need to get to the movie! I wonder how Iron Man would handle the likes of Hamas!"

～

Things had gone so well on Jake's first real date with Melody—concluding with a goodnight kiss—that he was especially glad that he did not have to return to Charlotte for another month, when practice began in earnest for the upcoming NBA season. He planned to make a concerted effort to nurture this relationship slowly and carefully.

What he felt about the situation was excitement—a kind of excitement he had never felt before in his life. This was not the kind of excitement one feels after tasting the thrill of victory, or the kind of excitement one feels after getting a great job, graduating from college, or the like. Nor was this the kind of excitement one feels when the hormones kick in. No, this was an excitement bordering on euphoria because it hinted that: 1) Jake might be able to enjoy a normal relationship with a woman without fear of being used; 2) he might be able to settle into America without feeling like an alien; and 3) he might be able to "walk the talk" by behaving like the Christian man he wanted to be. Amazing!

8 1

A Work for Art

MARISSA AND ART HAD found Nafplion so charming that they decided to stay overnight and enjoy the village a bit longer. In the evening the lights that hung in the trees around the *plaka* were turned on, and the center of the village really came to life with music and even dancing. They wandered into Aristotle's shop, splitting up to investigate all the nooks and crannies.

Art suddenly got excited. "Marissa, look what I have found! It's an icon of Christ by El Greco, a small version of his famous painting, *The Disrobing of Christ*, or *El Espolio*. See the carpenter making his cross and the soldiers removing his robe. I would love to have this for our home; that is, if we ever have a home!"

Aristotle was drawn to the couple. "Sir, how much for this little icon of El Greco's famous painting? Who is the artist? Such detail!" gushed Art.

"The workmanship is amazing, is it not! Athena is a local artist specializing in icons of all sorts—replicas and her modern interpretations. She has a studio outside of town. Ask anyone. Athena is well known in Greece, one of the very best of our artists.

253

This icon is very special; she made only this one replica, so moved was she by the image. Of course, the original dates to about 1579 and now hangs as an altarpiece in the Cathedral of Toledo. I could not accept less than $900. For this piece I will not haggle."

Marissa tactfully said, "I agree that the icon is beautiful. We would like to learn more about the artist before we make such a large purchase. Thank you so much for your time and explanation." At this, she steered a surprised Art out of the shop!

An angry scowl covered Art's face. "I really wanted that icon!"

"And you may yet have it. But I won't indulge in impulse buying! We will check out his story first!" For a moment, the two stared each other down, Marissa moving her hands to her hips. Art blinked first.

"Okay, you're right," Art agreed still disgruntled. Then he brightened up. "Say, I have an idea! Let's get in touch with my friend Barbara Zimmerman. Being an artist herself, she might know all about Athena the icon maker." The two found a café on the edge of the *plaka* and phoned Barbara, who was more than delighted to talk to Art and ramble on about icons in Greece. And yes, she was familiar with Athena and highly recommended her work as one of the best icon painters in Greece. She and Doug set a date to come by the Corinth site and inspect the summer's work before Art and Marissa had to leave. Barbara was always looking for new inspirations for her own artwork.

The icon was purchased, and Art learned a lesson. Marriage would require the meeting of *two* minds. This could be very difficult after years of thinking only about himself.

82

Hannah's Song

MANY OF KAHLIL'S RELATIVES and friends had rallied to support him in this difficult time. Grace, Manny, Sarah, and several cousins spent time at the hospital keeping vigil. Surprisingly, even a member of Yassir's family visited to say, "We are ashamed of what my brother was doing for many years and what he did to poor Hannah. Please believe we did not know he was alive. Please believe we are sorry for all the trouble Yassir created."

Grace was familiar with more than just the Torah, the first five books of what Christians call the Old Testament. The later books entitled 1 and 2 Samuel were also important historical documents, and part of the larger Hebrew Bible. In the waiting room, Grace encouraged Kahlil to read Hannah's Song from 1 Samuel 2. As a Muslim, Kahlil believed that Samuel was indeed a prophet. The Qur'an affirms this; however, reading these texts from the Hebrew Bible was new territory for Kahlil. More and more he was discovering that he, as a Muslim, along with his Christian and Jewish friends, shared one God. He began reading:

> Then Hannah prayed and said:
> "My heart rejoices in the LORD;
> in the LORD my horn is lifted high.
> My mouth boasts over my enemies,
> for I delight in your deliverance.

> [2] "There is no one holy like the LORD;
> there is no one besides you;
> there is no Rock like our God.
>
> [3] "Do not keep talking so proudly
> or let your mouth speak such arrogance,
> for the LORD is a God who knows,
> and by him deeds are weighed.
>
> [4] "The bows of the warriors are broken,
> but those who stumbled are armed with strength.
>
> [5] Those who were full hire themselves out for food,
> but those who were hungry hunger no more.
> She who was barren has borne seven children,
> but she who has had many sons pines away.
>
> [6] "The LORD brings death and makes alive;
> he brings down to the grave and raises up.
>
> [7] The LORD sends poverty and wealth;
> he humbles and he exalts.
>
> [8] He raises the poor from the dust
> and lifts the needy from the ash heap;
> he seats them with princes
> and has them inherit a throne of honor.
> "For the foundations of the earth are the LORD's;
> upon them he has set the world.
>
> [9] He will guard the feet of his saints,
> but the wicked will be silenced in darkness.
> "It is not by strength that one prevails;
>
> [10] those who oppose the LORD will be shattered.
> He will thunder against them from heaven;
> the LORD will judge the ends of the earth.
> "He will give strength to his king
> and exalt the horn of his anointed."

Immediately before these verses, Kahlil read the background to Hannah's prayer:

> Hannah stood up. Now Eli the priest was sitting on a chair by the doorpost of the Lord's temple. In bitterness of soul Hannah wept much and prayed to the Lord. And she made a vow, saying, "O Lord Almighty, if you will only look upon your servant's

misery and remember me, and not forget your servant but give
her a son, then I will give him to the Lord for all the days of his
life, and no razor will ever be used on his head."

God heard that prayer of Hannah, and granted her a son whom
she promised to dedicate to God. Samuel became a famous prophet
who anointed David as king over Israel. Kahlil pondered these stories,
and asked God to take care of *his* Hannah. Just then, Dr. Jacobi, looking
exhausted, came into the waiting room with some news.

"The fever has broken! The ventilator has been removed. She is
breathing comfortably, sitting up in bed, and complaining about the
gelatin. That is actually a *good* sign! Since she is beyond the contagious
stage, I will let you in to see her," announced Dr. Jacobi with a great deal
enthusiasm, despite being very tired.

There was a yell of approval in the room, and Kahlil shook the
doctor's hands saying, "I know this has been a trial for you as well. You
should go home and get some good rest."

"You are so right, but first, shall we go see Hannah?"

As Kahlil entered the now brightly lit room he could see the difference in his daughter. Though much thinner, her color was rosier,
and her hair was combed. Walking over to the bed, Kahlil instinctively
began singing like he had done so often with Hannah when she was a
child. Hannah responded with her first smile in a very long time.

"Father, it's nice to see you on this side of the glass wall! I feel
so much better today! By the way, I just had the most extraordinary
dream! I dreamed I was the Hannah mentioned in the Hebrew Bible!
Isn't that odd?"

Kahlil and Hannah finally had a long conversation about all the
traumatic events since that dark night in their antiquities shop. The
gonorrhea was gone; the flu was conquered. But Kahlil finally told her
about the possible pregnancy. "And while it is not certain yet, your husband may have left you an unintended gift before his demise—the gift
of a child."

"A child! A child!" cried Hannah. "After all I've been through I
might be pregnant!" Then going silent for a moment she calmed down
and said, "If so, there is only one thing to say in light of my dream: 'his
name shall be called Samuel, for the Lord has seen the plight of his

handmaiden and has visited her with his favor."' And with this, father and daughter praised Allah together.

83

Prophecies Fulfilled

As Art and Marissa drove the scenic route back to Corinth, they planned the rest of the summer's dig. Tomorrow, Nancy's team of locals was schedule to invade the site to clear away debris and, hopefully, provide some comic relief in the heat of the digging. Both scenarios were promised by Nancy! Next week, Doug and Barbara Zimmerman would arrive and provide yet another excuse to visit a local restaurant and maybe even party for a while at one of the bouzouki clubs in New Corinth, although Art wasn't much for paying for the obligatory bottle of whiskey! Maybe Doug could play the piano in exchange for something more palatable—like a great bottle of Grecian wine, say, Nemian Red! So much had happened this summer that Art had never fulfilled his promise to give Marissa a tour of New Corinth, still recovering from the earlier earthquake.

When Art and Marissa showed up for a later than usual breakfast the next morning, Mrs. Demetrios quietly handed Art the *Athens News*, Greece's oldest English-language paper. On page 4, along with other obituaries, was a familiar name—Spiros Spandexikos. The accompanying article detailed his death! Apparently, a friend, Nikos Alexandros, was speaking with Spiros who was driving somewhere near Athens, when all of a sudden there was a loud noise and then silence. The Athens police were dispatched and discovered that Spiros and his Mercedes were now under ten feet of water in a deserted quarry. A large crack across the road was attributed to a minor earthquake the city experienced at about the same time that day. Handing the paper over to Marissa, Art said, "Read this!" After doing so, Marissa ran back to her room and returned with a copy of the prophecy, which she read aloud.

HOW THE MIGHTY HAVE FALLEN,
THE WICKED FROM ON HIGH.
THEIR SECRET LIVES ARE DISCOVERED,
THEIR RUIN LIES NEAR BY.
INTO A PIT THEY WILL FALL,
NEVER TO BE SEEN AGAIN.
THEY WILL SLOWLY SINK INTO SHADOW,
THEIR SINS WILL DO THEM IN.

Mrs. Demetrios crossed herself in the Greek Orthodox manner from right to left shoulder. Marissa was visibly shaking. Art said quietly, "We need to call Kahlil immediately. Marissa, read the next verse of the prophecy."

MEANWHILE THE UPRIGHT SHALL SHINE
AND HEALING WILL COME FOR THE ILL.
THE PRAYERS OF THE RIGHTEOUS ARE HEARD,
THEIR REQUESTS GOD WILL FULFILL.

After about five rings, Kahlil finally picked up. "Kahlil, Art West here. How is Hannah doing?"

The deep melodious voice of Kahlil responded with joy. "The fever has broken. She is breathing and eating and sitting up and laughing! She has made an amazing recovery. Even Dr. Jacobi calls it miraculous. It must be all those prayers!"

Art was moved to recite from William Cowper's famous poem.

God moves in a mysterious way,
His wonders to perform;
He plants his footsteps in the sea,
And rides upon the storm.

Deep in unfathomable mines
Of never failing skill,
He treasures up his bright designs,
And works his sovereign will.

"And when I say 'mysterious ways' I'm not kidding," laughed Art. "Surely God has been merciful to Hannah, the prayers of the righteous have been answered, and our requests have been fulfilled!"

After Art hung up and delivered the news, Mrs. Demetrios was unusually quiet. Finally she spoke up. "There is more to prophecy. What is meaning of last two verses?"

TAKE NOTE OF GOD'S JUSTICE,
HIS COMPASSION AS WELL.
CLING TO THE SAVIOR,
IN HEAVEN YOU WILL DWELL.

Marissa gave Mrs. Demetrios a big hug. "Do not worry! We have seen God's justice and his mercy this week. If ever I have met a good and righteous person who clings to her Savior, it's you. What a blessing you have been this summer. In heaven you will dwell!"

84

Once Upon A Time VII

*P*AUL STOOD IN THE *middle of the courtyard with all those present circled around him, some holding the torches at various points so everyone could see. It was customary after the meal to enjoy another glass of wine while listening to the after dinner speaker. The invited refilled their goblets and settled themselves – they were prepared to listen to an entertaining speech. Nicanor really wasn't sure what to expect.*

Holding out his hand in the gesture of an orator, Paul began his speech with somewhat of a flourish.

> *"On this night of celebration and joy, it is only appropriate that we praise God by talking about one of his chief attributes. Yes God has virtues that he also instills in all those who believe in him. I am referring of course to agape, unconditional, free and gracious love. Agape is loving with no requirement of return. It is the love that many of us here have experienced in our relationship with the risen Lord Jesus. We long for you all to experience this agape love, for it is the one quality of life and relationships that is most enduring and endearing. Agape love can mold us into the image of Christ himself.*
>
> *"I myself have found this to be true, even in the midst of great personal loss and suffering. Indeed, agape love must be seen as the greatest quality and expression any life can exhibit. So I ask you to bear with me friends for a while, as I extol this sort of love!"*

With this dramatic introduction, Paul began to speak in a more lyrical, poetic manner.

"If I speak in the tongues of men or of angels, but do not have love, I am only a resounding gong or a clanging cymbal (like those made at the bronze works here in Corinth). If I have the gift of prophecy and can fathom all mysteries and all knowledge, and if I have a faith that can move mountains, but do not have love, I am nothing. If I give all I possess to the poor and give over my body to hardship that I may boast, but do not have love, I gain nothing.

"Love is patient, love is kind. It does not envy, it does not boast, it is not proud. It does not dishonor others, it is not self-seeking, it is not easily angered, it keeps no record of wrongs. Love does not delight in evil but rejoices with the truth. It always protects, always trusts, always hopes, always perseveres.

"Love never fails. But where there are prophecies, they will cease; where there are tongues, they will be stilled; where there is knowledge, it will pass away. For we know in part and we prophesy in part, but when completeness comes, what is in part disappears.

"When I was a child, I talked like a child, I thought like a child, I reasoned like a child. When I became a man, I put the ways of childhood behind me. For now we see only an imperfect reflection as in a mirror; then we shall see face to face. Now I know in part; then I shall know fully, even as I am fully known. And now these three remain: faith, hope and love. But the greatest of these is love.

"Look around you now friends, have you not seen and felt this love in this very household, and from this very family? Have you not experienced this love in good times and in bad, when someone was well or ill? When you have experienced such love as Christ pours into your life and into your very hearts, you know it and cannot deny it. It is so true, so real so pure, and it transformers those loving as well as those being loved profoundly. The love of human beings is fickle. Not so the love of God which he longs to share with us all. While we were yet sinners, Christ died for us, so that we might live in such love, live in newness of life. It is what God created all humans for—to be loved, and to love.

"And so on this night of nights, I appeal to your hearts—let love in, let Christ in. It is not merely the key to a joyful and genuine life, a life full of purpose and meaning, it is the key to eternity, to everlasting life. Amen"

And many in the assembly replied with hearty "Amens" as well.

Nicanor found himself moved beyond words by this oration, and he could see many wiping their eyes in the circle. Paul might look like an old shopkeeper, but his words moved even the skeptical and hard-hearted. Nicanor deeply and desperately wanted such love in his life, but this whole evening raised many more questions than it answered. Just when he thought everything was about to draw to a close, something else happened.

Both men and women started speaking in a language he had never heard before, and rather quickly Paul interrupted and asked, "Is there anyone here tonight with the gift of interpreting these tongues? If not, we must move on to the prophesying which all can understand so all may worship with both their spirit and their mind."

What surprised Nicanor most about what happened next was that prophecies would be directed to very specific situations and persons. For example there was a prophecy spoken about Erastos that said, "You have been spared for a specific reason. You will serve the Lord faithfully in the world, while not being of the world. Always remember your healing and remain faithful."

This, thought Nicanor, was apt, but at this point he felt more like an outside observer of someone else's religion. Suddenly, the crowd parted and Camilla walked straight up to Nicanor. She narrowed her eyes, cocked her head, grabbed his arm, and led him to the middle of the gathered meeting! He was mesmerized by her behavior.

Camilla then closed her eyes, opened her mouth, and spoke in a voice that seemed more authoritative than even Paul's. "Nicanor, thus says the Lord Jesus to you: 'It is time, time indeed, for you to repent of your skepticism. You have seen my works of healing in the life of Erastos. You have experienced my mercy as I watched over you when you travelled from Roma. You have enjoyed prosperity in lif -- but, your heart longs for love, and your house has no wife or children to welcome you home. You have a noble and honest character, but still there is a void in your soul which only I, Jesus, can fill."

Trembling, with his stomach all in knots, Nicanor broke down. He could not silence the questions in his mind, but his heart longed to respond in some way to the prophecy. Just then Nicanor felt a hand on his head, and then another, and then another, and then one on his right shoulder, and then one on his left shoulder. All around him powerful prayers were being said.

Suddenly, a tiny hand slipped into his, the hand of Julia, daughter of Erastos and Camilla. Nicanor bent over so that she could whisper in his ear. "We all love you here." And she gave him her biggest hug. Nicanor felt a huge warmth streaming through his body. He ceased trembling. Turning to Camilla and Erastos he smiled and said, "I would learn more of this Jesus. I have only known many gods, but now I have many questions. If Jesus is anything like your loving family, it will be worth all the time in the world to learn of him."

85

Nuptials Announced

For Art and Marissa, the summer ended with a whirlwind of last-ditch digging, meetings with Nancy, a visit from the Zimmermans, and poignant goodbyes with Elena Demetrios. The amphora was nearly pieced together, the mosaic floor was visible, and the rack was safely in the museum awaiting display. Their circuitous route took them first to Istanbul to visit Marissa's home and family, and then to Jerusalem to see Hannah, Kahlil, Grace, and Manny with a side trip to the monastery to visit a very surprised Mrs. Arafat. She plied them with handcrafted gifts to bring home to her son, Jake, and his new girlfriend. Their ten-hour flight from Tel Aviv to New York was cramped; clearing customs was tedious; and the flight to Charlotte was delayed. Marissa often said she loved to travel—except for the travelling.

Myers Park Church was looking fine on this late August day as Art and Marissa made their way to the pastor's office. A cold front had come through, and suddenly there was a foretaste of autumn in the air, as the temperatures dropped into the seventies with little humidity. Above them—Carolina blue skies—just the way Art liked it. James Howell was waiting to see Art and Marissa for some premarital counseling and planning.

"It's very good to see you both again," said James. "So how was Greece this summer?"

"Splendid," beamed Marissa leaping right into the conversation. "As you might imagine, being a Turk, I had serious reservations about digging in Corinth, but we had a grand time at the dig site at least. We'll dish out all the details at the news conference!"

"The media have been setting up all morning in Jubilee Hall. I announced the event in church last Sunday. I gather you two have settled on a general date for the wedding?" said James, getting down to business.

"Early next summer as soon as classes are over," replied Art. "But of course it won't be that simple especially since our families span two continents. In fact, Marissa and I are seriously considering having the ceremony in the Chora Church in Istanbul! Would you believe the church dates to the early fifth century? Of course, in the sixteenth century it was converted to a mosque, but today it's just a museum. I know this sounds like a strange venue, but I guarantee it won't need decorating! The mosaics and frescoes take care of all that. And remember what Christ said, 'Whenever two or more are gathered together . . .' Art was jabbering on like a child trying to convince his dad to let him go on a field trip!

James laughed and said, "Slow down, Art! Are you asking me to do the service in Istanbul? I must admit, I could be easily tempted! What a great excuse to see Turkey again! I'll bet that old church misses the days when weddings were held there."

"Fantastic! Of course the idea of my getting married in Istanbul is freaking out my mother. However, she is old-school enough to abide by the rule that the bride picks the venue."

"Before we get into planning mode, Marissa, how exactly did you become a Christian? There aren't too many of them in Turkey, are there?"

"In fact Christians have been a persecuted minority. But I came to Christian faith here in the US. I grew up in Boston and attended the famous Park Street Church near Beacon Hill and the Gardens. I will be candid and say it has been hard to nurture my Christian faith in Turkey. There aren't many churches in Ankara! But at least there are many historical reminders of Christianity's impact on my country. I especially love spending time in Capaddocia in the tufa cave churches, singing and praying."

"Cappadocia is a very spiritual place," admitted James. "I took a church group to Turkey five years ago. Normally tours hug the west coast with Ephesus being the highlight. But we added in sites in central Turkey as well. The whole group floated over Cappadocia's remarkable landscape in colorful balloons! But I digress. Art, I need to ask, are you really prepared to settle down? I mean, I can't see you becoming totally domesticated," mused James.

Art paused for a while, which made Marissa a little uncomfortable. "The thought of settling is unsettling. Marissa and I are both travel nuts and archaeologists. We've worked side by side now for two summers under the best and worst conditions. In that sense, I don't know what domesticated really means. However, if we decide to have children, that would change things dramatically. Whatever happens, our lives won't be very conventional. We will have to rely on the Lord continually for guidance."

"That's easier said than done," cautioned James. "I still think you have underestimated the sacrifices required to be a family and have a family."

Marissa added, "We are prepared to do whatever it takes to make this relationship not merely work, but grow and thrive."

"Excellent," replied James. "Let's have lunch before the news conference. Any hints about great revelations?"

"You'll just have to bide your soul in patience until two o'clock," said Art with a Cheshire Cat grin.

86

Art Begins The Tale

AN IMPRESSIVE CROWD WAS gathering in Jubilee Hall, and Joyce made sure her best friends got the good seats up front. Jake sat in the back row for two reasons: 1) he was missing Melody, and 2) he told Aunt Joyce he didn't want to sit with a "bunch of old ladies!" Joyce just sighed and let him off the hook, but not before introducing him to all her old girlfriends.

Because Art was on almost every major newspaper's speed dial for consultation, Associated Press (AP), Reuters, and even United Press International (UPI) would cover the event and send out instant news-wires to the major papers. The Christian Broadcasting Network (CBN) also set up shop, planning to record the whole event. The *Charlotte Observer* team was promised personal interviews after the conference.

Art and Marissa both planned to speak and answer questions, with James Howell acting as emcee. After tapping the microphone briefly to get the attention of the audience, James said, "We are ready to begin now. It is always a pleasure to introduce one of our favorite sons, Dr. Arthur West. For those who don't know him, Art is a Carolina man who received his PhD at the University of Durham in England, not to be confused with my alma mater, Duke University in Durham, North Carolina. Wonders never cease—this Blue Devil is looking forward to hearing from a Tar Heel! Please come to the podium, Art!" This produced a good-natured chuckle in the audience.

Marissa quickly whispered in Art's ear, "What in the world is he talking about? Who is this Blue Devil?"

"I'll explain later," whispered Art, bounding out of his chair. The applause rang out as Art, dressed in a navy suit with a Carolina blue tie, stood behind the microphone with his clicker and lecture notes.

"It is ever so good to be in Charlotte, my home town, and here at Myers Park, my home church. I want to thank James Howell for his hospitality, and reassure him that I'm pleased to call a Blue Devil my friend!

"It is also my pleasure to present Dr. Marissa Okur, my colleague and my fiancée!" Art smiled, paused, and turned to Marissa as the crowd buzzed and cameras clicked. "Dr. Okur received her PhD from Bilkent University in Ankara, Turkey. We have been working together the past two summers at two important archaeological digs, one in Hierapolis, modern Pammukale in Turkey, and this summer in Corinth, in southern Greece. Today I will talk about what we have learned about the culture of Corinth from our finds there. Professor Okur will then speak about the significance of archaeological work for the study of early Christianity.

"With the approval of Greece's Ministry of Culture, plus the help of Dr. Nancy Bookides, director of the Museum in Corinth, we were able to excavate a new site above ancient Corinth. You can be proud of the American School of Archaeology in Greece, which for over forty years has been digging at ancient Corinth with remarkable results. The upshot is that we now know more about Corinth as a first-century city than any other city in which Christianity was first planted. It was my intent to build on the previous good work and explore a new location.

"This new location sits on top of a little nob that overlooks the ancient city. From here, one can also see the Acro-Corinth as well. I think you will enjoy these slides—the scenery is beautiful.

"Note from this next slide that we are dealing with a large site. Several more seasons of excavations are in the planning stages. While there, we survived one of Greece's famous earthquakes, which actually helped us! A crevice opened up! Here you see small pottery and even glass objects we recovered from the pit. These next slides show the tedious process of piecing together a larger amphora or wine jar. But I'm not here to show you the usual finds. I am here to show you something surprising and novel.

"Here is a straight-on shot of the most interesting thing we found underground. What do you suppose it is?"

Someone in the crowd yelled out, "It looks like my mom's old laundry rack!" This produced some laughs in the crowd.

"That's a really good guess. It is a rack, but not a laundry rack. Indeed I had to wrack my brains to figure out what it was. Marissa discovered compelling evidence. Note here a magnified close up of little bits of animal hide and fur found on the rack. Now, with this additional clue, what do you suppose we found?"

A young lady a few rows back hollered out, "My aunt stretches fabric for quilt making on a gadget like that!"

"Yes, some things never change! This is a stretching rack on which animal hides would be stitched together and shaped into tents, which were often used as temporary shelters at the nearby Isthmian Games (think tent city at the Olympics). Now who in the New Testament do we know that made tents in Corinth and elsewhere?"

Hands went up all over the room. "St. Paul, of course, and Priscilla and Aquila," called out Gloria, one of Joyce's friends.

"Right you are!" said Art grinning. "Now I am not claiming that we found Paul's residence in Corinth. We found nothing that said 'Paul slept here,' but what we did find was a beautiful mosaic floor, and if we enlarge a corner of that floor on our next slide we find an inscription, which reads, 'DEMETRIOSTECHNOSPROSERASTOS.'

"Now for all you folks for whom this is indeed Greek, let me give you a translation. The inscription says, 'Demetrios, artisan, for Erastos.' There actually is a famous first-century Erastos, known from both Romans 16:24, which says, 'Erastus, the director of public works, sends you greetings,' and from the archaeological evidence in ancient Corinth. Here is a picture of an inscription about this man found in front of the ancient theater there in Corinth.

"Basically it reads, 'Erastus, for the office of *aedile* paved this parking lot.' Now since *aedile* is probably the Latin version of '*oikonomos* of the city,' which is the phrase we find in Romans, I am prepared to say with a high degree of probability that we are talking about one and the same person. Our Christian man Erastus, whom Paul probably befriended and converted during his first visit to Corinth, is the *aedile* or public works supervisor for the city. Now let me explain the significance of this.

"If I am right, then we have found one of the first Christian homes in any ancient city. We have found one of the places where Paul set up shop and made tents. We have found one of the villas where Christian worship services could be held, because the earliest Christians worshipped in homes. In short, this grand villa is the Myers Park Church of its day! While we haven't found any Pauline remains just yet, we have found the home of an elite early Christian named Erastos who had tents made on the back of his property. I am now going to turn this over to Marissa. Would you please welcome Dr. Okur!"

87

Marissa Has The Last Word

WEARING A SHORT-SLEEVED WHITE jacket over a dark green floral top and jade necklace, Marissa felt right at home in this Southern climate. Someday she would show Art her collection of nineteenth-century Turkish clothes. And wouldn't he be surprised if she wore a traditional Turkish wedding gown next June! She quickly put these images aside as she began her lecture.

"Archaeology is a tedious, time-consuming, patience-producing profession. And I love it!" smiled Marissa to a round of laughter. "If you remember nothing else I say, remember this—it is very rare to find a direct, or even indirect, correspondence between an artifact and an ancient person. For example, the stone cylinder with the Code of Hammurabi on it is a rarity. Why? Because it is an object that confirms the existence of a person we know only from texts. It is not common to find a correspondence between an inscribed object and a biblical text. As Art has just pointed out, we have probably found such a correspondence—a biblical referencee matched with an inscription in the city of Corinth, matched with yet another inscription at the villa. This triangulation can hardly be a coincidence. The evidence strongly suggests we are dealing with the same high-status, well-to-do Corinthian public works director named Erastus, or in Greek, Erastos. Most of the time, the stones we excavate as archaeological evidence are mute. But in this case the threefold testimony cries out for a plausible explanation.

"In all my years of archaeological work, I have never found a correspondence quite like this, and it gives us reason to trust that the biblical data accurately describes a historical man. Sometimes people get too carried away with the notion that 'archaeology proves the Bible.' More often than not archaeology simply supports that the biblical texts accurately describe the culture, the social setting, the conventions of their age. It does not prove that this or that person or this or that event happened. But in the case of the Erastus-inscribed stone, villa, and biblical text we can claim more. This is a very rare and precious find indeed.

"If I were to write the banner headline for this press conference it would read, 'Home of early Christian leader found. Tent making operation may connect villa with St. Paul.' Here is another clue that suggests that this headline is more fact than speculation. The animal hide fragment found on the tent rack was cilicium, a black or grayish goat's hair cloth. Now we know that Paul learned his tent making skills from his family, and we know he was from the province of Cilicia. One then has to ask, 'Who would be more likely than Paul to be making goat's hair tents in Erastos's backyard?' In my mind, Paul is the leading candidate. So it may well be that in this year of St. Paul we may have gotten a few steps closer to catching up with the Apostle to the Gentiles.

"As they say, archaeology is always a work in progress. I am going to ask Art to join me now at the lectern and we will take a few questions."

James Howell was standing below the stage, and handed Dick Osling, member of AP, the microphone. "Dr. West, do you think you might find evidence of the houses of Aquila and Priscilla or Stephanas in the vicinity of the villa of Erastos?"

"We would be thrilled to find those as well, but I doubt either of those folks could afford the high-rent district that Erastos lived in. Remember that Priscilla and Aquila were leatherworkers or tent makers by trade. They were not long-time Corinthian residents. As for Stephanas, we do know there were high-status Jews in Corinth, but whether they would live in an elite Gentile neighborhood is another question. Let's have another one."

The microphone was passed to a reporter for the *Observer*. "Dr. Okur, how difficult has it been for you to pursue your career in what is generally a male-dominated profession, especially in a male-dominated country like Turkey?"

Marissa nodded her head and sighed. "Ah yes, it is difficult. Professional, educated, women in Turkey must prove themselves, prove their worth, far more often than men have to. We are under closer scrutiny for sure. But I must tell you I am singularly blessed to be working with, and soon to be married to, a man who believes in the equality of men and women, not only in the sight of God, but in human society as well. Art West is a pretty rare evangelical scholar, in many ways." This produced a round of applause, particularly from the Myers Park Church women near the front.

James Howell had wandered to the left side of the room in order to allow another reporter a chance to ask a question.

"Dr. West, what would you like the members of the press to say about this conference today?"

"Please highlight that every time the New Testament has been tested against the archaeological evidence, it has been shown to tell the truth about real historical persons and the roles they played in early Christianity. And it tells the truth about the historical Jesus as well. But that is a subject for another day."

"One last question for Dr. Okur," cried a young reporter with CBN. "Are you a practicing Christian in Turkey? Is it safe for Christians to travel in Turkey? Can you have a Christian wedding in Turkey?"

"Whoa," laughed Marissa. "That's three questions. But I have three brief answers. Yes, there are Christians in Turkey and I can practice my faith without being thrown into jail. Yes, please come to Turkey, which is rapidly developing its Christian sites, like Pergamon and Laodicea and Ephesus! Christians are welcome in our democratic land where it is safe to travel with knowledgeable guides. And yes, we can have a Christian wedding in Turkey. Look for us in Istanbul next June. There will be further adventures of Drs. West and Okur!"

Author's Postscript

WE DO INDEED KNOW more about the social situation of Paul's Corinth than any other city in which early Christianity took root. For those wanting a lot more about Paul and Corinth we would suggest you pick up our *Conflict and Community in Corinth* (1996) and our forthcoming book, entitled *A Week in the Life of Corinth*. I myself (Ben) remain convinced that the Erastos in the inscription is the one mentioned in Romans 16, and I continue to be convinced by the thesis of Edwin Judge that early Christianity was led by a small but significant group of more well-educated, elite persons who provided the venues for house churches, for the writing down of Christian documents, for the housing of missionaries, and for the building of the social networks of the fledgling faith. The notion that early Christianity, even in its leadership structure, was a religion of the illiterate and non-elites is unconvincing based on all the evidence we have, including especially the evidence from Corinth, as well as from Rome (see Romans 16) and elsewhere.